THAT
PALE
HOST

L.G. McCARY

MONSTER IVY
PUBLISHING

For Caleb, my dance partner in the minefields.

In memory of Dr. Thomas Dowdy, who couldn't wait to buy my first book, whichever one it turned out to be.

One need not be a chamber to be haunted,
One need not be a house;
The brain has corridors surpassing
Material place.

Far safer, of a midnight meeting
External ghost,
Than an interior confronting
That whiter host.
Far safer through an Abbey gallop,
The stones achase,
Than, moonless, one's own self encounter
In lonesome place.

Ourself, behind ourself concealed,
Should startle most;
Assassin, hid in our apartment,
Be horror's least.
The prudent carries a revolver,
He bolts the door,
O'erlooking a superior spectre
More near.

-Emily Dickinson

ONE

THE BACK of my neck prickles with goosebumps as I watch the pregnancy test for any hint of a blue line. It is maybe a little too early to be testing, but I have to. I need that line.

David doesn't know what I am doing here in the bathroom. I doubt he even knows I'm awake. I left him playing video games with his online friends in the living room, laughing and talking through the headset as he blows away zombies with a shotgun. I don't want to get his hopes up again, so I have been pretending. Pretending that I haven't been charting my temperature and watching fertility tests turn darker. Pretending that I haven't been counting the days until the earliest a baby could be detected. To this day.

Technically tomorrow. I should test first thing in the morning, not 1 a.m. If the hormone is present, the test will detect it best when you first wake up. I know this, but I can't help myself. I can't sleep, and I won't be able to until I see the results of this test.

Is that blue? I think I can see the faintest hint of blue at the center of the circle.

A bottle clatters to the bottom of the tub, sending my

heart into my throat. I hate that tiny ridge at the back of the shower. Nothing stays where it's supposed to. I need to get a hanging shower caddy. In the orange light of the old bulbs over the mirror, the towels cast strange shadows through the frosted glass that look a little like a person. I jerk open the shower door to a tub cluttered with bottles and in need of a good scrubbing. Hard water stains and soap scum coat the cream-colored tiles. Nothing is hiding in here except a hairball on the drain. I have been jumpy all evening, but this is getting ridiculous.

I need to give this bathroom a makeover. I picture the cream tile and dirty grout replaced with a mosaic of pale green and blue glass squares. I shut the door and make a mental note to clean the bathroom this weekend. The house is not as well-kept as David would like. I know that. He hasn't said anything, but I've seen him doing my chores when he thought I wasn't paying attention. He knows this is consuming me. It's consuming him too. I look down at the pregnancy test.

Blue. The faintest possible hint of a blue line running from top to bottom, down the center of the first window.

God, please.

It isn't disappearing or fading. It's not my imagination, the creation of months of crushing disappointments. The soft blue tinge grows darker until it is unmistakable. My hands are shaking, and I ball them into fists. I smile at the mirror and try not to cry.

I have to tell David. But he's playing games with his friends. Zombies should not be involved when you inform a man he's going to be a father.

I'm a little dizzy. I close the toilet lid and sit down. It's been over two years. I know others who have tried much longer, but it has seemed like an eternity. We've been married for four years, and the gap a child is supposed to fill has grown with each passing month. I remember the first time we decided it was time to start our family.

"So we still want three kids, right?" David said as he did the dishes. I handed him my plate from the table and boxed up the leftovers from the dinner table—Chicken Parmesan with noodles.

"Three," I said.

"We ought to work on that." He grinned, his dark eyes devilish.

"Perhaps."

"Don't you think so?" David said. "I got the raise. Do you still want to quit your job?"

"Every day."

"This could be your excuse."

"I think you're right." I smiled as I put the leftovers in the refrigerator. "My doctor's appointment is coming up. I'll talk to him."

"When should we start trying?"

"My prescription runs out the same week as the exam."

"Perfect timing." David tickled my ribcage and pulled me into a damp hug.

"Perfect."

But it wasn't. It wasn't the next month or the next. I was disappointed. I wanted to be able to quit my job with grace, and every month seemed longer than the last. David told me to be patient. I've never been patient.

Six months blurred into a year. Every month brought another negative test until David made me promise to talk to my doctor.

"I'm surprised I haven't seen you sooner, Charlotte," Dr. Pressley said. "How are you doing?"

I burst into tears.

There's nothing physically wrong with me. At least, that's what they tell me. Doctors have poked and prodded for months. I must have given a gallon of blood by now. Every test has said my body is fine. No syndromes or diseases or imbalances. David is fine, too. I'm just not getting pregnant.

Until today. Until right now.

I have to tell David. He should stop killing zombies if I ask him to. It's late.

The pregnancy test is teetering on the edge of the sink. I hold it up to the light in case my sleep-deprived brain is seeing things. Two blue lines. Positive.

I set it on the counter again and pad through the darkened bedroom and down the hall to the living room. David is sitting in his gaming chair, laughing and mashing buttons. He's looking a little scruffy tonight, like he can't decide if he wants to grow out his five o'clock shadow. A grenade goes off in the surround sound speaker next to me, and I jump. He flips the microphone on his headset up out of the way and smiles between zombie kills.

"I thought you were in bed."

"Are you almost done?" I ask, brushing his short brown hair away from his eyes.

"Do you want me to be?"

"Yes."

"Then I am." He flips the microphone back down. "Guys, this is my last round."

I hear a chorus of disappointed men on the headset and laugh. I sit behind him on the faded floral couch and watch him blast through zombie hordes with ax and shotgun. His friends online trade insults and inside jokes I don't recognize. The test is burning a hole on the countertop in my mind.

I find myself staring at him as he plays. His big brown eyes caught my attention from our first meeting. My college roommate knew him from class. He was wandering the cafeteria looking for a table, and crazy Katie told him to sit with us. His tray held a burger, fries, and a glass of milk. This guy liked the basics.

I always said the wrong things. Especially around men. The more I liked a guy, the worse it was. When he told me he was an engineering major, I said the first thing that came to mind.

"So you're a nerd?"

Katie kicked me under the table. David laughed.

"But a nerd who will make good money," he said around a bite of hamburger.

"Nerd," Katie said, kicking me again. "Says the girl who paints spaceships for a class assignment."

"It was the Starship Enterprise, and it was awesome!"

David had to cover his mouth to keep from spitting his burger. Those big brown eyes were mesmerizing, and I found myself trying to save face and floundering.

"What? I love Star Trek!" I said.

Katie was going to leave bruises on my shins, but David kept laughing.

"It was the pop culture assignment. I got an A." I knew my face was turning red. Even my ears were hot.

"What's your name again?" David asked when he caught his breath.

"Charlotte."

"Charlie," Katie chimed in.

"Either one," I said with a shrug.

"Charlotte-slash-Charlie, that is amazing. Picard or Kirk?" he asked over his milk glass.

"We just met, and you're picking a fight?"

The milk shot through his nose. Katie's face contorted into a horrible *what-is-wrong-with-you* glare. I wiped the milk off of my tray with a napkin and handed him another.

"I think I may have found my new best friend," David said as he wiped his face with the napkin. "We both know the right answer is Picard."

I wanted to say something witty, but I laughed and dabbed the rest of the milk from the table. Katie gave me a weird look for the rest of dinner.

"I don't know how you managed that, but I think he likes you," she said as we headed up the stairs to our dorm room.

"Wait, what?"

"Seriously! I think you found your soulmate." She unlocked our door and flung it wide with dramatic flair. "Lucky. He's hot."

My husband dies of a zombie bite. He turns off the gaming system and puts away his headset and controller.

"Did I wake you up?"

"No, I was awake."

"Don't you have an early morning tomorrow?"

"I can't sleep."

He wraps his strong arms around me and kisses my neck. He smells like dandruff shampoo and the cologne I bought him for Christmas.

"I love you," I whisper.

"I love you, too."

"I want to show you something." My heart catches in my throat as I say the words.

"Oh, really?"

I punch his shoulder. I feel like I'm going to crawl out of my skin. He follows me into our bedroom, turning off the living room lights. I can feel him behind me, ready to pounce.

"In here." I pull him into the bathroom. I watch his eyes as he sweeps the room for something new. His gaze lights on the test, and his fingers squeeze mine.

"Charlie?" He picks up the test and squints at it. He looks at me.

"We're going to have a baby."

These last months I have cried more tears than I knew I had. David wiped them away with kisses and whispers of "I love you no matter what." "You are not broken." "This does not change us."

He has held my hand in doctors' offices as we awaited test results, never letting go until we knew our answers. He has made dinner and cleaned the house on nights when I couldn't cope. He has sat with me on the couch or laid next to me in our bed, reassuring me that I will be a mother someday. He has held me together in our shattered world without a single tear. I have seen his eyes turn red, but I have never seen my husband shed tears.

David is crying.

The room seems bigger and smaller at the same time. My chest shudders, and a sob rushes to my throat. He doesn't say anything. He wraps me in his arms and kisses my head. His tears mix with mine on the shoulder of my T-shirt, and I realize that for the first time, I am holding him up. We stand in the bathroom, covering each other with tears and kisses. Words would never be able to say what I see in his eyes.

It feels like a long time before we brush our teeth and get ready for bed. He checks my alarm clock for me while I finish washing my face. As I pat my face dry, I jump, caught off guard again by the weird shadows in the shower. I pull my towel off the rack and hang it on the back of the door instead.

"You're jumpy tonight," David says from the door.

"Just nervous. Something could happen, you know."

"Nope. We're not going there, okay?" David wraps his arms around my shoulders and kisses my ear. "I'm not letting you think like that."

"It's just where my brain goes," I say, turning to face him.

"And I'm telling your brain to hush. Worrying isn't going to do anything."

He flips off the bathroom light, and I follow him into the bedroom. I wonder for the hundredth time why I haven't painted and decorated. The room still feels like we're broke college students in an apartment. We really ought to get a headboard and matching nightstands.

"When do you want to tell the parentals?" David interrupts my thoughts. He pulls back the gray-and-white abstract, patterned comforter and flops onto the bed.

"I don't know," I say. I slide into bed next to him and put my head in the familiar hollow of his neck.

"Your mom is going to freak out," he says.

"So will yours."

"Our Sunday school will go nuts after praying for so long."

"Can we wait to tell them?" I ask.

"Of course. Whatever you want to do."

I don't want to think about all the attention I'll get, even though our church has been so supportive. There's such a fine line between encouragement and badgering when it's about having children.

David turns off the lamp next to the bed and sighs. "First grandchild for both sides. This kid is going to be so spoiled," he says with a laugh. "Mom will be out at every estate sale looking for toys."

"You don't think she'll try to take over, do you?" I ask.

"I'll reign her in if I need to." He pulls me tighter against his chest. "You should go with her some so she knows what you like."

"Mom and Dad will want to tell everyone they know immediately," I say. "Did I tell you Mom has been saving her vacation days specifically for me having a baby?"

"Sounds like your mom. She's just protective."

It's been so strange to be separated from them. I didn't really want to move two states away, but at least we're only thirty minutes from David's mom.

"I'm going to build all kinds of crazy stuff for him," David murmurs. "Or her! All the things I wanted to play with when I was little."

"And you're worried about the grandparents spoiling him or her?" I tease. "You and your projects."

"I'll have to push for that next raise in the spring," David says, kissing my forehead. "You'll call Dr. Pressley on Monday?"

"Yes."

"You're three and half weeks along, right?"

I smile in the dark. Why did I pretend today was just a normal day? Of course he knows. He has been counting the days with me.

TWO

"CONGRATULATIONS!" Renee crows and elbows her husband Casey in the ribs. "I told you they'd be next. I'm so happy for you!"

"Place your bets now: boy or girl!" Morgan says as she hugs me.

"I say boy!" Renee says.

I smile and whisper thank you. They've been praying for me for so long. It feels good to finally be able to tell them now that I'm used to the idea myself.

Our little home is bursting at the seams with members of our Sunday school class. It's a little awkward since the old ranch style isn't exactly open-concept, but we made it work. Renee and Casey brought extra chairs for the living room. It was David's idea to tell them about the baby at the fall costume party. We puzzled for weeks about what to wear until David thought of Galileo and made me the solar system with my belly as the sun and planets dangling from each arm. He found a black cloak and scholar's hat and made a fake telescope out of cardboard. I pat the yellow sun decorating my black turtleneck as

David kisses my cheek through a ridiculous gray beard made of cotton.

"How far along are you?" Renee asks, patting her own round belly beneath a fluffy orange pumpkin costume.

"Thirteen weeks."

Renee brushes the green vine dangling in her face over her shoulder. "I should have placed bets on it. I would have made a fortune."

"So, are you quitting your job?" another woman asks. I can't remember her name, but I know that's always the first question she asks when someone announces a baby.

"I don't want to work full-time anymore," I answer. "I'd rather be home and maybe work for myself some."

"Good luck. I'd go crazy at home," Renee groans. She points to her belly. "The school daycare has this kid's spot saved and everything. I'm already bored thinking about this summer."

"I'm glad you like your job," I say. Renee likes to argue, so I'm not giving her any reason to convince me to work. I'm still wary of her dinner parties after she made it her mission to get me to like fish and served salmon burgers. David always asks me if I have a granola bar stashed in my purse when it's their turn to host the monthly fellowship night.

"I told Charlie she should start painting again," David says from behind the kitchen counter.

"You paint?" Casey cocks his head in confusion.

"Yes, I did a lot of painting in college. Mostly oils and acrylic."

"I thought you were an accountant," Casey says.

David laughs a little too hard. I'm no accountant.

"No, I'm a graphic designer. I don't talk about my job much," I say. "It's boring, and my boss makes it miserable."

"Where do you work?"

"A small web design company. I basically design logos for a living."

"And she's criminally underutilized," David interrupts. "Charlie is amazing. Let me find her Enterprise painting."

"Ugh, David, don't. That thing is so old!"

"And amazing!"

Renee gives me quizzical looks, but our husbands are grinning.

"As in *the* Enterprise?" Casey asks.

"From the original series," David says with pride.

"My family watched a lot of Star Trek," I explain to the ladies.

"I've never seen that show," Renee says.

I would have been shocked if she had. David disappears into the garage and returns with my old painting. I know he's proud, but I hate showing it to people.

"Why isn't that on the wall?" Casey says.

"Wow, Charlotte," Morgan says, admiring the nebula behind the ship. "You're amazing."

"It's a really old painting," I sigh. The vivid colors are beautiful, but my more experienced eye can only see the clumsiness of the brush strokes and the flaws in the composition. "I should redo it. I didn't mix the colors properly. I could do so much better now."

"You should!" David says. "I could hang it at work!"

I laugh at him. "I don't know."

"That's your assignment after the baby comes: paint me a new spaceship!" he declares with a huge smile.

I blush and follow Renee through the curtain of orange and black streamers from our kitchen to the living room. Bodies crowd together on the couch and fireplace, and the room is a little warm. It's a bigger group than we expected, and I feel terrible that I don't know everyone's name. Our class has exploded with new married couples moving up from the "nearly-wed" class. I should probably introduce myself. I usually wait for Renee to help me meet new people.

Our teacher, Larry, is dressed as Martin Luther, complete with a brown cap and puffy pillow stomach. His wife, Grace, dressed as Luther's wife, rounds everyone up from our front room and the kitchen for charades.

"Couple of quick announcements before we get to more fun stuff!" Larry says. "We will have more people joining. Two more couples, from what I heard."

"We also have to say thank you to David and Charlotte for opening their home," says Grace. "And congratulations on the little one! More babies!"

My stomach knots, but I try to enjoy all the shouts of excitement and happy hugs from these ladies I don't know very well. It's the same questions over and over about my due date and baby showers and nurseries until Grace coughs and announces it's time to play charades.

The game becomes a comedy routine with Luther pretending to ride a roller coaster, a bumblebee tap dancing, and an '80s aerobics instructor failing miserably at making a milkshake. Before we know it, it's late. I'm exhausted from laughing. Or maybe it's the baby.

"I can't wait for Tori to move up to our class!" Renee says as she walks to the entryway.

"Who is she again?"

"She works nursery with me a lot," Renee answers. She picks up her purse from the side table behind our couch. "We're getting so big in this class. They better not try to split us."

"We'll stage a coup if they do," Casey says, raising a fist in mock rebellion.

"Come on, I'm sleepy," Renee whines.

The rest of our class trickles out the door. Larry and Grace help us with the trash and packaging the leftover food.

"I'm so excited for you," Grace says as they walk out to their car. "I love hosting baby showers."

"Thank you, Grace."

"Once you know if it's a boy or girl, we'll get planning."

"I'll let you know."

"I can't wait!" She squeezes me in a big hug and wipes away a tear. "I've been praying for you. Every morning. God is good."

I try to blink away the tears. "Thank you," I whisper.

"Just can't wait. We are going to celebrate this big, Charlotte. And you're going to let me. When God works a miracle, you celebrate!" she says with a decisive nod. I watch them pull away into the darkness and shiver. The cold October sky sparkles with stars. For a moment, I enjoy the beauty of the constellations and the cool wind on my cheeks.

"Get back in this house, woman! It's freezing!" David teases from the door.

"I'm just admiring your discoveries, Galileo," I say.

"I'm admiring my discovery, too," he says with a wink. I snort and plant a kiss on his lips.

"I need a shower," I tell him as I shut the door.

"Me too," he answers. "Let's share." I turn the lights out in the kitchen and living room and follow him to our room. He turns the shower on hot.

"Not too hot." I point to my belly. "Baby."

"I'm just getting it warmed up. You can set it when you get in."

"I think people had fun."

"Of course! Everyone had a blast. Larry is hoarse."

"Renee's Elvis was amazing. Please tell me someone got a video."

"I think everyone got a video."

We remove the planets and stars pinned to my shirt and leggings. David helps me pull off the turtleneck, so I'm left in black leggings and a tank top. He pats my belly and gives it a kiss.

"Can you put everything in the laundry for me?" I ask.

"Okay."

The bathroom fills with steam as the water heats up. I scrub away at my mascara and glittery eyeshadow while David gets undressed on the bed. The makeup remover sends the black and green melting down my cheeks until I look ghoulish and bruised.

Something catches my eye as I turn to look at David.

A dark place in the steam drifts. I watch the spot for a moment. It must be the old lights in the overhead heater casting shadows in the steam. I really need to get a new bulb.

It moves. No, the dark place *walks* past the shower to the toilet.

I fall back against the counter and yell. The shadow moves to the other side of the bathroom. My hands feel cold, and I clench them into fists.

"Charlie, are you okay?" David rushes in.

"Did you see that?"

"See what?"

"That!" The wisps of steam tumbles toward me like someone is moving through them. I run out of the bathroom and plow David over. "It moved. It moved!"

"Charlie, calm down. What are you talking about?"

"It looked like someone was walking through it!"

"What?"

"Like someone *not me* was walking through it!"

"Whoa, come here," he pulls me to his chest. "There's nothing there. It's okay."

"I'm telling you, it looked like someone was there."

David looks around the room with a frown. Then he grins and squeezes my shoulders.

"The heater."

"The what?"

"The heater. It has a little fan, remember?" He points to the heater coils on the ceiling. "I just turned it on."

"The fan?"

"Yeah, the fan is blowing it. Look, you can tell right there."

I watch the heating fan blow coils and puffs of mist out from the shower toward the mirror. Is that what I saw? My heart rate slows down as I watch the curls of steam. It makes sense.

"Here, look," David says, and blows a huge puff of air into the steam. It sends billows tumbling after each other. My cheeks are turning warm with embarrassment.

"It looked so creepy."

"My jumpy wife seeing things. Next time, I'll warn you before I turn the fan on."

"Yes, do that," I mutter into his shoulder. "It's all the hormones."

"So, what was your excuse in college?"

I poke him in the ribs where I know he's ticklish, and he hollers.

"You were mean," I say.

"Yes, I was very mean. And you were easy to prank. The spider was hilarious," he laughs. He leans in and kisses me to stop me from replying. I let him. "I love you, Charlie. You're beautiful. You know that?"

"Ha! Let me get this junk off of my eyes."

"Yeah, that's not so beautiful," he says. "That's downright terrifying."

"I'm a goblin. Boo!" I say, sticking out my tongue. "Go get that gray washed out of your hair. You look ridiculous, Galileo."

"As long as you're coming too."

My heart is still pounding a little, but I grin as he turns around and winks at me. I've got to stop watching creepy movies. I gaze at him in the mirror as he tosses his clothes in the hamper, avoiding looking at the place where the shadow used to be.

THREE

THE CLOCK READS 2 a.m. David is breathing steadily next to me. I'm not sure what has woken me up this time. I'm so tired of waking up to go to the bathroom. I spent the day finishing the last touches on the nursery and went to bed exhausted. At least it's finished. All the shower gifts are washed and put away.

I'm glad that the shower is over with. Having to open gifts in front of all the women in our class should be against the Geneva Convention. I wouldn't have minded just Renee and our teacher Grace, but I had to sit in front of a punch-sipping, chocolate-strawberry-eating panel of judges and wait for them to rate my reactions to each dress, bow, and burp rag. The worst part was all the questions. I'm still not sure why a wipe warmer is such a controversial registry item, but I know better than to ever bring it up again. When someone asked me if we were going to tell people the name we'd chosen, I thought this would be a fun surprise for everyone.

"We thought we'd wait until the baby shower, so today!" I said, grinning. "We're going to name her Rylie."

"Rylie? Isn't that a boy's name?" Renee said, her mouth full of quiche. I can't say I didn't expect that response from her. She always has opinions on names.

"It's for both, Renee," Morgan answered, giving me a look that said, "Ignore her."

"We chose it when we first got married. It means courageous or valiant," I said. "We played the newlywed game for a group date, and we got 'What would you name our first kid?' We both said Rylie for a girl."

"Wow, you knew just like that?" Morgan asked.

"When the ultrasound tech told us she was a girl, we both said, 'Rylie!'"

"Casey and I argued about Liana's name for months," Renee said. "He likes boring names like Anna and David."

I roll my eyes in the dark at the memory. David's name isn't boring. It's classic. I know Renee didn't mean to be insulting. She more than made up for it with her gift: a housecleaning service I can schedule any time I choose. I have most of what I need as well as special gifts I will cherish. Grace crocheted a baby blanket, and it seemed like everyone made bows for Rylie to wear. Our class also does a sign-up to bring dinner every other night for two weeks. I brought Renee lasagna when she had Liana. As long as Renee doesn't try to bring me fish, I'll be happy. Morgan said something about pulled pork, and Grace promised homemade enchiladas.

"I always come ready to hold the baby so Mama can shower before dinner," Grace said, bouncing an almost sleeping baby Liana from side to side. "So don't you dare do anything special before I get there."

"Grace is the baby whisperer," Renee said with a deep sigh. "Thank you for rocking her. I can hardly put her down at home."

"All babies know a grandma when they see one," Grace said with a wink. "Are her eyes closed?"

"Not quite."

"Goodness, she sure fights it, doesn't she?"

"She fights everything. Tummy time. Bottles. Sleep." Renee looked at me and wrinkled her nose. "You'll probably get an easy baby. Seems like everyone else does."

I shift from my right side back to my left. I doubt Rylie will be easy. She seems to enjoy kicking me in the ribs at inopportune times.

My legs are sticky with sweat. I push the covers back and waddle to the bathroom. A bubbling sensation in my stomach makes me unsteady. I suppose that must be what woke me. I shut the bathroom door and turn on the light.

Red. My legs are dripping with it. I'm sick to my stomach and lean over the sink as the panic strangles me. I can't think. I'm only 35 weeks.

"David!" My voice is thick with sleep. "David, help me!"

He's in the bathroom in moments, arms wrapping around me and looking at the floor.

"Honey, what happened?"

"I'm bleeding. The baby!" My heart pounds in my ears. I clutch my belly and breathe a prayer. It's one word over and over: Please. Please. Please.

"Are you hurting?"

"No."

"What happened?"

"I don't know." My hands are shaking, and nausea rises in my throat. "I don't know!"

"Do you need to sit down? What should I do?"

"I don't know!" Tears roll down my cheeks and hit the bathroom counter. The bright light hurts my eyes. David gently guides me to sit on the toilet seat. He disappears into the bedroom and comes back with his cell phone.

"I'm calling 911. Hold on, honey. Just hold on." He holds my hand as he gives our information. The dispatcher is asking him questions about how much blood and how far along I am and if I'm in pain, and that's when I realize I can't feel the baby moving.

"David, she's not moving."

"What?"

"Rylie. She's not moving!"

"They'll be here in a minute, honey. It's going to be okay." David's face is ashen. He grips my hand with white knuckles and grits his teeth. "I'm going to unlock the front door for them. I'll be right back."

He runs out of the room, still talking to the dispatcher on the phone. I'm left alone in our little bathroom, staring at the blood soaking my nightgown and my swollen stomach still and quiet. I hold onto the towel rack for dear life. The tears course down my cheeks in stinging streaks.

Then David is back, standing next to me and hugging my shoulder.

"Talk to me, Charlie."

"I feel so sick."

"They'll be here in a minute. They'll take care of you."

"She's not moving!" I whisper.

I feel like I'm strangling.

David holds me tight and listens to the operator again, answering questions I can't hear. My belly has not been this still in months.

I pray aloud this time. "Please. Please. Please."

I have no other words. My heart is going to rip into a thousand pieces. My little girl cannot die. She can't. And all I can do is beg God to protect her.

A blond-haired man wearing a paramedic uniform rushes into the bathroom followed by a red-headed man carrying a medical kit. They help me to the floor and work with quick motions, checking me and telling each other different things as they work. The flurry of medical terms makes my head spin.

"Ma'am, we're going to transport you to the hospital," the blond man says. "I'm going to give you some fluids and oxygen on the way there. Your husband can ride with us." He pulls a stretcher toward the bathroom door from the bedroom, and they help me onto it.

David squeezes my hand. "Honey, I'm going to call the doctor and then your folks."

He dials a number and steps away. He walks past a woman with dark-brown hair standing in the bedroom. She isn't dressed like the others, and her face reminds me of my mother's. She looks terrified.

"I found the baby's heartbeat," the red-headed paramedic says. "Hold on...it's a hundred." He looks worried, but I have a small piece of relief.

"She's alive?"

"Yes, ma'am. The heartbeat is a little slow, but it's strong."

"But she's not moving. She's not doing anything."

"You know you're having a girl?" the redhead asks. I nod as I wipe the tears from my eyes, and he smiles. "I have two girls myself. We're going to get you to the hospital right away. We're going to help you both."

I hear David on the phone with my mother as they roll me into the ambulance. The IV makes me shiver. I start to ask where the female paramedic went when pain stabs through my belly. My breath comes out in a wail, and David shuts his phone, diving into the ambulance with me.

"It hurts!" I scream.

Oh, it hurts. It hurts like fireworks exploding in my stomach, like knives carving me up. It came out of nowhere, and it won't stop.

"Where is the pain, Charlotte?"

I gesture to my stomach. I can't breathe.

The paramedics ask David more questions as the doors shut and the ambulance takes off. Pain tears through my stomach over and over. It sears across my back, refusing to let up. The blond man places a mask over my mouth and nose. I try to breathe, but it hurts.

"Charlotte, this oxygen will help you and the baby. I need you to breathe."

"Please help me," I beg.

I don't know who I'm talking to anymore. I gulp air in a brief moment of relief. The air from the mask is cold and smells sterile. The redhead says something, but I can't process his words. Everything blurs into a whirlwind of panic and pain. I can't think of anything except my baby.

The ride feels like hours, but I know it can't be more than a few minutes because the hospital isn't far. The pain must be contractions, but they can't be. It's too soon. The pain comes fast and furious, crashing through me like tsunamis. I can't stop crying. They wheel me down a hall where I watch the overhead lights flash past. It's like every horrible television episode I've watched where a character is going to die.

A nurse grabs my hand and smiles at me. "I'm Jennifer. Who is your doctor?"

"Dr. Pressley," David tells her.

"Well, he is on call tonight and on his way," she says as they keep rolling me down the endless hall.

"Help my baby, please."

"We're going to get you hooked up to the monitors right now so we can see how she's doing. It's a girl, right?"

I'm in a room. When we toured the hospital a few weeks ago, it looked much homier. Right now, it is a cave. My breath hitches over and over until I worry I might hyperventilate. This is not how it is supposed to go. I'm not supposed to be here yet. This is all wrong.

"I'm not supposed to."

"What, Charlotte?" the nurse asks.

"This isn't the way. What did I do?"

Jennifer grabs my hand and looks into my eyes.

"Sometimes things just happen," she says, her voice gentle and serious. "That's why we have hospitals and doctors and people like me."

"Is she okay?"

"We're checking the monitor right now." There are so many people in the room with me. It's supposed to be me and David and my doctor. David is signing forms in a chair next to my head.

"Heart rate is one hundred. No accels," another nurse says.

"Is that bad?"

Another contraction stabs me. This one spreads through to my back. Invisible crowbars are prying my spine apart. The scream that rips my throat in half sounds like it came from an animal. Jennifer grips my hand and puts a cold washcloth on my neck. David is holding my other hand and kissing it.

"Breathe, Charlotte," the nurse says. "Have you picked a name for your daughter?"

"Rylie," David says.

"Rylie needs that oxygen just like you do," the nurse says. "You have to breathe."

"Hurts." This is wrong. I've been practicing my breathing and how to be calm, but I can't.

"I know it hurts."

David whispers in my ear a hundred sweet things to distract me from the pain.

"When did the contractions start, Dad?"

"About an hour ago?" David says. I shake my head that it can't be that long, but it also feels like I've been in this hell for days. Jennifer talks me through another contraction. They're all running together now. Another nurse asks David something about the placenta. I don't know what she's talking about, but she looks concerned.

"Am I bleeding?" I say.

"We're taking care of you, Charlotte. I need to do an exam."

I don't want to think about it. I shut my eyes and bury my head in the sickly-sweet smelling hospital pillow. I want my own pillow. It smells like lavender.

"Where is my doctor?" I'm soaking the pillow with tears.

"He's on his way. And Dr. Casey will come as soon as he is out of surgery."

"Nurse, what can I do?" I hear David say from my hiding place in the pillow.

"You are doing great, Dad. Stay right there next to mom. Here, let's change out that washcloth." The cold, moist washcloth is more clammy than comforting on my neck.

"I'm going to throw up," I say. Another nurse shoves a blue bag underneath my chin, and I taste bile. There's little in my stomach. I heave with the contraction, my whole body almost seizing with the effort. It makes me see stars.

I know David is trying to help me, but all I can think about is the pain. My ears are hot, but the rest of my body is cold. The room is spinning like a merry-go-round. My guts twist, and something changes. I can't stop it. I can't think of anything else. I grunt through the haze around me as my body forces me to hunch over, and my muscles scream.

"Charlotte?" When I open my eyes, the look on the nurse's face scares me. Another contraction hits me, and again I'm carried along with a wave of pain. My body is pushing whether I want it to or not. The nurses are suddenly a flurry of motion, and someone says something about alerting the NICU.

"Where is my doctor?"

"Is she pushing?" David asks. "Honey, wait, the doctor is coming!"

"I've got you, girl," Jennifer says, squeezing my hand. "If you need to push, push. I have delivered lots of babies, and Dr. Pressley will be here any minute. You do what you need to do."

There are lots of other faces in the room, every one a stranger. Pain rushes through me, sending fire through my legs. I think I might tear apart. The faces swim in front of me.

"What happened?" David says, his voice tight. He rubs my hand. "That's a lot of..." his voice trails off. He is white as a sheet.

"Look at Mom, Dad," another nurse orders, moving David away from the foot of the bed. "Talk to her. We're taking care of her."

"I'm here, honey." David turns toward me and bites his lip. "I'm right here. Breathe." The nurses are talking to each other, but I can't understand the medical terms. Someone mentions calling a cart. That sounds bad. Jennifer leans up to me, her eyes focused and serious.

"Charlotte, I need you to listen to me," the nurse says. Her voice forms a knot of dread deep in my heart.

"I'm so tired." I have to close my eyes.

"We need to get that sweet baby out. Next push, I want you to push as hard as you can."

"What about the doctor?"

"Kelly and I will take good care of both of you until he gets here."

"I'm scared," I say to David. "Is the baby okay?"

"Baby is fine right now," the other nurse says, "but we need to get her out as soon as we can."

The pain rises, slow but sharp like the thrust of a knife through my back.

"Get ready, Charlotte. Push hard! Deep breath!"

"I'm here, Charlie. I'm right here," David breathes in my ear. The room is sharp and clear all of a sudden, and time stops. There is nothing but the pain and knowing that Rylie needs me. Rylie.

"Rylie!" I yell it at the top of my lungs. I cannot lose my girl. I can't. "Rylie!"

"That's it, Charlotte! Keep going!" the nurse yells. I'm screaming, and for a millisecond, all I can think about is how the sound echoes off the ceiling.

I am breaking into pieces. I gulp air and scream again. I know the nurse is trying to help me, but I can't hear anything but the rush of blood in my ears and my own screams of pain.

And then she's out. I look down to see her, but the nurse is cutting the cord and carrying her away. I'm supposed to hold her. I'm supposed to be the first person to touch her.

My arms are empty but somehow still heavy. My head dips forward. My whole body shakes until I wonder if there's an earthquake.

"Is she okay? Rylie!" I beg the nurses. "David, is she okay?"

I can't see her over the mess of bodies. I can't hear anything. David is pale next to me

The room fills with a silence that feels like death. Jennifer is busy at my feet. She's holding her breath. David bows his head on my shoulder and whispers a prayer. I don't hear the words. I'm straining to hear Rylie.

A cry. It's a tiny noise like a kitten. The nurses laugh.

"Good girl," I whisper. David squeezes my hand and says something to the nurses. My head grows heavy. I look down and realize that Jennifer looks worried. Another nurse is offering suggestions and saying she can put something in my IV. Someone else calls out numbers. Everyone is looking more worried. But I still can't see Rylie.

"I'm dizzy," I say to the nurse. I can't focus. It's so cold in the room. I can't think. "I'm really dizzy."

"I've got you, girl," Jennifer says. "Kelly, get the bed down now."

"I don't want the lights off," I say. I want to see my baby, and I can't if they turn the lights off.

"Charlotte, we're going to lay you down."

I'm colder than ever. I can't see David. Where is David? And why is it dark?

I don't have any strength to argue. The bed drops behind me.

"Please let me see her," I whisper. One of the nurses grabs my hand and squeezes it tight.

"She's getting some oxygen right now, honey. She's doing great." My baby cries again from the corner, and the nurse grins. "Hear that? Can you squeeze my hand, please?"

"See her, please." The words slur into a mess.

I'm dying. I see it in the nurses' panicked movements. I hear it in David's voice as he talks to Jennifer.

I'm going to die and never see my daughter. I'm going to

leave her alone without a mother. I'll never even get to hold her.

The earthquake in my chest begins again, sobs shaking me from head to toe. David is talking to me, but there's someone in his way. I don't understand what he is saying. There are so many people in the room, and half of them are around my bed, talking to each other about me.

Rylie. The nurse holds her against my face, but she is miles away. She is pink and bald and crying. The nurse has lifted Rylie's oxygen mask a few inches so I can see her face. She is transcendently beautiful. Her eyes are scrunched closed. What color are they?

"Can you give her a kiss, Mom?" the nurse says.

I try, but my lips are not working. Then my baby disappears into a plastic box, and the box vanishes. They've taken her away. The room fades into black and white, and swirls of shadows fill my vision.

The darkness drags me with icy fingers down a tunnel. I can't see the end, but I know when I reach it, I will never come back. One kiss is all my daughter will ever know of me. David's voice is fading. The nurses are calling my name. They sound far away. Another voice I should know says my name. It isn't David. Who is it?

"I can't see," I say. I am trapped in the tunnel. My stomach pitches and my head spins like I'm on a rollercoaster in the dark.

The rollercoaster is going to crash. I can't get off. I can't move or scream or breathe. I'm paralyzed in this spinning chaos with fireworks exploding around me.

I thought I would be at peace when I died.

FOUR

I JERK my eyes open and see the fan above our bed spinning slowly in the glow of the nightlight on our wall. My heartbeat thunders in my ears, and I force my fists to unclench the sheets. I can't take these nightmares much longer.

Rylie and I have been home one week now, and every time I fall asleep, I find myself back in the hospital. I dream of faceless nurses and doctors shouting medical terms that make no sense, and the pain making the room spin. It always ends with the darkness closing in as I scream for Rylie.

I turn to look at my baby in the bassinet next to me. I try to slow my breathing and gently touch Rylie's downy head. She has worked her left hand out of the swaddle blanket and holds it to her face. I want to hold her, but that would wake her up.

The alarm clock reads 1:00 a.m. I doubt I'll be able to fall asleep again, knowing Rylie will need to nurse soon. My stomach growls as I lie on the edge of the mattress. No one told me how my stomach would hurt so much waking up in the middle of the night. Maybe it's the medicines I'm taking. Every morning I've swallowed a nasty pill to replenish the iron I lost delivering Rylie.

Placental abruption with postpartum hemorrhage. Such strange clinical words for almost dying of blood loss. My doctor got the bleeding under control soon after I passed out, but I needed a transfusion. I still feel nauseated when I remember waking up to a red IV bag above my head. At least Rylie didn't need anything more than some extra oxygen for a few days. My girl is a tough cookie even though my body failed her.

Mom would be mad at me for thinking that. She demanded to stay with us a little longer so I can heal. She's been feeding me iron-rich foods, refilling my water bottle, and watching me like a hawk for dizziness. David treats me like I'm made of glass, about to shatter if he says or does the wrong thing. There's been a seemingly endless stream of messages on my phone of people offering food and other help. Renee told me the whole church has heard what happened and has been praying for me.

Part of me feels loved, but I'm mostly embarrassed. I hate that I need so much help. I just want to feel normal again, but I cannot shake this ugly feeling in my chest. There are so many things to remember, but I feel like I can't keep track of it all. Is Rylie eating enough? Is her cry normal? The first few days, I was supposed to track her diapers and feedings with a paper. It got lost somewhere between the hospital and home, and I couldn't stop crying. Mom finally printed me a new one she found online.

It seems so silly to cry over a diaper tracker, but how can I help it with all these nightmares waking me up?

"Don't worry," my mom told me this afternoon. "Everyone is nervous the first few weeks. And you're naturally a little nervous anyway." I keep telling myself she's right.

Then there was the ballerina lamp. David's mom was so proud of it when she brought it over this morning, but it doesn't match the nursery at all. I don't even like ballet. But it was a vintage find at an estate sale, and she couldn't wait to give it to us.

"It's my first 'Nana' gift," she told me. I don't know why I cried about it. I felt like an idiot. David looked at me like I lost my mind, and my mother-in-law said she could keep it at her house instead. David shooed her out of the room until I calmed down. I finally apologized for acting nuts. It was just an old pink ballerina lamp. Try as I might, I can't come up with any sane reason for crying about it. I can still see her smiling next to my mom on the couch.

"Don't worry, honey," my mother-in-law said, perched on the couch next to my mom. "When I had David, I cried when my mother baked me brownies. And then I cried when I ate the last one the next day. It's all hormones. I'm convinced they're of the devil!"

When I looked at it again this evening, I decided it wasn't that bad. It's actually a pretty lamp. And it's pink. If I change the shade, it will match the room. I hope David's mom truly isn't offended. It kills me to think I may have hurt her feelings.

I want a drink of water, but the bottle on my nightstand is empty. I slowly sit up and slide along the bed with the bottle, trying not to disturb Rylie.

Out of the corner of my eye, I see a dark shape standing in the doorway.

"David?"

David starts next to me in bed.

I stifle a scream as the shape vanishes like smoke.

"What?" David says, jumping out of bed, half awake. I can only point at the door.

"What is it? What's wrong?" He stands up and looks around.

"I saw someone," I say. "Mom? Mom, are you there?"

The doorway is a black void. Did I see someone?

"Hold on," he whispers. He grabs his softball bat from next to the bed and pads out of the room into the hallway. I try to follow his footsteps with my ears, but my heart is pounding so hard that I can't hear anything else. I glance back at Rylie and put a hand on her chest as it rises and falls. Then David is back in the room.

"There's no one there. It's fine."

"Was it Mom?"

"Your mom is asleep, Charlie. You must have been dreaming."

"But I wasn't!" I say over the blood pumping in my ears.

"It's okay, Charlie. I checked the whole house." He leans the baseball bat next to the dresser and climbs back into bed. I lay back against the pillows. David slips his arm around my waist and pulls me close.

"Are you okay?" he whispers. I make an affirmative sound, and he sighs. "It was just a scary dream. Go back to sleep."

"I thought I saw someone."

He squeezes my shoulders and reaches over to pat Rylie. He is asleep again in moments.

I'm still thirsty, but I can't move. If I move, David will roll over, and his arms are the only thing keeping me from falling apart.

FIVE

"AMAZING GRACE, HOW SWEET THE SOUND…" I'm not much of a singer, but Rylie doesn't seem to mind. She's only been in the world four months, so she doesn't know any better. She wiggles on my chest, rubbing her nose with her fist and sighing. She fights sleep as hard as she can, but she's starting to give up. The rocking chair always works.

It's working on me too. I'm exhausted, and the soft pink light from the ballerina lamp above her changing table is sending me into a trance. I should have had David rock her so I wouldn't fall asleep holding her in the chair. But I love rocking her. I love holding my baby and feeling her squirm against my chin as she tries to keep herself awake. She is only still when she finally falls asleep.

"Noisiest, wiggliest four-month-old I ever saw," my mother-in-law said last weekend. "Davy was busy, but this girl is biz-zy. No wonder you're tired, honey."

"You'd think she would have fallen asleep in the car since she wouldn't sleep during church," David said. He had stretched out on the floor next to Rylie, watching her kick and squirm. She flailed her arms at his face, smacking his nose. "Ouch. I guess the other babies in the nursery are too interesting."

"At least you can go to Sunday school again," Nana said.

"If only I could pay attention instead of falling asleep myself," I muttered and put a toy near Rylie's head. She cooed with delight and then grunted in frustration that I'd put it out of reach.

"You're going to have a time when she starts crawling, Charlotte," Nana said with a laugh.

I'm sure she was right. This girl is going to be a handful. Rylie wiggles again and sighs a huge sigh. I run my fingers up and down her spine, and her breathing slows. She's ready for her nap. If only she could be convinced that naps are the best thing ever.

Something moves by the closet.

It is made of shadows, almost like smoke or the after-image on your retina after seeing a bright light. I close my eyes and keep rocking. I know there is nothing there. I must be more exhausted than I thought. I pray my daughter isn't hearing my thundering heartbeat. Renee warned me I'd be so worn out that I'd hallucinate. I thought she was joking. The ballerina light doesn't seem so friendly anymore.

As I lay Rylie in her bed, I might as well have consumed fifteen espressos. The room is still and quiet, but I keep looking at the corner of the closet where the shadows from the window seemed to move. There's a tree outside. Maybe it was the wind? It had to be wind moving the tree branches.

I pull the door closed but leave a crack so I don't have to fight the squeaky knob to check on Rylie later. My heart thunders in my chest as I walk down the hall and find David on the couch, watching a reality show I don't recognize.

"I'm so tired I'm seeing things," I say. "But now I'm wide awake."

He mutes the television and grabs my hand.

"Go to bed, Charlie. I'll tuck you in."

I nod. I know I won't sleep. I'll lie there on the bed, trying not to think about how I'm seeing things that can't be there. David doesn't seem to be concerned, but I'm terrified. He guides me down the hall to our bedroom and watches me while I brush my teeth.

"You look like you've seen a ghost or something," he says.

"No!" I sputter around a mouthful of toothpaste foam. "I do *not* believe in ghosts. Ghosts do not exist, David."

"Good grief, calm down! I was kidding! You just look freaked out. What's the matter?"

I've been afraid to look in the mirror, but I can't avoid it now. This is like the one time I pulled an all-nighter in college, and all my professors thought I had the flu the next day. My hair is in a messy bun. I don't remember putting it up. The blue shirt I'm wearing has multiple stains on it that I didn't notice when I picked it out of the laundry. Did I pick this one out of the dirty pile instead of the clean, or did I manage to get that messy in one day? The deep circles under my eyes are almost like bruises. My shoulders hunch like I've been kicked in the gut. I bite my cheeks hard so I won't cry, but it does no good. David looks heartbroken behind me in the mirror.

"Sweetheart..." he trails off and seems to decide that hugging me is better than words. I can't slow the tears. I'm exhausted. Why can't I sleep?

"So tired," I say with hitching breaths.

"I know, honey. I know you're tired," he whispers in my ears. He rubs my neck and back with both hands, kneading the knots that have been there since Rylie was born.

"I feel like I'm losing my mind, David." It takes forever to get the sentence out, and he makes me rinse my mouth and put away the toothbrush.

He helps me into bed and sits next to me, rubbing my shoulders and back. "I'm sorry I can't feed her for you at night."

It's a nice thought to have him give her a bottle, but I don't want him to. After everything my girl and I have been through, I'm grateful to be able to nurse her. I'm exhausted, but I still want to be the one to hold her all night. Maybe I can make up for whatever went wrong when she was born.

"It's okay. I don't mind that. But the house is such a mess today."

"It is not a mess. It's fine."

"The laundry is still in the washer."

"I'll get it. Go to sleep, Charlie." He massages my back for a few more minutes and pats my arm. "I love you. You're a wonderful mom."

He walks out, and I'm left alone to watch the shadow of the tree in our back yard illuminated by the sunset. It is still and silent outside. No wind.

My phone buzzes next to me. Renee wants to know if I'll be coming to fellowship night. She's hosting this time, and our whole Sunday school class will be there for a meal and games. The screen glares at me in the dark room like a grumpy school teacher. I don't want to open the floodgates by responding right away. Renee goes a little nuts with events during the summer.

I leave the phone on my bedside table and try to ignore the second accusing alert. She's been hounding me for a playdate for weeks. I'm not sure how a playdate is supposed to work with a four-month-old and seven-month-old. Liana can army crawl, and Rylie can barely roll over. I suppose she's trying to get me to leave the house more. It is so much work to get Rylie into the car, and it's hot by early morning.

When was the last time I went somewhere besides the grocery store and church? Or Nana Tanya's house. My mother-in-law loves her granddaughter. We've been to her house several Saturdays for dinner. It's easy since she has a crib set up in the guest room and even keeps diapers for us. But going to a party? I don't know if I can do that.

My phone buzzes again.

Don't leave me hanging, Charlotte! You can bring the drinks. I just want to see my bestie.

Bestie. Are we besties? I don't know.

Why isn't there wind? I wish there was.

SIX

"WELCOME, MISS LIANA!" I say to the curly-headed girl streaking like lightning through our front door.

Liana runs past me to Rylie and the basket of toys behind the couch. Renee laughs and shuts our front door behind her.

"Mommy time! Tell me you have coffee, woman," Renee says. "Liana, ask first!"

"She's fine," I say. "I have bubbles we can play with outside later."

"Fabulous. Missile loves bubbles."

I laugh at Liana's nickname. It fits. She streaks from toy to toy in our living room. Rylie watches Liana for a moment before running to her book basket next to the fireplace.

"So we need to do Fourth of July at your house this year, lady," Renee says, adjusting her sandy brown messy bun. "We can just walk down from your back gate to the park for the fireworks."

"Yeah, I guess." We put Rylie to bed early, and I'm not sure she'd like fireworks. But honestly, I don't want to deal with cleaning up after everyone. Or having a gazillion people in my little house.

"You have the perfect back yard for the kids to play. I'd totally help you plan," Renee says.

She totally wouldn't, so I change the subject. "Are you officially done with school?"

"Yep! No more teaching for me!" Renee laughs and pats her belly. "This one is going to be a boy. I can feel it."

"I was really surprised that you decided to quit."

"Oh, I love being home with Missile. She hated daycare anyway."

I can't help but snort. I doubt Renee remembers how she tried to convince me to go back to work part-time and use that same daycare. I cover my laugh with a cough and smile.

"Well, Morgan and I didn't expect you to quit." I can't help but poke her a little after all the comments she made when I left my graphic design job. That feels like a lifetime ago. How have two years flown by so quickly?

"I came home one day from class so tired that I couldn't remember what day it was," Renee is saying. How long was I not paying attention? I don't think I missed much. I'm so spacey lately. I keep forgetting stuff at the grocery store, and I find so many unsent messages on my phone. Maybe I need stronger coffee.

"Missile had a bad day at daycare," Renee continues, "and I ordered pizza for dinner. Casey walks in and tells me he got the promotion, and I told him I was *done* working."

"Oh wow. How did he take that pronouncement?" I say. I can already guess it wasn't pleasant.

"He was mad, but he got over it," Renee says, her voice thick with sarcasm. "He knows when he won't win the argument."

I keep my face the neutrally pleasant mask I have carefully crafted for conversations with Renee and nod. I'm sure Casey definitely knows when he won't win an argument. I think anyone who spends a lot of time with Renee figures out it isn't worth it with her. I wonder if Casey's version of the story will be similar. It's not like he and David talk about their marriages while they play video games, but I've heard some complaining on Casey's end.

I jerk out of my thoughts at the sound of wood hitting Liana's skull.

"Rylie, no hitting!" I say. Liana runs crying to Renee. Rylie frowns defiantly at her, wooden block in hand. Then she takes off into the kitchen and hides behind the counter. Heat creeps into my cheeks.

"I'm sorry, Renee. Is she okay?"

"She's fine. Missile, you're okay, aren't you?"

Missile sniffs and nods. She goes back to playing with the blocks. I try to convince Rylie to apologize, but she says no. I feel nausea creeping through my insides. Renee must think I'm such a pushover not making Rylie obey, but I'm trying. I just don't want a tantrum on top of everything else.

"So, are you going to tell me why you flaked on fellowship night at our house?" Renee says, drumming her fingers on the arm of the couch.

"I wanted to come," I falter. Why does she have to bug me about this every time we talk? This is why I didn't want to have her over, but she wouldn't let it go and I caved.

"You're missing a lot of stuff, girl."

"I go to Sunday school and worship every week," I say.

"Not *every* week." Renee gives me a look.

"Almost every week," I answer with an embarrassed shrug. "But if David is out of town, it's so stressful getting everything ready by myself."

"Well, you need to stay for Sunday school every week,

not just when he's home. Morgan and I miss sitting with you," Renee says. "I'm going to keep calling you out on this, girl. You can't escape me!"

I laugh. As if anyone could escape Renee. She smiles and winks.

"See, there's the Charlotte I know. You need to laugh more," she says. Her eyes soften, and she picks at the handle on her coffee mug. "Mom life is weird, you know? I feel so lost sometimes. I wonder if I'll wake up some morning and wish I was still working."

I nod, unsure how to answer her.

"Do you ever wish you were working?" she asks, her voice quieter than I've ever heard before.

"No," I answer. "Definitely not. Rylie is my job now."

Renee shakes her head as if clearing cobwebs and raises an eyebrow. "Of course, you love it. You're Supermom."

The sentence is tinged with sarcasm, but I don't have time to think about it because I have to break up another toddler fight. It is clear the girls will play better together outside, so Renee takes them to the back yard while I go to the garage for bubbles.

The overhead light is flickering again. David keeps forgetting to change the bulb. I step into the shadows next to the car to rummage in the outside toy box. Digging tools, water play buckets, and bubble wands abound, but the bottle of David's special bubble solution has vanished. I finally notice it on the cement next to the door. I must have forgotten to put it away last time.

There's a shadow on the floor as I walk into the kitchen.

"Renee?"

I round the corner to find an empty dining room. Renee is outside watching the girls from our patio. I shake myself a little and walk back out. I'm seriously seeing things. Rylie has got to start sleeping better at night.

"Did you ever get so sleep-deprived you saw things?" I ask as I set the bubble mixture on our outdoor table. Renee swallows her sip of coffee.

"I totally did. I thought I'd done the laundry one time. I zoned out on the couch and had this weird half-awake dream where I put it all in the washer and dryer. And then I cried when Casey came home and it was all still sitting there on the floor in the laundry room. He made fun of me for weeks!" She rolls her eyes. "He did the laundry that night. And he slept on the couch."

"I keep thinking I'm seeing something out of the corner of my eye, and when I look, it's nothing." I can't believe I said that out loud.

"Like something moves and freaks you out, but it's nothing? Totally normal," Renee says, waving a hand carelessly. "I had spit up on my glasses for two hours once. Thought I was getting cataracts!"

"How did you not notice that when it happened?" I laugh.

"No idea!" Renee says. "I'm all freaking out that I might be going blind, and then I got to look in the mirror. Would have got me right in the eye if I wasn't wearing glasses."

"Gross!"

"Motherhood makes you lose your mind, Charlotte," she says, tapping the side of her forehead with one finger. "Seriously does."

SEVEN

THE MUGGY, cloudy afternoon drags on as I snuggle Rylie in the window seat in our front room. Relaxation is impossible. Every corner of my house is laughing at me. The dust, dirt, smudges, and stains mock my pile of clean laundry. Rylie has knocked three of the five yellow and blue pillows on the floor. She flips through the picture book on my lap and points at the bunny on each page. Her cheek is still red from where she napped on her hand. The pile of laundry on the seat next to us is nearly as tall as she.

"Mama, bunny!"

"Yes, bunny. Can you find it on the next page?"

"Issa brown bunny." Her hair is a halo of messy blonde curls. She wiggles higher onto my lap and raises the book up to my nose. "See? Brown!"

"Yes, brown. What is he doing?"

"He eating."

"What is he eating?"

"Salad."

I nod at the bunny munching lettuce. "Yes, that's basically a salad."

She turns the page and shoves it into my face again. "Bunny!"

"Lots of bunnies! Can you let Mama fold some clothes while you show them to me?"

She solemnly nods. I listen to her narrate each picture as I sort the washcloths from the bigger towels and stack them in a neatly folded tower. If I can get this done, I'll have two chores off my list. Grocery shopping this morning was miserable, but at least I got what I needed. If only Rylie hadn't seen that little pink pony toy when we walked in. My stomach churns as the memory replays for the thousandth time.

The older woman had dyed black hair and thickly drawn eyebrows, and the thick-rimmed glasses on her hooked nose made her look like a vulture. "My girls never behaved like that."

"She's been a little grumpy this morning," I answered as I tried to maneuver around the rice pilaf display next to me without letting tantruming Rylie close enough to a shelf to knock something off. She still managed to kick a box of rice off the display and nearly kicked me in the face as I bent to pick it up.

"You need to give her a good spanking," the vulture lady said with a sniff and walked away, perfectly manicured nails clicking impatiently on the cart handle. Why did the stupid store have to put a toy display on the end of the aisle right where Rylie could see them?

My mother told me to ignore the old lady when I called her from the car. "If she's old, she probably doesn't remember how naughty her kids were, honey," she said.

I sobbed that I would never go to that grocery store again, and my mom laughed.

"Don't be silly. Just don't go if Rylie is having a bad day."

"But she's always having a bad day!" I wailed.

It seems like Mom has to talk me down from crying every week lately. Rylie wrote the book on stubbornness. I'm so tired that my days seem to be blurring together. I don't know how Renee handles two kids.

"Mama, bunny! See black bunny!" Rylie hollers, shoving the book into my face again.

"I see. With a red hat!" If she can stay distracted with the book for a little longer, I'll be done with the towels. The garage door creaks, and Rylie throws the book.

"Daddy home!" She stands up on my lap, slamming her head into my jaw.

I see stars and reach for the towers of washcloths and towels as they topple to the floor. She runs to the kitchen, leaving me sitting in a mess of formerly folded laundry, biting back tears from my bruised jaw. Her tiny hands are noisily fiddling with the garage door, but I know she's not tall enough to open it yet.

"Daddy home! Daddy!" The door creaks, and Rylie squeals.

I rub my smarting jaw and stare at the mess of towels.

"Where's Mama, Rylie?" David says from the kitchen.

"In the front room," I call.

He comes in from the kitchen carrying Rylie like a sack of potatoes over his shoulder. Something in me cracks like thin ice on a pond at the beginning of winter.

"Honey, what happened? Are you okay?" He puts Rylie down and sits down next to me on the laundry, knocking the last folded towel onto the floor.

The tears come unbidden. "I just folded those."

"Oh no! I'm sorry." David throws his hands in the air and looks crestfallen. "I'll help you."

"Owie, Mama!" Rylie pats my arm with all the gentleness of a bulldozer. "You have owie!"

"Mama has an owie?" David asks.

I can't stop crying, so I point to my rapidly swelling chin.

"What happened?"

I nod toward Rylie and keep crying. Rylie's eyes well up with tears, and she pats my knee with her chubby little hand.

"I sowwy, Mama."

"Oh dear, did you bonk Mama?"

"I sowwy!" Rylies cries and buries her face in David's work shirt.

The thought of yet more laundry to wash and dry and fold sends me into a fresh shower of tears.

"Charlie, what's wrong?"

"It was a bad day." I leave the ruins of my clean laundry to find a cold pack for my chin as Rylie follows me, crying and saying she's sorry.

"It's ok, baby," I hitch between sobs. "You didn't mean to."

I know I'm being ridiculous, but I can't stop crying. My little girl pulls on my jeans, still apologizing. David picks her up and helps her give me a kiss on my sore jaw.

"Got to be more careful, silly girl," David says and blows a raspberry on Rylie's cheek. "Be gentle! Like Daddy!"

He calms Rylie's tears while I try to get ahold of my own. The cold pack helps a little. I wipe my eyes as I stand at the kitchen sink and notice a purple stain on the windowpane.

"You have got to be kidding me," I growl at the chunks of blueberry dotting the wall, the window, and the corner of the curtain.

"Whoa, what is that?" David asks.

"Blueberry smoothie. She asked for it and then she

threw it." I rub the dried purple mess furiously with a sponge while I hold the cold pack to my jaw with the other.

"Naughty girl," David says, frowning at Rylie. She huffs and hides behind her lifted elbow.

"And then she threw a tantrum in the grocery store over a toy pony."

"She did? Rylie, were you being hard on Mama today?"

"No!" she shouts and wiggles to get away.

He lets her down on the floor, and she runs to the living room and hides behind the couch.

"I'm sorry, honey."

"And then she wouldn't eat her lunch when we got home." I slosh soapy water on the windowsill to scrub yet another purple dot gone unnoticed. "She fought her nap forever. I barely got the laundry in the dryer, and then she woke up so I couldn't fold anything."

"Hey, do you need this?" David says. He picks up a white recipe card from the floor, and my chest tightens.

"I forgot the chicken." I sit on the floor, put my head in my hands, and cry. It's dumb, but I can't stop myself. "I forgot the chicken."

David is saying something about needing to calm down, but I can't. I don't have what I need to make our dinner, and now that I'm on the floor I see more smoothie spots on the woodwork below the cabinet. I feel so stupid crying over chicken, but I can't help it. A cold shudder goes over me, and I lean my head against the cabinet door.

David tries to help me up, but I don't want to get up.

"The one thing I actually *needed* I forgot because there was this old lady who said I should give Rylie a spanking. I just wanted to get out of there."

"I'll get us some pizza."

"I don't want pizza. I want teriyaki chicken."

"Pizza!" Rylie hollers. She comes bounding into the room from her hiding place behind the couch but stops when she sees me on the floor.

"I can get takeout then."

"But the budget. We're trying to be more careful."

"Charlie, it's okay. We can get something." He kneels next to me and wraps his arms around me, holding me gently, like I'm about to shatter into a million pieces. Maybe I am. "It was a bad day, but it's okay."

I cry into his shoulder.

"Mama, pizza!" Rylie hollers in my ear.

"Rylie, go get your shoes," he says, patting her head.

"No!"

"You and I are going to get Mama something to eat."

"Eat?"

"Yes, go get your shoes so you can help Daddy."

I hear her little feet slapping against the cold tile as she runs across the kitchen for her shoes.

"It was a really bad day," I whisper to David.

"Good grief, there's more smoothie down here!"

"It was on the ceiling, too."

"We need more secure sippy cups," he says. "You'd think someone would have invented one."

"That one was supposed to be unspillable," I snort.

"I should have gone into children's cups instead of aerospace engineering," he says. "I'd make a truly unspillable sippy."

"It would have to be pink with bears," I say. "That's the only acceptable design in the whole universe."

"Her Royal Highness the Empress of Madsenia has issued a decree?"

"She has. Most vehemently."

"Rylie! Bring me your shoes, little girl!" he yells to the other room.

Her tiny feet slap on the tile as she runs into the kitchen.

"Mama, pizza!" she hollers. She dumps a plate of play pizza on my lap and sits on the floor.

"Thank you, Empress of Madsenia," I say.

"Mama eat!" She picks up the plastic pizza slice and holds it under my nose expectantly.

I wipe my eyes and pretend to take a bite.

"All done!" She throws the slice back onto the plate and throws her hands in the air.

"Rylie, shoes. Go get your shoes," David reminds her gently.

"I wuv you, Mama!" She says, patting my cheek. "I wuv you."

"I love you, too, baby. Go get your shoes." My breath is uneven from crying, but I manage to smile and kiss her hand. She runs around the corner to the shoe basket in the laundry room. David picks up the pizza slice.

"I think she's sorry, Mama," he says. "How about I get us teriyaki from the Chinese place on Seventh? We haven't gone there in a long time."

"That's too spicy for Rylie."

"I'll get her something else. Why don't you go wash your face while I take her with me to get the food?"

He kisses my forehead and waves me away to our bedroom to clean up as he carries Rylie out to the car.

I slowly walk to our room. Nothing makes sense today. When I think about it, nothing truly terrible happened. Why am I so upset over small things? Maybe it's "death by a million paper cuts," like Morgan says. All these little things piling up until I lose it.

I wet a washcloth and listen to the bathroom clock tick

as I dab my swollen face. My eyes are red from crying, and my jaw has an ugly welt. I notice a purple spot on the elbow of my shirt. More smoothie. I went to the grocery store with smoothie stains on my elbow. Renee would think that's hilarious, but I don't think I'll tell her.

I hang the washcloth on the shower door to dry and walk into our bedroom. There's so much to do. If I fold the laundry first, I might have time to vacuum the living room before David gets home, but the blueberry smoothie stains are gnawing at the back of my mind. I can almost feel them seeping into the woodwork until they're permanent.

The water doesn't want to warm up and sends chills down my arm as I soak the sponge. Outside, the sky is growing darker, and the wind has picked up. I flick on the overhead light, and it glows a sickly green. The smoothie spots make a purple trail from the underside of the counter next to the sink and down the side of the cabinet where the door meets the frame, pooling under the bottom of the cabinet.

The dried magenta mess reminds me of alien blood in some terrible science fiction movie. I end up on my side, cheek nearly against the tile floor as I try to get the best angle. My nose is running from all the crying, and I sniff.

Feet.

I see someone's stocking feet on the floor next to my hand. I scream and jerk away, kicking. I blindly run to the living room, gripping the sponge and screaming.

"Go away!"

I'm afraid to look back at the intruder. My stomach lurches as I wait for them to respond, but I hear nothing but the blood rushing in my ears.

I peek into the kitchen. It's empty and silent. My feet are heavy as lead, but I force myself to walk back into the room, past the kitchen table, to the other side of the counter.

The pantry is empty. The garage door is closed and locked. I steady myself against the counter and try to get my heartbeat under control.

Rylie's play pizza. Two of the pieces are wedged against the cabinet at an odd angle. I kneel down next to them and put my head close to them and laugh out loud. I must be losing my mind because they don't look anything like a pair of feet.

Pizza feet. Dull giggles spill out of me.

"I'm such an idiot," I mutter to my daughter's toys.

I toss the plastic pizza over my shoulder into the living room and scrub the purple spots furiously. At least David wasn't home to see me act like a psycho.

Crash!

Lightning rips across the sky, and the thunder rattles the windows. I watch the dark boiling clouds outside the kitchen window from my spot on the floor, and my fingers ache as I scrub harder.

Another flash lights up the sky, and suddenly the overhead light goes off. I hear the electricity click and blink out.

"Stupid house!" I groan. Why does the power always go out when it storms?

I finish scrubbing the smoothie stains by the light of a flashlight and go to the front room to refold the clothes. So much for vacuuming. The power is off for who knows how long. I call David to warn him he won't be able to open the garage door. Rylie is screaming in the background. Good. At least she's being terrible for Daddy, too. I don't care if that's a terrible thing to think.

I sit on the window seat and finish the towels, Rylie's clothes, and half of ours as the rain pours. The wind whis-

tles in the chimney and makes the windows creak. The thick
wet air is suffocating, and every flash of lightning makes me
jump.

I grope the walls as I walk down the dark hall toward our
bedroom with the basket of towels. My familiar house is
shrouded in alien shadows. I'm being silly. This is ridiculous. Why am I afraid to go into my own bedroom?

Lightning slices across the room from the backyard
window. The stark shadows look like someone sitting on my
side of the bed.

I swallow a scream and run to the living room, abandoning the basket in the hallway as thunder shakes the roof.
I curl up on the couch with Rylie's blanket, still shaking. The
storm rages outside, and I put my fingers in my ears. I'm sick
to my stomach. Every flash of lightning hurts my eyes.

"Charlie, are you there?"

David shakes my shoulder. I jerk away from him and
grip the back of the couch.

"I...I don't..."

Rylie is throwing a fit on the hallway floor behind him. I
put my fingers in my ears again to block out her screaming.
David gives me a look.

"Why didn't you open the door when I knocked?"

"I didn't hear you," I say.

"You didn't hear me?"

"No."

"Were you asleep or something?" he demands.

"No."

He looks angry, and I realize his hair is wet. He hands
me the take-out bag and goes to the hallway to grab a
screaming Rylie.

"What happened?"

"We got soaked waiting for you to open the door," he

says over Rylie's tantrum. I hear a clicking noise, and the lights blink back on.

"I'll get a towel," I say. "I'm sorry, David. I didn't hear you at all."

"How? You were right there."

"I just didn't."

I retreat to the hallway, flipping on lights as I go, and grab a clean towel from the basket in the hallway. Our room is silent and empty through the open door. I walk back to the front room, gather Rylie up in the towel, and carry her to her room to get dry.

After a struggle, I walk out with a very grumpy Rylie in dry pajamas to find David has set up the table with our dinner.

"I think you need to talk to Darren," he says.

"What?"

"From church. You know, the counselor?" he says, buckling Rylie into her toddler chair. "I think you need to talk to him. Or maybe a doctor."

"Why?"

"Because you're shaking like..." he stabs a piece of chicken with his fork and rolls his eyes in frustration, "Like my cousin's chihuahua that's scared of everything on the planet."

"I am not."

"Look at your hands."

"I'm tired," I say, balling my hands into fists.

"Did you drink one of my energy drinks or something?"

"No! Those things are gross."

"I'm worried about you," David says. "I come in to find you cowering on the couch—" I give him a sharp look, and he raises both hands. "Fine. *Sitting* on the couch under a blanket. With your fingers in your ears. You were freaking out, Charlie. Don't try to tell me you weren't."

I want to contradict him, but I remember the pizza feet in the kitchen. I hand Rylie her chicken nuggets instead.

"And this isn't new. You are on edge all the time. You can't focus. Even when Rylie's sleeping, you never sleep."

"If I don't do chores while she naps, they never get done."

"Who cares about the chores! I don't!" David says a little too loudly. He bites his lip and shakes his head. "You need to talk to someone. You were up the whole night last night, weren't you?"

I keep my eyes fixed on my teriyaki chicken. "I'll be okay," I say, my eyes on Rylie's curious face, watching the two of us.

"You need to talk to someone or at least get something to help you sleep."

"I don't want to." All those pills have a million side effects, and I feel yucky enough already. Every time I shut my eyes, I wonder what horrible thing will happen while I'm sleeping. When I do fall asleep, I wake up in a panic like I did this morning, looking for Rylie. David squeezes my hand.

"You need to," David says, his eyes on Rylie. "Darren's number is on the church website."

"I know."

"Charlotte, what is it? Please tell me."

I don't want to remember, but I do. It was so blurry in the hospital, but once we came home, the memory crawled back and took me prisoner. That awful moment when I felt myself bleeding out on that hospital bed. I fix my eyes on the floor and bite my tongue hard. I have cried enough today.

But once I think about it, I can't stop replaying it. The agonizing pain in my stomach and the spinning colors like fireworks going off in my skull. I remember David's terrified eyes being the only thing I could recognize. And then Rylie being taken away by the nurse. Her soft cry as she disappeared out the door, and the hospital room door shut behind her. I can't handle this memory anymore.

"Charlie, please," he whispers. "I want you back."

"I'm right here," I say angrily.

I want to eat my teriyaki chicken. Rylie is still watching us as she eats her nuggets. I don't like the way she's looking at me. Like she's afraid for me. Or maybe afraid *of* me.

"Please call Darren."

"Okay. Tomorrow," I say, hoping it's enough to make him leave me alone. I don't want to scare Rylie any more than I already have. I'll probably forget. Or maybe I'll actually call. Maybe he can help me without me having to talk much. Maybe we can talk about the Bible or whatever and leave seeing things because I'm sleep-deprived out of it.

EIGHT

MY SKIRT WON'T LIE flat no matter how much I smooth it. I'm early, but I wish I'd sat in the car for a few more minutes. The lobby chair is stiff against my back. I wish Darren didn't have a secretary. I still feel naked sitting in this office, as if all my life were spread out in front of her.

My phone vibrates. My mother-in-law has sent me a picture of Rylie playing in our back yard. Rylie is showing the camera a large dandelion. I should get out there and weed next week. Another photo pops up of Rylie grinning from ear to ear, running toward the camera. I'm so glad Nana Tanya wasn't busy this afternoon. I wouldn't want to leave Rylie with a stranger, and she loves her grandma.

"She has my schedule. I think next Wednesday or Thursday?" I hear Darren's voice from the hallway.

A woman's voice says something unintelligible. It's familiar. I strain to recognize the voice even though I know I shouldn't.

It is Tori Butler. She comes around the corner into the lobby. Her eyes are a little red, and she startles when she sees me. I can't believe Tori is here. She teaches preschool

Sunday school and helps with the children's choirs. I wonder what she could be talking to Darren about. I wave while wishing a hole in the earth would open up and swallow me. What if she tells people she saw me?

"Hi, Charlotte," she says, brushing her blonde waves behind her ears. She smiles, but she looks drained. I know from the decorative mirror on the wall behind the secretary that I'm wearing the same anemic smile.

"Hi." What else can we say? I can't ask her what is wrong. She can't ask me.

The last time I talked to her was at my front door when Rylie was born. She was the first person to show up with a casserole. I wonder if she remembers how I cried. I've been embarrassed to talk to her ever since.

"Rylie is getting so big," Tori says.

"Yes, she is!" I answer a little too enthusiastically, but I'm grateful she's given us both something to say. "She's so talkative now."

"I love playing with her when I work in the nursery."

I can't say it out loud, but I hate putting Rylie in the nursery. I've been keeping her with us in service most of the time because it feels safer. Is that normal? The thought makes my stomach curdle. Maybe David is right. I busy myself with my purse to keep myself from crying.

"I need to go," she says gently.

Maybe she has seen my tears. Maybe not. Either way, she is leaving. I try to work up a smile to say goodbye. But she stops and turns back to me. She looks me straight in the eye and nods to herself.

"You should come to the women's Bible study on Tuesdays with me, Charlotte," she says. "Grace is a great teacher."

"Oh, I didn't know she taught." How did I miss that my

Sunday school teacher's wife is teaching the women's Bible study? I'm a bigger mess than I thought.

"You can sit with me," she says.

"Isn't the sign-up closed?"

"I'm in charge of the list, so I can add you when I get home," she says. "We always order extra materials, too."

"When does it start?"

"Two weeks from Sunday. Renee is coming now that she's not teaching. And Miss Georgina runs the child care."

That's Rylie's favorite Sunday school teacher, and I think Tori knows it. It makes me feel terrible that she seems to care so much about me and my daughter when I know so little about her. I should be more consistent. I've been making so many excuses to stay home. She must think I'm an unorganized mess, but she seems genuinely excited that I might join her. I've been so lonely that I swallow and nod.

"That would be great."

"Awesome! I'll tell Grace. Do you have my number? Never mind, just tell me yours. I'll put it in right now and text you all the details." She hunts in her purse for her phone. I'd protest, but she looks so happy I can't argue. She taps in my number as I recite it. "Gotcha! I'll see you on Sunday. I'm not working in the nursery this week."

Tori disappears out into the normal world, and I fiddle with my purse again to avoid looking at anyone. I don't know why I'm so flattered that she invited me. Tori does that with everyone. She's on the greeting team in the morning, and she helps in the nursery all the time. I remember Renee joking that she's everywhere at once.

"Charlotte?" Darren is standing in the hallway ahead of me. "I'm ready when you are."

The walk down the hallway seems to take longer than it should, and I almost chicken out. I want to go home, but I step through the doorway into his office. He shuts the door and gestures to two chairs opposite the desk. Darren's office is simple, but I notice it has that unusual quiet of extra insulation.

"Would you like some water?" he asks, adjusting the collar of his blue polo shirt. His dark mustache and thinning hair make him seem almost grandfatherly.

"Yes, thank you."

He hands me a bottle of water from a box behind his chair as he sits across from me.

"So. What would you like to get out of this appointment?"

"I guess I need help."

"Is there something specific?"

I examine my fingernails. "David thinks I need help."

"Do you think you need help?" He folds his hands in his lap and leans back into the chair.

"I don't know. Maybe. I don't like talking about myself."

"Is that what you think you'll be doing?"

"I guess." I pick at a hangnail. I feel like I'm in an interrogation room, just waiting for him to shove a lamp in my face to get a confession.

"You know, you are not the first person to be nervous about seeing me," he says. He walks over to the desk. He pulls out a Bible from a drawer.

"It is hard to trust someone enough to open up, especially in church. We all have holy faces we wear on Sunday. I know I do." He looks back at me. "We don't want anyone to see that we are hurting. Because godly people don't have problems, right?" He opens the Bible to a page that looks well worn and hands it to me.

"Read verse nine out loud." He has handed me the first chapter of Ecclesiastes.

"What has been is what will be, and what has been done is what will be done, and there is nothing new under the sun," I read, my voice breaking.

"Charlotte, there is nothing new under the sun. I'm here to listen, to pray with you, and to be an objective voice for you. Godly people *do* have difficulties and pain and suffering, and we all need help sometimes. And if it's something where you need medication, I work with several Christian psychiatrists for referrals."

"I don't want to take any medicine," I say quickly. "Side effects and stuff. I just don't want to."

"I have lots of options that don't involve medicine, depending on what your concerns are," he says, leaning forward with open hands.

I don't think people who see shadows move are the kind who show up in this office. Maybe if I tell him my other "symptoms," he can help with those. It won't be lying, right?

"I'm having a hard time sleeping." It's the truth.

"How long have you had a hard time sleeping?"

"A long time."

"Can you point to a time when it started to bother you?"

"I guess about a year ago," I lie. "Rylie was sleeping through the night, but I still couldn't."

"So she isn't waking up, but you're still waking up?"

"I can't fall asleep. And I wake up all the time."

"Why do you think that is?"

"I'm scared." It comes out before I can stop it. But I am. I'm terrified. I can't tell him what I'm terrified of. He sits in his chair with his hands folded in his lap, waiting for me to continue. The silence is oppressive. "I'm scared of everything."

"You're feeling anxious."

"Yes. I can't go to sleep like that. I feel like..." Maybe it wouldn't give me away to say this. "I feel like someone is watching me."

"Like who is watching you?"

"I don't know." Truth. I have no idea who the figure is, or if it is anyone.

"You feel like someone is watching you."

"That sounds crazy," I say.

"Why do you think that sounds crazy?"

"Because who would be watching me? It's ridiculous."

"Tell me about that feeling."

"It's horrible." I wait for him to respond, but he is content to listen. "I hate it. I'm scared something bad will happen and that someone is waiting for me to mess up. It's making me nervous just sitting here talking about it."

"It sounds overwhelming."

"Yes. It makes it impossible to sleep."

"What kinds of thoughts go through your head when you can't sleep?"

And now I know I have to lie. He's going to ask me questions I can't answer.

"It's like if I sleep, something awful will happen. I don't know what. Just something awful."

"Do you think about Rylie?"

"Sometimes." I think about shadows that move when they shouldn't and how I'm going crazy. Why does he have to ask me all these questions? "I don't want her to be afraid too."

He smiles and nods. "How old is Rylie now?"

"Two and a half."

"Wow, she's getting big."

"Yes, she's growing every day. She talks constantly now."

"What does she talk about?"

"Dancing. She wants to be a ballerina. Or a pirate. A dancing pirate." I giggle despite the lump in my throat.

"A dancing pirate. That's very creative." Darren grins. "Can I make you aware of something? You're happy talking about her. You are smiling, and you sat up when you said that. Your body language completely changed."

I slump a little.

"Do you feel happy most of the time with her?"

"I think so." Is that true? I think it's true.

"But you are still scared of something, and I sense from what you've said that this has been a problem for awhile. Maybe since Rylie was born?" How did he know that?

"Yes."

"Do you remember me coming to see you when you were in the hospital?"

"Yes."

"I'd like to talk about that for a minute. Can we do that?"

"I guess."

"Can you tell me what happened when Rylie was born?"

"I had a placental abruption. I was bleeding out." I hate telling this story. "They took me in an ambulance. It was horrible."

"I'm sure it was," he says.

"It was the worst thing that's ever happened to me." I focus on the floor and try not to cry.

"You must have been terrified."

"I felt myself dying."

"Do you still remember what that feels like?"

"Yes."

He watches me, his hands clasped in his lap.

"Has that feeling ever gone away?"

Until he spoke the sentence, I would have said no. Now I see it in everything. That fear has seeped over every part of my life. I am cloaked in its shadow. Have I ever been able to enjoy my daughter? Have I ever been joyful with her?

"No. I didn't think about it, but it never has," I answer. "I'm so scared Rylie will get hurt or lost or something bad will happen to her. And me."

"Is that the same feeling that you get when you try to sleep?"

I nod, because I can't stop crying.

"It's making you anxious right now, isn't it?"

"Yes. It's been that way ever since Rylie was born. It's like there's a bomb, except I can't see the timer, and I don't know when it's going to go off."

The longer I think about it, the thicker that cloak of fear becomes. It all makes sense. The tears spill over. Renee has called me overprotective, but it's more than that.

"I didn't realize. I didn't see how bad..." It's too hard to speak. All the moments where I've thought I was seeing things fill my mind, and I can see how silly they are. I'm always on alert for something that wants to hurt me, but there's nothing there. Those stupid pieces of play pizza in the kitchen and the shadows on the walls in Rylie's room were just normal, everyday things. "No wonder I can't sleep." I wipe my eyes and lean forward. "How do I stop it? How do I stop being afraid?"

"I think that will take some time, and we'll want to keep talking about it. But we should start with 2 Timothy 1:7."

"God did not give us a spirit of fear..." I look away from him self consciously. "I learned it in Sunday school when I was little."

"Then finish it."

"But of power, love, and of a sound mind."

"Let's grip tight to that, okay? Power, love, and a sound mind. That's what He wants to give you. I'd like you to meditate on that verse. Put it on your bathroom mirror or the sink in the kitchen. Keep it close. Say it to yourself often." He stands and rummages in his desk. "On the practical side, I have some suggestions that might help you sleep."

He gives me some handouts about sleep hygiene, which is a thing, apparently. Then he teaches me a calming breathing pattern that seems like it could help. He suggests supplementing with melatonin. That's better than telling me to take one of those sleeping pills that can make you act crazy. The suggestions are good, but I'm overwhelmed. This fear has consumed me. How can I get out from under this? He catches my eye again and smiles.

"You were hoping to fix it all right away, weren't you?" he says. "I can't tap you on the head with a magic wand and make everything better. I wish I could. Sometimes God sweeps in and miraculously heals, but more often, He works slowly."

NINE

"CHARLOTTE, HI!" Tori says, waving at me as I walk into Sunday school. Her blonde hair falls in soft beach waves, and she has a new pale pink manicure since I saw her on Wednesday. It seems like there is an extra weight to her voice. Am I imagining it?

"Good morning," I say around the lump in my throat.

She sent me a text message with the women's Bible study information after she saw me at Darren's office, but seeing her in person is different. Her smile is genuine, and the hug she gives me is strong and friendly.

"Where's your hubby?" she asks, gesturing for me to follow her to the front row.

"Seattle," I say.

"I've always wanted to visit Seattle!" She pats the chair next to her.

I hate the front row, but I sit because I don't want to hurt her feelings. "I guess Greg is working, too?"

"Yes, every week, it seems like."

I feel exposed with my back to everyone else. She fetches us both cups of coffee, and I wonder as I stir in the sugar and creamer why we haven't spent more time together before now.

"Charlotte, you're actually here!" Renee says as she walks in. She grins deviously, her brown messy bun bobbing with her steps. "I'm going to sign you up to bring donuts so you have to come next Sunday, too. Hi, Tori!"

"Missile go to nursery okay?" Tori asks as she hugs Renee.

"Ugh, I don't want to talk about it," Renee says. "So you're abandoning me and Morgan, Charlotte?"

"Um..." I can't think of anything to say. I'm never sure if Renee is joking or serious.

"She's been promoted to the fabulous row," Tori says, gesturing to the two of us. "There are rules, you know. On Sundays, we wear pink!"

She points to my skirt, and I laugh. My flouncy pink skirt and floral blouse match her pale pink jumpsuit. She still looks much more put together with her manicured nails and floral sandals.

"I didn't know this row was exclusive," Renee says with mock offense.

"Very," Tori says. "Invitation only."

I laugh and push my hair back from my face. The memory of Darren's office feels like a cloud hanging over me as Renee complains that she hates pink.

Tori would have to admit to being at Darren's office herself to talk about it, so maybe she'll keep quiet. I silently pray she won't mention it. I don't want to explain myself to Renee. Or anyone.

"Maybe you can get Charlotte to actually talk in class," Renee says, poking me in the shoulder.

"Prayer requests! What's going on in everyone's life this

week?" Larry announces before taking a bite of a jelly donut.

Renee sits down a row away with Casey, Morgan, and Morgan's husband. Tori elbows me, and I stiffen. Is she expecting me to ask for prayer seeing Darren?

She holds up her coffee cup and points for me to do the same.

"To pink," she whispers and taps her paper cup against mine.

"To pink," I whisper back. The knot in my chest feels a little looser.

I wait for a bomb to drop, but Tori doesn't say a word during prayer requests. The knot loosens further, and I lean back into my chair.

"Charlotte, I see you're alone this week," Larry says. "Is David on a trip?"

"Yes, he's in Seattle eating lots of fish and chips and trying out every coffee shop he can find."

Tori leans toward me. "Gross," she whispers. "I hate fish."

"Me too. That's why he's eating it far away from me."

"Are you free for lunch today?" she asks. "We can go somewhere Greg and David wouldn't like."

"That would be fun!"

"It's a date then."

Larry clears his throat. "Do I need to separate you two?"

"Don't interrupt," Tori declares with a dismissive wave of her hand. "We're bonding over a mutual hatred of fish."

"You're both going to hate the lesson," Casey says from behind his coffee cup. "It's Jesus feeding the five thousand."

Tori swoons in horror. "Fish! We would starve!"

"No, we could fill up on bread," I laugh. Who am I right now, laughing and joking with my class? It feels good, like I've set down a heavy backpack at the end of a hike.

"It's too bad that kid didn't have lasagna or something," Larry says with a grin. "That's the version from the Message Bible: Jesus feeds the five thousand with never-ending trays of lasagna."

The joke brings the house down, and we finally start the lesson. Putting Rylie in the nursery usually makes me sick, but the nausea hasn't come today. I wonder if it is Darren's advice or Tori's one-liners. Either way, I enjoyed myself. Tori and I agree to meet at a restaurant with a playground, and I head to the nursery to grab Rylie. My girl has fallen asleep in the teacher's arms. She barely stirs while I carry her to the car, but she rears back when I set her in the car seat.

"Mama!" She scrubs her eyes with her fists and pulls at the elastic holding her soft curls out of her face.

"You woke up!" I say to my sleepy toddler. "Are you hungry?"

She launches into her usual toddler rant about the unfairness of life. I even understand a few words. Mostly "no," "nap," and "chicken nuggets." The drive to the restaurant is all excited chatter about chicken nuggets and Daddy coming home.

"Hi!" she screeches through the window when she sees Tori waiting for us.

"Miss Rylie, did you have fun this morning?"

Rylie hugs Tori's legs and babbles as we head inside and order lunch. She gets her beloved chicken nuggets and proceeds to tell the entire restaurant about them at the top of her lungs. She is so loud. I wish she could sit quietly for a few moments and eat without having to tell the world about it. It feels like everyone's eyes are on us, and I want to hide under the table.

"She's adorable, Charlotte. No one cares," Tori says with a smile. My discomfort must be written on my face.

"I'm sorry she's so loud."

Tori winks. "You should see Liana."

"Ha! Yes, Liana comes over a lot."

"Does she sing for you?"

"Of course."

"I sing!" says Rylie. "I'm a teapot short and tout. Here my humble! Here my pout!"

Tori sings along with Rylie and convinces her to finish her food while I eat my own. I finally let Rylie run into the play area and watch her through the window. She tosses her church shoes into a cubby, and I wince as her white tights hit the gray playroom floor. Those will need stain remover as soon as we get home.

"You're a great mom, Charlotte," Tori says, interrupting my laundry concerns.

"Oh, I don't know about that."

"You are. Take the compliment with a smile, lady," she says with a tone of giving orders. "So tell me about yourself! We've never really gotten to talk, have we?"

"No, we haven't," I say.

I'm not sure what to say. I'm too distracted by Rylie climbing the stairs. Tori sits forward and sips her iced tea. I feel so scatterbrained right now. I've never been good at introducing myself to people.

"How about I start?" she says, taking a sip of her tea. "I came here for college at Northern because I wanted a Christian school."

"What was your major?" I ask.

"Marketing with a minor in fashion design."

"That explains why you always look amazing."

"You're a sweetheart." She flips her hair back from her

face with a grin. "Anyway, I was saved in high school, and I wanted to go to college somewhere that would help me grow. Rylie is up in the airplane," she interrupts herself, following my eyes in the busy play place.

"Sorry," I say. I feel my cheeks burning. I'm just waiting for Rylie to fall or hit another kid or do something where I have to take her back home. "I can't turn off the mom radar."

"Does she ever sit still?"

"When she's sleeping."

Tori laughs and leans back against the booth. "So, where was I? I met Greg in the college group, and we dated for a little while. First relationship I ever had with a Christian guy, and I ended up marrying him!"

"Did he go to Northern, too?"

"No, State. And it was all up in the air until he graduated. He wasn't sure where he'd work, and he 'didn't want to string me along,' he said." She rolls her eyes. "Then he got the job at RHL and proposed with a ball of string."

"What?" I'm confused, but she's grinning.

"He said, 'I decided to return all that string,' and handed me this massive ball of yarn." She laughs and holds her hands out as if she's holding a basketball. "And then he said, 'open it.' Girl, I had to unwind that stuff for almost half an hour."

"Oh no!" I laugh. It sounds like Greg has a goofy sense of humor.

"He put little notes on it that I had to read in order as I unwound it. Then in the middle was the ring box."

"That's so cute."

"Except when I opened the box, the ring was another loop of string," she says, laughing again. "He had the ring in his pocket the whole time. Just wanted to make me unwind all that yarn," she says, looking down at the marquise-cut diamond ring on her hand. "I kept it, too. I figured I could do something cute with it someday. So what about you?"

"We moved here for David's job, and we loved Larry and Grace's class at Fellowship so much that we stayed."

"So, how did you meet?"

I tell her about meeting David in the cafeteria and our nerdy argument. I lean my head on my hand, unable to keep from grinning at the memory.

Tori looks up into the playground. "She's so funny. Have I mentioned she's my favorite?"

"Your favorite?"

"In the nursery. Rylie is my favorite to watch."

"You're sweet to say that."

"I'm never bored if she's there. She has so much energy."

"That gets her into trouble," I say. "I'm sorry she's such a handful. I feel like I'm not doing a very good job."

"Okay, stop it."

"I'm sorry?"

Tori drills me with her perfectly lined brown eyes, and her words are crisp. "Stop beating yourself up. You're a good mom."

The words sting. I should leave. I start to reach for my purse, but Tori's voice stops me.

"Look at her. That young lady in there is the cutest thing on two feet, and you get to be her mom."

"I don't...I'm not..." Words choke in my throat, and I look through the window at Rylie, a blur of purple on the playground.

"I'm sorry if that came out a little snippy, but I don't like it when gals talk bad about themselves. You are a good mom."

Tori sure seems perfect. She's beautiful and funny.

Tears sneak out of the corners of my eyes, and I fumble in my purse for a tissue. "Thank you," I whisper.

"Oh, I didn't mean to make you cry." She bites her lip.

"No, I needed to hear that."

Tori smiles until it crinkles the corners of her eyes. "Good."

"I thought having kids would be so much different." The words are catching in my throat, but I'm determined not to cry. I take a bite of my lunch and wipe my eyes. "Rylie wears me out."

"She needs gymnastics. Or ballet!" Tori says with a big grin. "There's a dance studio next to where I work. I wonder if she's old enough?"

"You sound like my mother-in-law," I say, rolling my eyes. "She gave us this ballerina lamp for Rylie. It totally doesn't go with the room. Every week Nana says something about putting her in dance. But Rylie would have to obey a teacher for that to work."

"I'll check that studio for you," Tori says. "But don't feel obligated!" She points at the top of the play place. "She's in the airplane again."

Her phone buzzes. She nods and points without looking at it. "That's Greg. I'd better head home."

She packs to leave and hugs Rylie goodbye.

"I'll see you next Sunday. Or maybe earlier in the week?" she asks.

My stomach drops as I realize she's talking about seeing Darren. I fumble a noncommittal answer, and she hugs me. She smells like some kind of floral perfume. I imagine it's expensive.

"I'm glad we got to talk," she whispers.

How did I end up friends with Tori? I would never have thought she would want to talk to me, much less invite me to lunch. Is she worried I'll tell people I saw her at Darren's office? Maybe she was just spending time with me to gauge if I'll gossip about her.

My mom would tell me to stop overanalyzing things and just be glad for a new friend. But if I'm so uncomfortable knowing that someone else has seen *me* at the counselor's office, I can't imagine how nervous perfect Tori Butler must feel.

TEN

I'M SITTING in my car in the parking lot of the church, but I'm not sure if I want to be here. Rylie is pretending to read a book in her car seat behind me. The Bible study starts in ten minutes, but I haven't turned off the car. I don't know if I belong here.

I jump at a knock on my window. Tori waves at me through the glass and waits for me to roll down the window.

"Sorry I scared you! I forgot something in my car and saw you. I'm so glad you came! Come on. We can sit together."

I gather my Bible and Rylie's backpack and follow her into the church. Rylie dashes into the nursery before I can even say goodbye. I hand the teacher her backpack.

"I have my phone with me if she gets upset," I falter.

Rylie doesn't give me a second glance as she searches for toys. The nursery worker's fluffy gray hair doesn't move a millimeter as she nods and shoos me out. Tori beckons me down the hall.

"I am so glad you came. I told my boss that having Tuesday mornings off is non-negotiable. I never miss!"

"Where do you work?"

"I'm the assistant manager at Pepper's. You know it?"

"No." I shrug.

"It's home goods. Fancy vintage stuff I can't afford," she laughs. "But I get to make it look pretty and sell it to other people. We don't open shop on Sundays, so I get to go to church."

I follow her meekly into the large room the youth group uses on Sunday mornings. A large wooden cross stands on the side of the short stage, and the walls are covered with bad fake graffiti that makes me cringe. They need a better color scheme.

I imagine everyone's eyes on me as Tori leads me to a seat close to the front next to the middle aisle next to Morgan, who is busy on her phone. I sit between them and watch Tori gather her Bible and study book. Her long blonde hair flows over her shoulders in perfect waves. Her jeans and gray blouse are casual with the effortlessly cool vibe I have never been able to master. Even her nails are painted a soft gray to match. I wonder more than ever why she would ever be in Darren's office.

"Renee is running late." So Renee comes, too. I stare at the floor. Renee is right. I've been a hermit. No wonder David has been worried about me.

I don't hear much of the announcements. I have no idea how they do things here, and the lack of familiarity has me on edge. Grace asks us to get into groups of five or six to share prayer requests and get to know each other. We flip our chairs around into a group. I recognize Debbie, an older woman who teaches in the youth group.

"I'm the old lady here," she says with a laugh. "Nice to meet you, Charlotte. Aren't you Rylie's mama?"

"Yes, she's my ball of energy."

"Y'all, Missile is going to be the death of me," Renee sputters as she flips another chair around and dumps her purse on the floor. "I could not make her get clothes on this morning. What did I miss?"

"You're up for snacks next week," Tori tells her.

"Of course, I am," she answers and sticks her tongue out.

"Just bring goldfish," I say, raising an eyebrow.

Renee hides her head in her hands. "That was for the children's museum," she says. "I forgot to take it out of my bag."

"Likely story," Morgan says, teasing.

"We met at the park a few weeks ago," I say, "and she pulls this massive bag of goldfish out of the diaper bag. It was as big as my head!" I rarely have a reason to tease Renee, and it feels good.

"It was for a big group!" Renee protests. "Plus, I keep snacks around for emergencies."

"Hoarder," Morgan says in a sing-song voice.

"That's called being a mama," Debbie laughs. "I was the same with Cheerios way back when. Always had a bag of three."

"Ok, let's do prayer requests. Renee's hoarding is already on the list," Tori says, still giggling. Her laughter makes me feel a little more at ease.

"You wait until it's you, woman," Renee says to Tori, wrinkling her nose.

"My son is taking an MCAT practice test this weekend, so pray that he does well and that it helps him get ready for the real thing," Debbie says. She turns to me, "He's going to be a doctor like his daddy, but he has to get into med school. Oh, and my sister's friend has been diagnosed with some thyroid disorder."

She continues with more details, and I'm tempted to

look up the symptoms on the internet and figure out what disorder she is talking about. I hear David's voice in my head, saying, "*Don't do it, wife. Don't ask the internet if you're dying again.*"

Renee sarcastically raises her hand and sighs a dramatic sigh. "Pray for me to find something to occupy the Missile. Liana is wearing me out, and I need some kind of physical activity for her."

"That reminds me!" Tori says. "There's a dance studio near where I work, and I saw they have beginner ballet classes. I was talking to Charlotte about it the other day. I checked, Charlotte. Rylie is old enough for them! They let you do one trial class for free. "

"Charlotte, we should sign our girls up!" Renee says, almost too enthusiastically. "They'd get to do something together."

"I don't know."

"Come on! It will be fun. It's free, right?"

I try to smile. I hate when Renee puts me on the spot. "I guess a trial class could be fun. I'm not sure if Rylie will follow instructions."

"That's why we take them together," Renee laughs. "That way they'll be troublemakers together!"

I end up agreeing to the trial class. It's probably a bad idea, but at least I don't have to go alone. I thought I wanted to be alone, but sitting in this circle, I realize that's the last thing I want. I've always been jumpy, but church used to be my safe place. My friends were safe. I didn't realize how much I had been holding them at arm's length. I've missed them.

"You're going to keep coming, aren't you?" Tori asks as we gather our things.

"Of course she is!" Renee says as if she's giving orders.

Tori follows me to the nursery and then to my car with Rylie.

"Did you have fun?" she asks as I buckle Rylie into her car seat. "I really hope you'll come back."

"I think I will," I say.

"Wonderful! I knew asking you to come was a Holy Spirit nudge. I'll see you next week then." She gives me a light hug as I shut the car door. "Or maybe tomorrow if you'll be at the church again." She says the phrase slowly, and I know she is asking if I'll be going to see Darren.

I smile weakly. "Probably."

"If you want to go to lunch or something after, we probably could."

"David's mom watches Rylie for me, so I'd hate to leave her too long," I say. David is coming with me tomorrow, too, but I don't want to admit that. Not yet.

"Let me know if you change your mind."

"Of course." I want to ask her why *she* is seeing Darren. Maybe she'll tell me without me asking.

"Come by Pepper's any time! I'll sell you all kinds of things you don't need." She laughs.

"David will love that!" I say, the sarcasm a little thicker than I meant. Her blonde waves bounce behind her as she walks to her car and waves goodbye.

I look down at my bare nails and boring blue T-shirt. Do I really belong here? Rylie demands lunch from the back seat, and I breathe in slowly. I hope getting more involved isn't a mistake.

ELEVEN

"ARE YOU EXCITED, RYLIE?" David says next to me. Rain is coming down in sheets as we drive to the studio. I hope we can get into the building without getting too wet.

"I dance, Daddy!"

"I can't wait to watch you," he says. "So, how long will this be?" he asks me.

"Not long. It's two songs. Then she'll have them do their skill practice."

Rylie has been in the ballet class almost two months now, and I am amazed at how much she has learned. Her teacher, Miss Colleen, was right that she is a natural dancer. I'm still trying to get used to her dancing around the house and yelling ballet terms in French. She wanted to wear her leotard to Mother's Day Out a few days ago.

"Think she'll behave?" David asks.

"I'm sure she will." Rylie picks at the velcro on her shoe, her leg bent and foot stretched up almost up to her face. I snap a picture with my phone, and she frowns.

"What are your songs, Rylie? Tell Daddy about them."

"No."

When she takes that tone, it's better to back off. I don't need a tantrum right before a parent showcase. David drops us off by the door, and I cover Rylie's head with an extra jacket from the back seat so I can carry her inside while he parks the car. His coat is completely soaked by the time he makes it into the studio.

"Is this Rylie's daddy?" Miss Colleen asks, extending him a hand. "I'm so glad to meet you. Rylie has progressed so quickly."

I'm always mesmerized by how elegantly Colleen moves. She's tall and thin with deep brown skin and wide dark eyes. She loves glitter, too. Her black hair always has rhinestones stuck in it somewhere. Tonight her cheeks and collarbone are dusted with a subtle shimmer, and her leotard sparkles blue and green. Rylie says she's a fairy princess, and I almost believe her.

"Nice to meet you," David answers. He glances around the room. "I appear to be one of the only dads who could make it."

"I know Rylie is excited to show you her routines."

It's not a large audience since Rylie's class has only five kids. She sits on her mat at the side of the room, rocking back and forth with nervous energy. I wave at her, but she frowns and looks at the floor. I try to tell myself she will be fine, but my stomach is tying in knots. Will she throw a tantrum? Will she cry?

"Good evening, parents! And a few grandparents," Miss Colleen says. "I'm so glad you braved the bad weather tonight so that our baby ballet class can show you what they have learned this semester! We're going to show you two songs. The first one is our warm-up dance that we start with every class. The second is called 'Pretty Ballerina' and lets them show off their skills. Okay, ladies, up!" She claps her hands twice, and the girls hop up from their mats at the side of the room.

Except for Rylie. She frowns at her pink shoes and hugs herself. The other girls line up on the pink tape in the middle of the room. David elbows me in the arm and gives me a look. I want to run up and make her obey, but I can't.

"I'm not supposed to do anything," I whisper. "I'll get in trouble. We're supposed to let Miss Colleen handle everything during classes. She'll get up."

David frowns. "I don't think she's going to, Charlie."

I take a deep breath to calm my wildly beating heart and press my still-icy hands against my cheeks to cool them. Rylie is definitely not moving.

"Miss Rylie, time to start," Miss Colleen says firmly. Rylie shakes her head and pulls her knees to her chest, hiding her face. It's a standoff. I'm stuck. I can't intervene because of the rules, but she's holding up the whole showcase.

"Rylie, are you going to follow instructions, or are we going to dance without you?"

"No!" Rylie yells and dives behind the pile of mats behind her, hands over her eyes.

Miss Colleen looks at me, and I mouth, "I'm sorry." She shakes her head at me, her face calm and in control. She nods to the other teacher, and music fills the room. The other little girls stretch, twirl, bounce, and crawl around the room behind the teachers. One little girl with black hair giggles loudly the whole time, and the audience can't help but laugh with her. Everyone except us. David stares at the wall behind the dancers, his face deadly serious. I don't know if he's angry, upset, or annoyed at having wasted his time. I fidget in my seat, willing Rylie to stand up and join the group. The song ends, and the audience applauds politely.

"No clapping!" Rylie yells from her hiding place behind the mats. She stomps her foot and dives down again.

I have walked into Sunday school with baby vomit in my hair. I have been humiliated by grumpy old ladies in the grocery store. I have dragged a screaming Rylie out of church while our music minister tried not to make it worse by laughing. I have had to bandage a screaming Missile's bloody knees from Rylie shoving her on our concrete porch.

This is still the most embarrassed I have ever been.

"Miss Rylie, are you going to follow instructions and dance?" Miss Colleen says. When she runs a class, it is so easy to forget she is barely out of college. I'm amazed at how calm she is while Rylie kicks her feet against the mats. I grip the chair to keep myself from getting up and carrying my child out of the room.

The next song plays, and the girls begin their adorable routine. I don't watch a moment. All I can see is Rylie, or rather Rylie's tutu sticking up from behind the practice mats. David glares at me. I raise my hands helplessly, and he rolls his eyes.

The pretty ballerinas dance back to their mats and bow.

"Thank you so much for coming!" Miss Colleen says. "I hope you had fun tonight." She continues a short speech about learning skills and trying new things, but all I can see is Rylie hiding behind the mats.

"We'll see you after Christmas!" Miss Colleen says.

The rest of the parents mercifully retrieve their daughters and leave without saying anything to me except for the woman behind me. She pats my arms and winks.

"Been there with big brother," she whispers. She points to the little boy holding her hand, who looks to be about four. "Don't be embarrassed."

I wish that made me feel better. I trudge toward where

my daughter is still hiding behind the mats. Miss Colleen kneels next to her.

"Rylie, can you please look at my face so I can talk to you?" she says.

"I'm sorry, Miss Colleen," I say.

"Come here, Mama," Colleen says. Her voice is gentle but firm. "Rylie, I'm very sad you didn't participate tonight."

Rylie jumps up and runs to me for a hug.

Miss Colleen watches her in my arms for a moment. "Rylie, were you scared to dance?"

"I scared. I scared!"

I snuggle Rylie close as she sniffs and hides her face. Poor baby.

"I thought so. Stage fright," Miss Colleen says to me with a sad smile. She gestures for me to turn Rylie to face her, which feels like a wrestling match.

"It's okay to be scared," Miss Colleen says once Rylie looks at her. She nudges Rylie's shoulder. "But is it ok to yell or throw a fit?"

Rylie shakes her head and covers her eyes with her arm.

"Next time you get scared, you can tell me or your mama, okay? But it's not nice to your friends to yell and stomp your feet and make it hard for them to hear the music. Being scared is fine. Distracting everyone by misbehaving is not. Do you understand?"

Rylie nods her head.

"Can we try again next year, Rylie?" Colleen asks.

Rylie doesn't answer, but she doesn't hide her face.

"You'll be brave next time," I say, planting a kiss on her tear-stained cheek.

"That's right! Because we don't give up, right? Keep, keep trying. Don't give up!" her teacher chants the phrase I've heard many times in class.

"Keep, keep twying," Rylie says. She tries to make herself as small as possible in my arms.

"This is just a speed bump," Colleen says to me. "Happens all the time. Even my teenagers have freakouts."

"Thank you," I say, but I can't hide my embarrassment.

I rejoin David in the hallway as the last other family walks out into the rainy parking lot.

"Stage fright," I whisper over Rylie's head.

He nods, but he doesn't seem very sympathetic.

"But she's going to try again, right?" I say. "Right, Rylie? Keep, keep trying?"

Rylie nods and reaches for David. "I want Daddy."

David kisses her forehead and smiles.

"I'm going to get the car, okay? You wait with Mama."

"I want Daddy!" she cries as he heads out into the rain.

"It's okay, baby. He'll be right back." I heft her up against me again. She's getting so heavy. She covers her face with her arms again. I catch a glimpse of my face in the lobby mirror. My ears are bright red, Rylie has tangled my hair on one side, and I look like I'm about to cry. Why is it always so obvious that I'm a mess inside?

Another gust of cold hits me as the last family disappears into the parking lot. I am a little unsteady on my feet, but I can't put Rylie down. I watch our reflection in the mirror and try to count to ten. Rylie's ballerina bun is quickly turning into a ponytail.

I need to get out of this studio. Now. Where is David? I breathe in through my nose and slowly out through my mouth, trying not to lose it. I need to be away from this room. The mirror seems to shimmer like a mirage. Blinking seems to make it worse, so I close my eyes.

I'm about to have a panic attack or cry. Why isn't the breathing technique helping? Where is David? The corner of the front desk gouges my ribs as I realize I've been backing away from the mirror.

I force myself to open my eyes and see our car is at the door. I rush outside, covering Rylie's head with the sleeve of my jacket. David takes her and shoos me into the front seat. I press my head into the back of my seat and wiggle my fingers and toes slowly. I am not going to freak out over a ballet recital. It's ridiculous, and I'm not going to do it.

My heart doesn't seem to care about what my brain is telling it. It keeps pounding as if it wants to jump out of my chest and run to the next county. I jump when David's door shuts.

"That was ridiculous," David says to me, his voice low.

"I don't know what happened. She was so excited yesterday," I whisper.

I don't want Rylie to hear. We should wait until we get home to talk about it.

"Charlie, are you okay?"

"Yes," I say, lowering my head to my knees.

"Then why are you leaning over like that?"

"I'm upset," I say. "Trying to calm down." I am *not* panicking. I refuse to panic. I am just upset that my child hid her head behind a stack of practice mats with her hind end in the air like an ostrich.

"I want to do ballet," Rylie hollers from the back seat. I roll my eyes and look at David as we come to a stoplight.

"You missed your chance, kiddo," he answers blandly without taking his eyes off the road.

"No!"

I put my hand on David's arm, trying to warn him not to respond. She's asking for an excuse to throw a tantrum.

"Too bad."

The tantrum begins. I cross my arms and shrink myself

down into the seat, trying to focus on breathing slowly and ignoring the screaming and kicking in the back seat. David grips the steering wheel tighter and sighs loudly. I tried to tell him.

It seems like ages, but we make it home. Rylie's bun is now a messy ponytail. She's also missing a shoe.

"We'll find it in the morning," David hollers over her screaming.

He carries our kicking and crying daughter inside while I collect my purse and Rylie's shoe that I know I'll forget about in the morning if I don't find it now. When I finally make it inside, she is sniffling but willingly getting dressed for bed.

"Good night, baby," I say, kissing her wet pink cheek.

"Night night, Mama. I sowwy," she says as she grabs my neck and plants a teary kiss on my chin.

I leave David to finish the rest of the bedtime routine and change into pajamas.

"She said she had stage fright?" David asks as he walks into our room, pulling off his shirt.

I nod.

"She's not scared of anything though," he says. "You've seen her at church. She's a daredevil."

"Colleen says it happens all the time. Even to teenagers."

David tosses his shirt in the hamper and stretches his arms over his head with a sigh.

"It might be a funny story someday," David says. "At least that's what Mom would say."

"I don't think I've ever been so embarrassed in my life," I say. I shouldn't be so upset. It's a parent showcase, not *Swan Lake*.

"I'm going to go play some games with the guys," David

says, pulling on a faded T-shirt. "They're getting online about now."

"I'm sorry she didn't dance for you," I say. "She's so good."

"I believe you," David says.

He pats my shoulder and disappears into the living room to kill zombies, leaving me alone in our bedroom. I curl up in a ball on my side of the bed.

TWELVE

RYLIE RUNS from one end of the playground to the other. I have been waiting for good weather so we could go to the park, and she could not be happier. My five-year-old follows the strips of black stuff from the edge of the monkey bars around obstacles and past the swinging bridge until she comes to a temporary victory stop next to the swings. She throws her hands in the air.

"Yay! I did it!" she yells. She rushes off to the starting line again. I'm tired merely watching her, but she completes the circuit a dozen times without stopping for breath.

"Mommy, are you watching me?" she says, hands up in victory next to the swing. "I'm going to do it again now!" My shoulders are shaking with suppressed giggles. I'd hate for her to think I don't take her races seriously.

I'm trying to treasure these moments of just the two of us. It seems like yesterday she started ballet. This fall, she's going to preschool two days a week at Fellowship Christian School with Missile.

Her dark-blonde curls are flying behind her in a tangled mess. I may be forced to cut them if she won't let me brush her hair more often or at least keep it in a ponytail. I hate to do it. Those curls are my last piece of her babyhood.

"Mommy, can I have a drink?" She reaches for my water bottle and guzzles for a long minute. I realized a few days ago that her r's don't sound like w's anymore, and it makes me sad. I miss her asking for a "dwink."

"We're going to go home for lunch soon, sweetie," I say before she disappears into the castle again.

"No! I don't want to!"

I don't want to either. If I wasn't starving and worried about sunburns, we'd stay here all day. Just the two of us.

"Rylie, I think we should have a smoothie with our lunch. What do you think?"

"No! I'm not going to have lunch! I'm going to run a race again!" She ducks under the swinging bridge and runs as far from my chair as the fence allows. "I'm not going home!"

"But Mama is hungry! We have to go home before my tummy monster starts growling!"

She's not buying it, and I don't feel like fighting this battle. She will tire, and her own tummy monster will growl.

A shudder runs down my spine, and I look over my shoulder. There's no one around this time of day. The windows of the houses across the street are all empty and quiet, but I can't resist searching them for eyes.

I rub my fists against my temples and count like Darren taught me. The sky is scrubbed clean from the light rain last night, the flowers are springing up, bright with color, and some birds are arguing in the tree behind us. But I'm still miserable.

I'm usually able to slow down and take control of my thoughts before they overwhelm me. It's taken a long time to feel like I'm not always on the verge of losing it. I still have trouble when David isn't home. I found the source of the creaking in our bedroom fan, and that helped some. David pointed out yesterday how little I'd been home. I get out of the house as much as possible. Bible study. Wandering the mall. Taking Rylie to the park. Grocery shopping. More wandering the mall. More Bible study. Sometimes I make a sack lunch to save some money.

I have to admit that I'm avoiding the house. How stupid is that? I'm afraid of my own house. Every time I turn around, something startles me. I'll go for weeks, even a month without an incident, and then a shadow will move while I'm on my way to bed. Last time, I could have sworn I saw a second set of eyes in the mirror behind me after my shower. And then there are those flashes of blue at the corner of my eye. It's almost always blue. My eye exam was perfectly normal, so it's not something wrong with my retinas. I shudder again.

I've got to get out of that house. That's the solution. We need to move! Why didn't I think of this before? I've never seen any moving shadows or creepy faceless eyes anywhere but our little personal haunted house. I am so sick of the creaking, the annoying shadows from the tree in the back yard, and the constant power outages when it storms. It's hindering my progress, as Darren might say.

A thought sends every other plan for the day scampering into the back of my mind. I'm going to look for open houses and listings online. Why didn't I see this before? If I can get us moved to a different house, it will all go away. No more shadows that look like hands, no more fuzzy outlines behind me in the mirror.

"Mommy, I'm hungry."

The tummy monster has attacked her.

"You are? What should we feed your tummy monster today?"

"Peanut butter and jelly!"

"Sounds delicious, Rylie-Girl. Let's go home."

"I want a smoothie."

"Then we'll have to make a smoothie."

"Don't forget! Pinkie square!"

"What did you say?" Her face is so serious that I know I shouldn't laugh.

"Pinkie square!"

"You mean pinkie 'swear?'"

"Pinkie square!" She crooks her little pinkie and points at the flat of her knuckle. "See? Pinkie square!"

I can't help it. The laughter bubbles over, and she frowns at me.

"Mama, no!" she yells indignantly. "No laughing! It's not funny!"

"I'm sorry, baby," I say, biting back giggles. "Okay, yes, I pinkie square. I won't forget your smoothie."

We head home to lunch and chores in my creepy house. I know I'm acting a little weird, because David looks worried about me when he gets home. I can't help it. I don't know how he'll take this idea of moving, and my mind keeps running scenarios of different ways to convince him.

"So I was thinking," I say over the bubbles and dirty dishes in the sink, "maybe we should start looking around at some other houses."

"You mean moving?" David sets his glass in the dishwasher. "Why?"

"I don't know. We're kind of outgrowing this house."

"I thought you loved it here."

"I guess." Love? I am terrified of this house. "It's kind of creepy, though. All the creaking at night. Reminds me of a—"

"Creepy?"

"Sometimes it feels a little..." the next word oozes off my tongue like acid, "Haunted. Or something."

"Haunted?" David laughs out loud. "Since when do you believe in ghosts?"

"It's so creepy when I'm home alone with Rylie!" I say. "And the power going out during storms."

"Okay, you're right about that. We need to get that fixed. I'll get Casey to come help me this weekend," David says.

"No. No, I..." I scrub at stuck-on lasagna. I need a sand-blaster. "I think it's getting a little small for us. And I don't like being here all by myself when you're gone."

"Why don't you show me some of these creepy spots in the house, and I'll see if I can fix them."

"I was joking, David."

He raises an eyebrow at me. "Didn't sound like it."

"Yes, I was. Mostly."

"I'll bet I can fix it. I'll get out my ghostbuster kit."

"You're making fun of me now." I give him a face, but he laughs.

"You need to quit watching scary movies."

"Fine." I scratch at a burnt piece of pasta on the corner of the pan. "I'm serious about moving, though. I'd like two sinks in our bathroom, and I don't like the guest bedroom. It's hot in there all summer."

"Yes, but why all of a sudden?"

"I don't know. Feels like the right time, I guess."

He leans against the counter and frowns. "I am pretty happy here," he says.

"Well, I'm not. I think we need something bigger." My pan is clean. I set it in the dish rack and my gloves next to the sink. He regards me for a moment. I can tell by the look on his face that he's not convinced.

"I guess I'll think about it," he answers slowly.

"There are some great houses closer to church!"

"We'd have to specify no ghosts with the agent," he says, tickling my ribs.

"Very funny," I glare at him, and he kisses me as if it's a peace offering.

"I'm sorry," he says. "I won't tease you anymore."

"Pinkie square?"

"Pinkie what?"

"It's pinkie square, according to Rylie." I show him my "square" pinkie, and he snorts.

"Alright yeah, I pinkie square that I won't tease you anymore."

"Good."

"Can you pinkie circle? Or pinkie triangle?" He gets that mischievous look that Rylie inherited. "I've got it: pinkie dodecagon!"

"I'm not the authority on these things." I laugh. "You'll have to ask Rylie."

He pulls me close and kisses my neck.

"She's asleep. I'll ask her tomorrow," he murmurs.

"Want to watch a movie?" I ask.

"Actually, no."

"Oh."

THIRTEEN

"I SHOULDN'T HAVE VOLUNTEERED for this," I mutter to David over the cluttered kitchen countertop. He gives me a look and shakes his head.

"It's great, Charlie. Your food is great, and everyone is having a good time."

I wish I could agree. I rearrange bottles of soda, a stack of napkins, and mason jars filled with utensils for the hundredth time and check the clock above the oven. Tori and Greg should have been here by now. Renee and Casey are sitting outside on our patio, chatting with the new couple, Yvonne and Reuben. Their four kids are playing with Rylie and Liana in the back yard. Their middle daughter, Hannah, is in Sunday school with Rylie. I hope they're getting along. They seem to be.

"I don't know if I have enough food without..."

"Tori is coming." David pats my hand. "She texted you, right?"

"Yes. Twenty minutes ago."

"Then she'll be here any minute. I'm going to check the grill." He heads toward the patio door. "They'll be here.

Relax." In a moment, he's outside chatting with the other guys.

I know these people. They know us. Why am I still so miserable? The salad sits covered in plastic wrap on the counter. Renee's brownies are next to the sink. I avoid looking at the blank spot on the counter where Tori's hash-brown casserole and veggie tray are supposed to go.

Thank goodness, the doorbell. I race to the front door and yank it open. Tori and Greg are standing empty-handed.

"Hi!" Greg says. "Sorry, I was late getting home from work."

Why is he lying? Tori told me she was going to have to stop for the veggie tray. I plaster a polite smile on my face anyway.

"Hi, guys." I wave them in, wishing for the third time tonight that David had been able to paint the entryway last weekend. The test swatches are so obvious next to the mirror.

"Oh, I love your living room!" Tori says with a frozen smile. Greg strides into our kitchen without another word. "Sorry, honey," Tori whispers to me. "They were out of veggie trays at the store."

"Ha! Of course, they were." I throw my hands up and laugh because I worried that exact thing would happen. Fourth of July weekend means the grocery stores run out of everything.

"And...I burned the hash browns," she says through gritted teeth. "I hope we'll have enough food. I couldn't find anything that would work in the deli aisle."

"Oh no! That's too bad!" I head toward the kitchen, hoping no one minds steamed mixed vegetables, and try to laugh it off. "I've got something. It's fine, Tori." Greg is pouring a cup of soda. His tanned skin has obviously spent a lot of time in the sun this summer. He's wearing a red muscle tee and gray shorts. I edge behind him at the counter and look at them both as I consider what to do. They are a study in contrasts: he with blue eyes and dark hair carefully gelled and shaped, her with brown eyes and blonde, care-free waves.

"I'm so sorry," Tori says, adjusting the neck of her blue tank top with one hand and her gold hoop earring with the other.

"Should have taken it out sooner," Greg says over his cup of soda, which foams and drips onto the counter.

"I've blown up baked potatoes in the oven before," I say as I dig in my freezer for the vegetables. "The whole house smelled like french fries for a week!"

"I'm so sorry, Charlotte," Tori repeats, her tone flat. Greg pours more soda in his cup and walks out to the back yard, a trail of bubbles spilling after him.

"Good thing she had a backup plan, Vix," he snaps. The door slams behind him. Tori grabs some paper towels and blots at the soda on the carpet with an apologetic frown.

"We're both grouchy. They scrapped one of his projects."

I set the microwave for the vegetables and join her in cleaning up the soda.

"It's fine. Don't worry about it."

"No, it's not fine! I had the casserole all ready! And then I got distracted."

"You can bring it next time." I hate to hear her apologize again. She wads up the paper towels and stuffs them in the trash can.

"I was sad you didn't drop by the store this week while Rylie was at dance class," she says. "Is that the new wall color?" She turns on the overhead light in the hallway and stands back with a critical eye. "That's going to be gorgeous, Charlotte."

"You think so?"

"With that mirror? Perfect. I can't wait to see the finished product."

"I hope it works."

"You'll love it so much you won't want to leave," Tori teases. I wrinkle my nose at the thought, then laugh at my face in the mirror.

"Why don't you do this for a living, Tori?" I say.

She winks at me. "Maybe I should."

"Miss Tori!" Rylie dances into the hallway and pirou- ettes into Tori, almost knocking her over. Missile is behind her, followed by the new couple's middle daughter, Hannah.

"Hi, Rylie-Girl! Where are you going?" Tori asks.

"To get more toys!"

"You have to put them away, though," I say gently.

"We'll help!" Missile says and runs past us into Rylie's room. Tori laughs and follows me from the hallway into the front room.

"Have you found a house yet?" she asks.

"A few ideas on the internet, but we still need to get an agent."

"I knew it! They're in here talking about the house." Renee has come in from the patio with Yvonne, who is rubbing lotion on her hands as she walks. She reminds me of a cat, in a way, constantly watching her surroundings with aloof suspicion.

"Sorry," Tori says with a grin. "I can't stop myself. Hi, Yvonne! I'm so glad you came."

"So, are you guys hoping to need a fourth bedroom?" Renee asks me with a raised eyebrow. The question hits me like walking into a wall. "We're all wondering when the next Madsen baby is going to show up."

"I don't know." I can barely get the words out. I wish I could hide under a chair like Rylie.

"Rylie is five now, so time's a-wastin'!"

"Remember she had a rough time," Tori says gently.

"Oh, that's true," Renee says, hands over her mouth. "Sorry, Charlotte."

"What happened, if you don't mind me asking?" Yvonne asks. Everyone always wants to know. I know it's normal, but I wish people wouldn't ask.

"Placental abruption. There was a lot of bleeding." I still hate talking about it. Darren helped me see it can be helpful to others, but it doesn't make it fun to relive. "Rylie was 35 weeks. She was fine. I wasn't, though."

"When did the abruption start? Were you on bed rest?" Yvonne asks. She puts a hand to her cheek and shakes her head slightly as if she's irritated with herself. "I'm sorry. Did you know I'm a nurse? Not trying to be nosy."

"I didn't." My cheeks are hot. I need to write down details like this so I don't feel so awkward. "We had to call an ambulance. I had a blood transfusion after she was born. I passed out for some of it, so I don't remember a lot of details."

"No wonder you're gun-shy," Yvonne says.

"We'll see what happens," I say. Tori gives me a reassuring smile and changes the subject. I'm preoccupied with Renee's questions, though. I hadn't thought about more kids in a long time. Our lives are so full with Rylie. She takes up everything. Our time, our emotions, our conversations.

I see a flash of bright blue in the corner of my eye, and instantly my heart rate is sky-high. I carefully step to the side as if I'm adjusting the hall mirror and count to ten. We have got to get out of this house. It's turning me into a paranoid crazy person!

"Yeah, Charlotte went off and abandoned us," Renee says. I've missed part of the conversation.

"What?"

"We were going to do gymnastics together, but no. Rylie's doing ballet," she rolls her eyes. Except I never said Rylie was going to do gymnastics. Why does she say things like this? Renee's guilt trips are starting to get to me.

"And she loves it," Tori says. She turns to Yvonne. "Ask her to show you. She dances all the time in children's church."

"How sweet," Yvonne says, wrinkling her nose.

"You could do ballet *and* gymnastics, you know," Renee whines. "I don't know anybody at the gym yet."

"I think that would stretch the budget a little further than we can manage."

"I totally forgot: Greg is applying for a new job!" Tori says.

"Wonderful! Where?" Renee asks.

"It's that firm on Elm. I don't remember the name. You'll have to ask him. He thinks they would have better hours, and the pay is about the same."

"I don't blame him," Renee says. "He's hardly ever at Sunday school."

"He's made it to Sunday night service a few times lately."

"Oh, good!" Renee says, twisting her hair up into a claw clip and fanning her neck. "I never know who is around in the evenings because of children's choir. You two need to have a kiddo so I see you on Sunday nights, Tori."

Tori laughs, but I barely manage a smile. Renee really needs to think about what she says.

"Food is done!" David calls as he carries the serving plate full of steaming grilled chicken into the kitchen.

"So, when do the fireworks start?" Greg asks, following David inside.

Casey picks up the rear with a sleeping Gabby in his arms. He passes her off to Renee and stretches his arms. "After dark, so probably an hour or so?" he tells Greg.

"Do we need to send someone to stake a claim at the park?" Greg asks.

David frowns. "We usually sit in our back yard. We can see the fireworks from here."

"We don't want to walk down to the park?" Greg looks frustrated, and Tori gently pats his arm. Her mouth smiles, but her eyes don't.

"We have the citronella candles and stuff in the back yard," I say, dishing up chicken and veggies for Rylie. She, Missile, and Hannah have disappeared back into the playhouse outside.

"We don't want to see the fireworks over the water?" Greg says. "I thought that was the plan."

"It gets crazy crowded at the park, so we started watching from here," David tells him.

"And Missile almost got lost that first year," Renee says, patting a passed-out Gabby on her shoulder. Gabby's sandy-brown pigtail is bouncing on Renee's upper lip like a mustache, and it's too ridiculous to ignore.

"Renee, I mustache you a question," I say, pointing to my lip. Tori snorts, and Casey raises an eyebrow.

"Wait," he says, "you get to grow a mustache, but I can't have a beard? Not fair, wife!"

"Oh hush, Sandpaper Face," Renee says. "You'll wake her up."

"You know, you look good with a mustache," Casey

teases. "Maybe *you* should grow a beard."

"Maybe you should sleep on the porch," Renee says.

"This chicken looks delicious," Greg says. "I need to get a new grill so I can cook out more often, Tori."

"You do?" Tori says. She looks confused.

"Yeah, of course. I've always wanted to try grilling ribs."

"Sounds like fun," she says. She gives me a look that tells me Greg doesn't cook. I hand her a plate with a knowing smile and head outside to convince Rylie that food is a good idea.

The evening light gives me some peace even though I keep seeing flashes of blue in the middle of playing hostess. When the fireworks finally start, I'm grateful for the distraction. These moving shadows aren't scary. The bright flashes create wild afterimages in my eyes that remind me of that blue. Maybe that's all it is in normal circumstances: afterimages. I don't know a lot about the science of eyesight, but the thought is comforting.

With a bright finale full of silver, red, and blue explosions and loud booms that shake the windows, the fireworks show ends. I breathe a small sigh of relief. My house will be my own again.

"Thank you so much for everything, girl," Tori says. "We had a blast!"

"Can't believe Rylie could sleep through the end of the fireworks," Greg laughs as he walks past me to their car.

"She wore herself out playing."

"Did you put her in bed?" Tori asks.

"David did. She must have been exhausted to stay asleep through him actually putting her in bed."

"Well, thank you for everything. We had a wonderful time. Maybe next time I won't burn the side dish," Tori says with a sad smile. "You're still coming over, right?"

"Just let me know when. I'll have to ask if Nana can watch Rylie."

"Oh no, please bring her. I miss seeing my Rylie-Girl now that she's out of my class." She opens the car door. "Is next Saturday okay? Greg has to work, so it would be us girls. Nothing fancy. Sandwiches or something."

"I would love to."

We work out the time, and I convince her to let me bring some salad to go with the sandwiches. The memory of her fake smile as she walked into our house needles me.

"I hope I didn't make you feel bad earlier."

"Of course not." She waves away the apology like an errant fly, but there is hurt in her eyes. "I got distracted and didn't get it out in time."

"Hey, I have work in the morning," Greg says from behind the wheel.

"I'll see you Saturday," I say. I wave as they drive away, and an empty feeling settles into my chest. I slowly walk through my dark, messy house to find David in the back yard.

"Can you get the trash out while I finish cleaning the grill?" David asks, scrubbing the grill grate with a wire brush.

"Sure." The bag in the kitchen is almost overflowing. I tie it up and hoist it over my shoulder like one of the seven dwarves with a knapsack. I wink at David as I come back out onto the patio and whistle, "Hi ho," like one of the seven dwarves. He laughs.

I grab a red plastic cup marked with Greg's name on it from behind one of the lawn chairs and march around to the side of the house to the garbage can, still whistling. The night is beautiful. Rylie actually behaved. Tori likes my paint colors. The chicken was a hit. I toss the bag of party refuse into the can and savor the end of a successful evening for a moment. The moon is bright and full over our rooftop, and I hear the neighbor's hot tub rumbling in their enclosed porch next door.

"Thank you for a lovely night," I pray aloud. "It was fun."

Hands, more like claws, reach for me out of the darkness on the side of the house. I stumble against the wood planks of the fence and cover my head with my arms. I keep batting at the air. It's going to get me. Why is it after me?

Nothing. I slowly put my hands down and look at the wall of our house.

It's my shadow. The moon is so bright that I have a clear black shadow that is larger than life. The angle of the moon sends my movements snaking over the brick in a creepy caricature. It looks like a monster with claws if I spread my fingers.

My heart thunders in my chest.

I'm such a dork. I wiggle a hand in the moonlight and watch my shadow dance over the brick. It's so ridiculous that I can't stop laughing.

"What's so funny?" David asks. I hear him shutting the grill.

"Scared myself half to death."

"What?"

"Come here and see!" I say as he pokes his head around the side of the house.

"What? Your shadow?"

"I thought it was trying to grab me." The giggles grip me until I'm practically hysterical. All the fear has to go somewhere. David laughs at my laughing, and the next thing I know, we're both pretending to be Peter Pan against the house wall.

"Okay, we need sleep!" I say, trying to stop giggling.

He kisses my cheek, still laughing. "Let's get to bed," David says. "Should we get Rylie into her pajamas?"

"Let her sleep." We walk inside the house and flip the lights off. David heads to the bedroom while I turn on the dishwasher and rinse the last dish.

"Mama?"

Rylie is standing in the doorway from the living room, looking confused, her arms wrapped tightly around her worn pink blanket.

"Did you wake up and not know where you were, sweetie?"

"I want my jammies."

"Let Mama finish washing the dishes. Daddy can help you. He's in our room."

"Where is Liana?"

"She went home."

"Is she going to come play again sometime?"

"You'll see her at church, baby."

"Okay." She sits down in the doorway and wraps the blanket around her shoulders. I can't help giggling a little. My sweet little girl looks two again instead of five. I turn back to the sink to finish rinsing the dishes.

There is someone in our yard.

A yelp escapes my throat as I run to grab my daughter. I trip over the kitchen chair and fall headlong into Rylie. I'm scrambling and flailing to get off of her as her screams jolt me like an electric shock. I pull her into the kitchen and hold her tight, pressing my back against the half wall between the kitchen and the living room where we can't be seen from the glass patio door.

"I'm so sorry, baby! Did I hurt you?" I whisper, trying to quiet her screams. I landed on her hand, and she can't stop crying. My heart feels like it will burst as I try to calm her without showing myself to whoever is in the back yard. David rushes in from the hall.

"Rylie?" he says. "What happened?"

"Can you check the back yard?" I beg him, but he's only looking at Rylie.

"Mama hurt me!" Rylie says, pushing away from me to jump into David's arms.

"I tripped and fell on her," I say, my voice thick with fear. "I saw something in the yard. Could you check?"

"Mama hurt me," Rylie cries into his shoulder. The room seems to press in on me from every side as if to smother me.

"David, please. Just check."

He gently sets Rylie on my lap and goes to the door to the patio. Rylie doesn't want me to hug her, and I have to hold her back from running after David.

"Shh, baby. It's okay. Mama's so sorry," I whisper in my little girl's ear. I cradle her against me, praying she stops crying.

I grit my teeth as the porch floods with light behind us. I can't look at the kitchen window.

"Shhh," I say as she struggles against me.

"No, Mama!" she says. "You hurt me!"

The porch light turns back off, and I close my eyes. My stomach feels like I've been kicked.

A hand on my shoulder sends me scrambling with Rylie, and I knock over the kitchen chair.

"Charlotte, it's fine!" David says, grabbing the chair before it hits the tile. "There's nothing there." He lifts Rylie out of my arms and carries her to the kitchen sink. "Are you okay?" he says, setting her on the countertop and looking her over.

I follow him, wincing at the pain in my hip where I hit the chair.

"Did Mama hurt your hand?" I ask Rylie.

"You hurt me!" Rylie says, pointing to her fingers. There is a red welt on the side of her hand next to her pinkie finger from where I landed and pinched her hand between my knee and the tile.

"I'm so sorry, baby," I say. My whole body feels shaky. "I fell, sweetie. I'm so, so sorry."

"Mama didn't mean to hurt you, Rylie," David says, kissing her hand. It takes a few minutes to calm her down and convince her I didn't mean to hurt her.

"I'll get her to bed," David says, sending me to our room.

"Are you okay, Charlotte?" His voice is suspicious, almost like when he made me go see Darren the first time. I hate that tone. It's even worse because it's deserved. "What happened?"

"She came in while I was finishing the dishes, and then I thought I saw something in the yard."

"How did you fall on Rylie?"

"I was running to get her, and I tripped on the chair." I sit on the bed and grip the comforter in both fists with white knuckles. "I couldn't catch myself. I'm so stupid."

"It was an accident," David says. "She forgives you."

I look him in the eye and feel my lip quiver.

"I could have really hurt her," I whisper. "Just because I freaked out."

"Everything is okay though," David says. "You didn't hurt her that bad. Just a bruise."

But I could have. The thought pierces through me like a million needles.

I could have really hurt Rylie.

FOURTEEN

"THANKS FOR COMING OVER," Tori says, ushering us into her newly renovated entryway.

Barely a week after the Fourth of July, and she has already redecorated. The front door is hung with a floral wreath of dogwood flowers and a buffalo plaid bow. Sunlight reflects from the second-floor window onto the stairs. The elegant gray and white rug runner contrasts with the dark refinished wood floors. A farmhouse-style entry table next to the stairs reminds me of something I've seen in a magazine.

"You're sure you don't mind Rylie? I would have left her with David, but he's working on a project with Casey."

"Of course not!" Tori says.

She scoops Rylie into her arms and tickles her until she screams with laughter. The house smells like chocolate.

"I made yummy sandwiches, Rylie-Girl. You like peanut butter and jelly, don't you?"

"Yes!" Rylie yells and claps.

"Then come with me. We'll have peanut butter and jelly."

I linger for a moment as they head to the kitchen and admire her front hall. The textured white walls are covered in framed photos and artwork. The sun shines through the cut-glass windows on either side of the door. Tori is gifted. It looks like I've stepped into an elegant bed and breakfast. The last time I saw her house was the Sunday school Christmas party last year. It looks like a different house without the red and gold holiday decorations.

There is a large framed photo of Tori on her wedding day as I walk down the hallway to the kitchen and living room. She looks like a model from a magazine, her blonde hair in perfect beach waves, half pulled back with an orchid pin.

"You were a beautiful bride," I say as I round the over-stuffed couch to the island and set my salad on the bright white countertop.

"Thank you for saying that," she says. "I was sick that day."

"You can't tell at all!"

"I can," she says. "The photographer made my nose look less red when he edited everything, but I can tell."

"Tori, you look like a model all the time. Isn't Aunt Tori beautiful, Rylie?" I ask.

"Beautiful!" Rylie shouts around a bite of peanut butter and jelly sandwich.

"You're so sweet," she says.

The kitchen table is spread with Rylie's plate, club-style sandwiches for us, and a pitcher of iced tea, which makes me feel even more like I'm visiting a bed and breakfast. I look out through the wide windows at her back porch, a planter full of bright pink flowers, and the lawn of thick, lush grass.

"Wow, what do you do to the lawn? That is amazing!"

"It's Greg's thing. He's got it down to a science," she says, waving me to my seat at the table. "Does Rylie drink milk?" she asks, holding up a gallon from the refrigerator.

"Milk, please!" Rylie says.

"Sweetie, don't talk with your mouth full," I tell her. I turn back to Tori as she pours the milk. "He'll have to tell David his secrets. We have bare patches at the back fence. I don't want it to look bad when we have an open house."

"I'm sure he'll be happy to spill," Tori says as she pours milk into a small, worn plastic cup covered with bears and hearts. I can't help wondering when we're going to talk about what I came to talk about. The subject is there under the conversation, like a crumb under a tablecloth. Tori sips her iced tea.

"Thank you, Aunt Tori," Rylie says, spewing sandwich crumbs from her mouth.

"You're welcome," Tori says. "She's such a sweetheart," she says, turning to me.

"Dance has helped her so much. She gets her sillies out so she can listen better, don't you, Rylie?" I say.

Rylie nods and nearly spills her milk.

"I'd love to see her all dolled up," Tori says.

"Her class is supposed to participate in the full recital this year, but I don't know much about it yet."

"I'm gonna dance!" Rylie says, throwing her hands up in the air.

"Yay! Keep me in the loop when it's recital time. I want to see this girl shine," Tori says. "You must have so much fun watching her."

"I do," I say quietly, watching my little girl bouncing in her chair. "It's a lot of fun."

"Why don't you and I sit on the couch?" Tori says suddenly. "We'll be more comfortable. Rylie, if you watch really carefully out that window, I'll bet you'll see the squirrel that's been eating all my birdseed."

We relocate to the overstuffed olive green couch and set our food on the round marble-topped coffee table. I bite into deli lunchmeat, crunchy bacon, and crisp lettuce, and sigh. Everything Tori makes is so good.

She takes a sip of iced tea, shifts one leg underneath her, and leans her chin on her hand as if she's finally ready to talk. She glances at Rylie, busy watching the window for squirrels.

"I'm not sure," she says. "About kids." Her voice is so low I can barely hear it.

"What do you mean?"

"I mean, I'm not sure I want them," she says. Her cheeks are turning red.

"Have you had problems?"

"No, we aren't trying yet."

"Oh." I don't know what to say. I thought she wanted to talk about infertility.

"It's such a big responsibility. We never seem to have everything ready."

"I don't think you can," I say. "I don't have a clue what I'm doing, you know."

She laughs and takes a bite of her sandwich. "Yes, you do. You're a great mom. But I'm not sure if we'll ever be close to ready. Things seem to keep coming up."

"Maybe if he gets that other job," I say.

"Maybe. He's never home, and he hates it," Tori says, studying her plate. "And I hate it because he's so miserable and it keeps him from coming to church. You know this is the sixth job he's applied for this year? It never works out. He puts in so much, and it's never appreciated."

"We're always praying for him."

"Sometimes, I wonder if it's God saying to not have kids."

"I'm done, Mama!" Rylie interrupts us, jumping up from her chair.

Tori stops me from getting up. "Can she have a c-o-o-k-i-e?"

I nod. "I thought I smelled some."

"Here, Rylie-Girl," Tori says, walking to the counter with a sneaky look on her face. "Come look inside this owl. There's a surprise." She slides a brown, vintage, owl-shaped cookie jar to the edge of the counter.

Rylie clambers up on the stool next to it and opens the jar. "Cookies!" She grabs a large chocolate cookie studded with white chocolate chips.

"You didn't have to make cookies," I say. I wish she would have let me bring more than a salad.

"Any excuse for cookies is a good one," Tori says, waving away my words.

"Tank oo!" Rylie sprays cookie crumbs out of her mouth.

Tori rounds the couch with a cookie for each of us. She watches Rylie dipping her cookie in her milk.

"I know children are a blessing. And we want to be parents," she says. Her jaw hardens. "But I don't feel a hundred percent about it. Ever."

"I think you'd be a wonderful mother."

"I hope so," she says. I have never seen her look so doubtful. "I want our kids to see their dad in church every week. To see both of us." She looks at her hands and frowns. "My Dad wasn't a Christian, you know. My brother isn't either. I think my mom believes, but she has so many health problems. We never went to church except Christmas. And Easter egg hunts."

"I didn't realize that."

An ugly worry nags me. Is Greg a Christian? I assumed so, but now I'm not sure. Surely he is. I shouldn't be so quick to judge. But Tori's face makes me wonder.

"Does he want to be there with you?"

"Oh yes! Yes, he does." She pushes her salad around on her plate. "He got out of the habit of going in college, but he was raised in it. His parents were always there when he was a kid. But they've had such a hard time. The church they went to when Greg was growing up split a few years ago."

"That's awful," I say.

"They voted the pastor out! I didn't even know you could do that."

Rylie has finished her cookie and decides to bounce through her tap routine in front of the French doors to the porch. She has more tile to tap on here than at home, but the noise makes me cringe.

"I have some coloring pages and crayons," Tori says. "I'll get her set up at the kitchen table."

At first, Rylie doesn't stop dancing. She has to finish the number. My stomach curdles around my salad and sandwich as I watch her tapping from the cabinet to the window. The bruise on her hand next to her pinkie is starting to fade, but it's the only thing I can see. I have got to get out of that house.

I sink into the couch after Rylie settles in with the crayons.

"Anyway," Tori says with a sigh, "it took Greg's parents several years to find somewhere they were comfortable after that split. They didn't find a new church until Greg was in college."

"Wow."

"I think..." Tori looks away from me for a moment and then whispers, "I think it's made him reluctant about church, you know? I know work has him busy all the time, but I think sometimes he worries that if he gets really involved, he'll be disappointed again."

This is not at all what I was expecting.

"I can see why he might have a hard time," I say after a moment. "Those kinds of fights can get ugly."

"I didn't know it was such a problem. I thought churches were families, and seeing how mean Christians can be to each other—"

I hear the automatic garage door opening, and Tori jumps up.

"He's home early," she says, rushing into the kitchen. "Sorry, I thought it would be just us girls. But I guess that's a good thing. He must be done with his project."

She pulls sandwich items and a can of soda out of the refrigerator and spreads mustard on a slice of bread. Rylie jumps out of her seat and starts to quietly tap back and forth next to the windows.

The garage door opens, and Greg steps in, humming a song I don't recognize. He drops his bag on the floor next to the door. "Hi, Charlotte!"

I smile and wave. He turns back to Tori.

"Hello, wife!"

"You're home early," she says, handing him the soda.

"Finished quicker than usual," he says. "You two didn't leave me any lunch?"

"I'm making yours right now."

"Please and thank you," he says and kisses her cheek. He cracks open the soda and says something in engineering-speak that David would probably understand. Tori finishes making his sandwich, and he turns back toward me.

"I see you brought Miss Rylie!" He says. He sets his sandwich on the table, leans over, and pats Rylie's curls. "Why don't you come out to the front hallway and show me your tap routine where it won't be so loud?" She follows him to the doorway of the living room and turns back to look at me.

"I'll be right here, honey," I tell her.

She bounces her way to the front of the house, and I hear her tapping her way to the other side of the entryway.

"I'm sorry. I didn't think he'd be home until this afternoon," Tori says as she puts away the food.

"No biggie." I bring my food into the kitchen and stand in the other doorway that leads out to the formal dining room. I can lean out a little and see Rylie in the entryway this way.

"Are you coming to the retreat next month?" Tori asks.

"Probably not."

"You should come! We've planned so many fun things."

"I don't know if I can leave Rylie that long," I say, fiddling with the hem of my shirt.

"It's only overnight."

I know she's right. Rylie is five. It shouldn't be a big deal. I shrug and pick at the last bite of my sandwich.

"I don't like to leave her."

"David will be home, right? He seems like a great dad." She says the words as if she were stepping onto thin ice.

"He's a wonderful dad," I say. "She loves her daddy so much."

"You are so blessed," she answers. She looks down at the counter and says something I can't quite hear.

"What?"

"I said, 'David is such a godly man,'" she says as she looks up into my eyes. I hear my daughter sing "On the Good Ship Lollipop" and lean out of the doorway to watch.

A chill on my spine makes me shudder. I see something in the entryway next to Rylie. Something moves, flickering like a flame in the wind. I make out a blue shirt and dark hair, but the eyes are what terrify me. They are terrifyingly familiar: blue-green and wide in terror. They're *its eyes*. It moves toward the stairs, and I realize it's a woman. The ghost, *my* ghost, is a woman. In a heartbeat, she vanishes like a candle blown out. My throat tightens, and I grip the countertop and close my eyes. I have to leave. I have to leave right now.

"Charlotte?" Tori's voice breaks behind me.

"I need to go." I can barely make myself look at her. "I'm sorry. I have to go."

I run through the kitchen to grab my purse in the living room and stumble into the entryway.

"I'm sorry, Greg, but I need to go home. I forgot something important I need to do."

"But she didn't finish her dance yet," he says.

I hear myself sputtering apologies as I pull Rylie to the front door. Tori is going to think I'm crazy. They're both going to think I'm crazy. I jerk open the door, but Tori stops me and wraps me in a big hug.

"It's fine, Charlotte. I will see you on Sunday." She pulls back and looks me straight in the eye, her face urgent. "Why don't I help Rylie get buckled in?"

Fear burns on my cheeks as I hurry out to the car. Tori settles Rylie in her car seat despite the beginnings of a tantrum. She wanted to sing the lollipop song to Greg. Tori shuts the door and grips my hand through the open window.

"Text me when you get home, okay? I understand. It's fine."

I nod. The car is too warm, and Rylie's tantrum builds as we drive across town in the Saturday lunchtime traffic. I try to calm my wildly beating heart. She said she understood.

How can she understand when I don't know what is happening myself?

I put Rylie in her room for some quiet time, and in a miracle from God, she goes without a fight. She hasn't taken a real nap since she turned three. The bathroom needs to be scrubbed, so I grab my tray of cleaner and gloves. Mindless tasks help me think. The bathroom fills with the smells of bleach and glass spray.

It's a she. My ghost is a she, and *She* isn't confined to my house. And she was wearing blue. The thought makes me nauseated. She can follow me. All our discussions about finding a bigger place are a waste of time. She can follow me, and something tells me she *will* follow me. I can't escape. This thing is going to stalk me everywhere I go.

I can't have more children. The thought crashes over me like a wave. What if I'm losing my mind? Rylie is already going to be warped by these ridiculous fears. How could I bring another child into the world, knowing that? Would I be a danger to them?

The house doesn't matter. It's not about the house. It's about me. I can't act like moving will fix everything.

My phone buzzes on the counter.

Did you get home okay, honey? Tori asks in a text message.

Yes, thank you. I'm so sorry.

What am I sorry about? I'm sorry I saw a ghost in her house and ran out of there like a crazy person?

Or thought I saw a ghost. Maybe it was the curtains. Maybe what I saw was the shadows from the curtains. I'm going to manage this somehow. I'm going to get over it. The tile in our bathroom needs a good scrubbing. I'll start there.

Don't apologize, Tori's text message says. *I understand. Want me to help you get Rylie into Sunday school tomorrow?*

I'll be okay, I answer.

I finish cleaning the bathroom and move on to dusting the living room. I need to stay busy. If I'm going to figure this out, I have to keep myself occupied.

I should get out my oil paints. It's been weeks, but I've noticed things seem calmer when I paint. I don't remember the ghost appearing at all when I have painted. I haven't seen Her since we got home. Maybe making me look crazy to my best friend was all the fun she needed for the day.

Who is she? Something about her eyes feels so familiar. I'm terrified to get a better look at her, but maybe it would help. Maybe I would know who she is.

This is crazy. I'm not going to think about it anymore. I gather my supplies at the kitchen table and pull out the easiest thing I can think of. In a moment, I'm gliding watercolors onto thick art paper. I haven't used watercolor in years. I don't have a plan. I start with flowers and hearts and simple patterns. Things that make me feel calm.

I will beat her. I will paint her away until she never comes back.

FIFTEEN

"SO, I found another house you might like at lunch today," David says behind me as he changes into his bed T-shirt. "It's over on Broad by the other park Rylie likes. Four bedrooms."

I stare at myself in the mirror. I can't tell him what happened at Tori's house today. That means he's going to freak out. He had so much fun with Casey that he barely noticed I was quiet at dinner, and what I have to say will be like a grenade in his lap. The thought makes my stomach hurt.

"It has a porch," David. "We could go look at it tomorrow."

"We could, I guess."

"What do you mean, 'I guess?'"

"I've been thinking about it." I brace for it. "I don't want to move anymore."

"What?" David throws his hands in the air, then drops them at his sides. "Hold on, what happened?"

"We're fine here. It's fine."

"But I thought you wanted more space."

"I know what I said. But this house is fine. We are fine."

"Charlie, what is going on? You've talked about moving every single day for months now. This makes no sense."

"I don't want to leave anymore. We're close to church, and the park, and the lake. We're close to everything here. And you're right. We can't afford it right now."

"Honey, I never said—"

"I would rather stay here, David! That's all, okay?"

"No, it's not! Why on earth have we been painting and changing things and talking to the agent?"

"I changed my mind. This is our house, and I want to stay."

"But what if *I* want to move?"

"Well...we aren't."

David looks like I've slapped him. His mouth twists into a suspicious frown. "And how I feel doesn't matter? What about needing the extra bedroom?"

"We have an extra bedroom. The guest bedroom is right there."

"Until we need it for a nursery. Then we'll need another one."

"No. We won't."

"Wait, are you thinking we move Rylie into the guest room?"

"No!"

"But I thought..." he sits on the bed, hands limp in his lap. "I don't understand."

"We don't need another nursery, David. We're fine." I go back into the bathroom to brush my teeth and leave him sitting on the bed. He doesn't say anything until I come out of the bathroom.

"I thought we wanted three," he says, hands on his knees.

"I don't anymore."

"But I still do, honey."

"You're not the one who has to be pregnant."

"Slow down for a second," David says. "This is all coming out of nowhere. Since when do you not want any more kids?"

"Since I nearly died!"

I can't read him. I don't have any idea what he's thinking right now, but I don't really care. My mind is made up.

He says nothing for a moment that feels like eons, looking at the wall behind me with no expression. A chasm opens between us as he looks me in the eye again, and I see anger.

"Didn't your doctor tell you it would be okay?"

"He said it raises my risk of a second placental abruption. And I won't risk it."

David covers his eyes with his hand, and I see his jaw muscles flex. "But we have always wanted more kids."

"Before I almost died!"

"But you didn't! You're fine!" The quiet words slam against me like a brick wall.

I scream back. "No, I'm not fine! I will never be fine again! Do you have any idea how terrifying it is to go unconscious, believing you will never wake up?"

"I was right there with you, Charlotte."

"But you weren't bleeding to death!"

"You didn't bleed to death! You are right here with me! But you know what? In your mind, you're still there in that hospital bed. And you're dragging Rylie and me there with you every single day. Like it's our fault somehow."

"How dare you." I run away from him into the bathroom. My chest burns until my eyes water, and I sit on the closed toilet as far away from the bedroom doorway as I can get. I can barely breathe through this white-hot anger.

But he's not done. He appears in the doorway and glares at me in the mirror.

"Do you realize what you are saying to me? I have a right to be upset. We've said for years we wanted three kids. I thought that was why you wanted to move. You kept talking about needing more space!"

"You hear what you want to hear."

"So, what am I supposed to hear?"

"That we are staying here. And I'm going to ask the doctor to make things permanent!"

The silence fills the room until it chokes me. He grips the doorpost and clears his throat.

"Don't you think I should have a say in that decision?" His words are crisp but calm. I want to tell him no, that he doesn't get a say when I'm the one who would have to endure another pregnancy, terrified of dying. But I say nothing.

"Were you even going to tell me?"

"Yes!"

"When?"

"I'm telling you right now."

He rubs his hands through his hair and breathes through his nose.

"I..." he falters. "I don't know what to say to you. I don't know."

He says nothing else, but the silence is accusation enough.

"I just made the decision today." Since seeing a ghost in Tori's foyer and realizing that I'm losing my mind. Since realizing he doesn't see how I'm falling apart. Or he does and he doesn't care.

He looks at the floor, his fingers interlaced on top of his head.

"You just decided today."

Any desire I had to be diplomatic evaporates at his tone. "Yes, today. Do you have a problem?"

"Charlotte..." He drops his hands to his sides and looks me in the eye. "I don't believe you. I don't think you were going to tell me at all." His eyes are sharp and accusing, and my stomach writhes. The look on his face stings, like touching a butterfly and discovering it's an angry wasp.

"Fine. Don't believe me. I've told you now, so why does it matter?"

"It matters! It matters a lot! I can't trust you anymore. How can I trust you with other things if you were making a decision this huge without me!"

"I wasn't!"

"Yes, you were. You are!"

"David, you are being selfish."

"We both wanted three kids from the beginning!"

"And then I almost died!"

"But. You. Didn't." The words are quiet. Cold. I don't know this man anymore. I don't know how he can ignore that I still relive those moments in my nightmares. I don't know how the man who held me close when I was hurting the two years before we had Rylie can be so determined to have more children, that he would risk my life.

"I won't take the chance again," I say.

"And you don't care what I think about it at all."

I say nothing. I do not owe a stranger an answer, and that is what he is right now.

"Well, at least you're not lying to me," David says, his face contorting with disgust.

"Lying? You are—"

"Stop. Before you say something you regret."

"Don't tell me what to do!" I want to scream, but it comes out more like a hiss. David picks up his pillow.

"We are both too upset to be productive in this discussion."

"Don't you dare talk down to me."

"I'm not!" He holds a hand up. "This is me calling time out, okay? Time. Out."

"Fine. Go ahead, ref," I say, turning off the bathroom light and hugging myself next to my side of the bed. He has moved to the door to the hallway. "Running away to shoot zombies?"

"I'm going to the guest room," David says, his voice dripping acid. "I need space. I need to think."

"Fine. Go." I pull the covers open on my side of the bed and dive under them like a barricade in a war zone.

"We are going to talk about this again."

"Go!" I keep my eyes firmly on my nightstand. I am not looking at him again.

"We are going to talk about this again. Without yelling."

I don't care if I was yelling. This is something worth yelling about. I hear the door shut and turn my light off. My eyes slowly adjust to the dark as I study the outlines of my dresser and nightstand in the dim glow of the alarm clock. The air conditioner shuts off, and the silence makes my ears ring in protest.

I hear a crying sound and sit up instinctively. Rylie must have heard me shouting. I shrivel into a hunched ball of shame on the edge of the bed. She didn't need to hear that. I move to the door to comfort her, but I stop with my hand still on the lock. It's not Rylie. It's David. David is sniffing and talking to himself in the guest room next to our bedroom.

"I love her," he says. "Help me talk to her. I'm so confused."

Every ounce of shame evaporates. I hate him. The part of me that should feel sorry is suffocated by the anger building in my chest. How dare he make me choose between what he wants and being there for Rylie? I'm the only mother she has. I don't care what we wanted when we first got married. I don't care if he cries all night long. He's clinging to a version of me that ceased to exist after Rylie was born. He loves the woman I was before, not me right now. He doesn't even know me. And I don't know him.

I'm so sick of this false sympathy. He should be grateful for what we have and stop acting like he deserves more. I jump back in bed and turn the fan to its loudest setting. The minutes on the alarm clock melt into hours.

I find myself walking down the hallway in a daze. I'm at Rylie's bedroom door.

She's not there. I run from room to room calling for her, but she's gone. David follows me, saying it will be fine, but I'm panicking more by the minute. My mom is outside on the doorstep, and I rush her inside, begging her to help me find Rylie. She rolls her eyes at me.

"Honey, I'm sure she's fine." She turns away toward the kitchen.

"She's not fine! She's gone!"

"Is she playing hide-and-seek?" My father asks from behind me.

"I'm telling you, she's gone!"

The room spins, and I run back to her room. I can't find the light switch to turn it on. I can't find it. My hand searches, but the wall is empty.

"I found her, Charlie!" David says behind me. I turn back to see him standing in the hallway, holding a little girl's hand. But she isn't Rylie. She isn't. A scream wells up in my throat.

"I found her! See? She's fine!" He smiles and pats the little girl on the head.

"That's not Rylie!"

"She's fine! See, she's right here."

"That's not Rylie! How can you say that?" I scream, clawing myself forward to shake him by the shoulders. "You don't even know your own child!"

SIXTEEN

THE WORDS CHOKE out of me as I sit up in bed. I can hear nothing but my heartbeat, and I squeeze my eyes tight.

It was a dream. A horrible dream. I rub my cheeks and neck with my palms and wait for my heart to slow down before opening my eyes. The sun is peeking through the blinds. Our mattress is lumpier without David's weight on the other side, and the room is too cold from the fan.

I roll over to look at my alarm clock, and suddenly I'm wide awake because we're going to be late for church. I jump out of bed and grab a blouse and pants from the closet. I don't have time for a shower, so I spray my hair full of dry shampoo and coax it into a messy half-ponytail. I'll have to do my makeup in the car.

I run down the hall to wake Rylie, but her room is empty. I hear laughter in the kitchen and follow the noise to find her sitting on David's lap, eating pancakes.

"Mommy!" She jumps down and runs to hug me. "Daddy and me made pancakes!"

"I see that!" I scoop her up in a bear hug and spin around next to the kitchen table. "Oh, you're sticky! Don't get it in Mommy's hair, sweetie. We need to hurry! We have to get ready for church."

"I made this one," she says, running back to David's lap to hold up a deformed blob of a pancake. She takes a bite and grins. "All by myself!"

"Daddy just had to flip it, right?" David says. He sets Rylie in his chair and moves behind the counter to the griddle.

"I was waiting until you woke up to make the rest."

"We're going to be late," I say, looking in the cabinet for cereal. I don't want him doing anything for me today. I refuse to owe him anything.

"Go sit with Rylie."

I glare at him.

"I want to wear my purple dress to church," Rylie says, kicking her feet back and forth beneath her at the table.

"Silly girl, you wore it last week," I say.

Sometimes her chatter wears on me, but today I'm grateful she is here to fill the silence with talk of pancakes, ballet, and Bible verses. The pancakes hiss on the griddle. David checks the color and flips one over.

"We're going to be late," I say.

"Here," he says, handing me my plate. I jerk it from him and dump the plate on the table in disgust.

"We'd better hurry and get ready for church, kiddo," David says, tickling Rylie and scooping her up over his shoulder. "Let's let your mama eat her pancakes in peace."

"I didn't get her dress out yet," I say.

"I can handle picking it out," he says. "There's butter on the counter if you want it."

I want to say something mean. Something that will cut him to ribbons and make sure he never speaks to me again. I hate him. But he's gone to Rylie's room before I can think of anything. The pancakes smell like cinnamon and vanilla, and they are perfectly cooked. Better than I have ever managed to cook them. Another way he's so superior to me. Another way to show me he's the better parent.

I carve the pancake with my fork and stab a piece of oozing butter and syrup. The pillowy cake tastes like my grandmother made it, but my tongue takes to it like glue. I wash it down with a swig of milk and push down the rest before I can talk myself into eating cereal instead. No sense in wasting them, and I have to finish getting ready. David comes back to the kitchen wearing a clean polo. Rylie follows him in her purple dress.

"David, she wore that dress last week!" I say, sighing. "And her hair is a mess."

"Blame me for the fashion faux pas," he says, grabbing his Bible. "I'll get the car ready."

I bite my tongue and squeeze my hands into fists. There is no time for Rylie to change. I rush her to the bathroom and brush her hair into a quick ballerina bun, hiding the messy bobby pins with a purple bow. Hopefully it will hold through Sunday school.

The drive to church is as silent as the grave. Rylie must have picked up on the tension. I barely finish my makeup before we pull into the parking lot. We rush inside and find a seat before the end of the first worship song.

The music is too loud and grates on my ears. I can't focus on the sermon because I'm trying to keep from touching David. I wish I had stayed home. I wish the earth would open up and swallow me off this pew. I want to scream or cry, but I have to pretend to be happy. My Bible feels like a lead weight on my lap.

The service ends, and we drop off Rylie in Sunday school and walk to our own class. David finds us seats in the back, and we keep to ourselves, an island of misery in a class full of laughter.

Tori and Greg come in late and wave to us, taking their usual front seat. I force myself to smile and act normal, but my stomach writhes.

How am I going to survive this at home? I have to drive home with this man and sleep in the same bed with him. My nausea grows as class drags on. I keep my face buried in my Bible or my purse. Every muscle is stiff and sore. Then the class is over, and I can finally run home to hide.

"I was worried about you yesterday, Charlotte," Greg says a little too loudly as he walks up from the front row. Tori gives me an apologetic look and whispers in his ear.

"Oh, sorry," he says with a grimace and lowers his voice. "I just wanted to say I'm glad you're okay this morning. Did you get some rest?"

I nod and mutter that I have to go. Tori seems to want to talk, but I can't face her. I turn and follow David at a distance into the hall.

I don't know what really happened yesterday. Maybe I panicked like I used to when Rylie was a baby, and my mind filled in something to be scared of. Or maybe it was the spots of a migraine aura.

We finally escape to the parking lot with Rylie.

No matter what I come up with, the memory is stubborn. It defies being anything other than the foggy outline of a woman. The clammy feeling in my stomach seems to be on its way to being permanent.

"What was Greg talking about?" David demands as I stomp to our car.

"It doesn't matter."

"Excuse me?" David says.

I whirl around to face him. Rylie wiggles her hand out of my grasp and opens her car door.

"So now you care about me and how I'm doing?" I say, my voice rising to a shriek.

"Lower your voice," David says, waves his hands in front of his face like I'm a fussy toddler.

"Excuse me, you suddenly care about how I feel because Greg does? Is that it?"

"Charlotte, that is not fair. Stop it."

I tilt my head to one side and smile bitterly. I don't care if it's fair.

"What was he talking about?" David asks, each word crisp.

"Greg was there when I left their house yesterday," I say, every inch of my skin bristling. "I rushed home because I forgot something, and he must have thought I was upset."

"And that's all?" David says.

I turn to help Rylie with her seat belt and glare daggers at him. David chews on his lower lip. He looks up at the sky.

"No lightning bolts. I guess you're not lying," he says, raising his eyebrows at me. "This time, anyway."

SEVENTEEN

MY SIX-YEAR-OLD VANISHES underneath a small mountain of blue tulle and sequins. Her head pops through the top of the costume after a lot of wiggling and giggling. The student recital is in November, so we have a month to make sure this costume fits perfectly.

"It's itchy!" Rylie says.

"I know, baby. Show me where it itches, and I'll try to put something over it."

The blue and green chevron-patterned leotard shimmers in the sunlight. I help her loop the elastic band at the end of each wing-like sleeve around each hand and adjust the puffy tulle skirt.

"My headband!"

I wrap the soft lacy band behind her ears with the pompoms settled on top.

"Do you like it, Rylie?"

"I'm a peacock!"

The sequined feather pattern on the back of the tulle skirt flashes as she arabesques to the window.

"Now we need that blue and green eyeshadow," I say. She giggles and bounces up and down.

"I want my music! Turn on the music so I can dance."

I turn the music on and watch her prance and strut around the room.

"Hey, look at this!" David says from the kitchen doorway.

"You're home early," I say, edging away from him.

"Is that your new costume, Rylie?"

"I'm a peacock! Watch, Daddy!"

David leans against the doorframe and grins as she taps around the room. She ends with a dramatic bow, runs, and jumps into his arms.

"I'm a peacock."

"Yes, you are. Unfortunately," he says with a raised eyebrow and looks at me. "She's a peacock. Not a peahen."

"What?"

"Peacocks are the boy birds. They're the ones with the big fancy tails. Girl birds don't look like that."

I grit my teeth and give him the evil eye.

"It's a costume," I say, my voice a warning that Rylie hopefully won't notice. "Who cares if it's biologically accurate?"

"They should have made that boy in the class the peacock and the rest of them peahens."

It doesn't matter that Rylie loves it and looks adorable. He has to criticize. Rylie is frowning, pulling at her tutu.

"Get over it," I growl. "It's a dance routine, not science class."

"Charlotte, I wasn't picking a fight." We are squared off against each other with peacock Rylie in the middle.

"Mama, it itches!" She tugs at the back of her costume.

"I'll fix it, baby."

I leave them in the living room to find the pack of moleskin I bought after the last time tulle rubbed my girl's skin raw. She'll be the loveliest little peacock in the recital. The dance teacher has come up with far weirder costumes than a gender-bent bird anyway.

"Charlotte, I wasn't picking a fight." David startles me while I'm digging through the cabinet.

"Why do you have to nitpick every single thing about dance?" I say. If he doesn't want me to bite his head off, he needs to stay at arms-length. "This is her favorite thing in the world, and every single recital, you make some snide remark."

"That was not a snide remark! It was an observation!"

"It was nitpicking. Again. Are you going to make fun of her purple princess costume, too?"

"I wasn't saying the costume was bad."

I am done with this conversation. "Where is Rylie?"

"She's dancing. I turned her music back on." He stands next to the bed, arms folded.

"Maybe keep your opinions to yourself from now on. Or at least don't say it around Rylie. You're going to ruin it for her."

"Charlotte, what is this about?"

What is anything about anymore? He still wants more kids, and he won't stop trying to talk about it. But there is nothing to say, and I won't let him get started.

"You have to ruin anything dance-related when it's the best thing she's ever tried, and she loves it."

"Well, I think this is about you, yet again, getting angry about something tiny as an excuse to pick a fight."

As if I needed any excuses. I finally find the moleskin and leave the bathroom without responding to him. He shouts something after me as I go find Rylie.

"Here, sweetie. Where is the itchy spot?"

I cover the scratchy bits with moleskin, and now Rylie doesn't want to take the costume off. She dances around the living room again and bows dramatically at the end.

"Very pretty. You're a beautiful little peacock, Rylie-Girl," David says from the hallway. He's changed into a T-shirt and jeans.

"Yes, you are."

"When is the recital again?"

"Two weeks from Saturday."

"Are you doing your homework, Rylie?"

Rylie's face instantly falls, and she rumbles like a storm cloud. "I don't want to."

"You don't dance unless homework is done."

"Grrr!" Rylie says, stomping her heel.

I wish he hadn't brought up this battle. So often lately he starts the homework battle and leaves me to deal with it while he messes around with something in the garage. Something in me snaps. He will not do this to me again. Not today.

"I'll bet Daddy can help you with your homework tonight if you get stuck."

His eyebrows furrow, but Rylie brightens a little. "Will you, Daddy?"

"Sure. I guess I can do that. Unless you'd rather Mommy helped you?"

"I think Rylie wants you to help her," I say, giving him a look. *You start the battle, and you finish it, Mister.*

He nods. I won this one for now.

"Why don't you go get in your regular clothes, and we'll get your homework finished?"

"Okay!" she says as if homework is suddenly the most wonderful idea she'd ever heard of. I help her get the top of the leotard off, and she runs away to her room to change.

"I hope it's worth it this time," David says, gesturing to the costumes on the floor.

"She is good, David. This is worth the time."

"How many times has she run off the stage now?"

"She gets stage fright," I say, gathering up the purple princess costume for her ballet routine. "But Colleen has been prepping her. She's going to be fine."

"I hope so."

"She loves tap and ballet, and she has both routines down cold, David," I shout. "She will do great!"

"She's been doing this for over a year now. You spend hours on these expensive costumes and all the private lessons and videos that she's not even in because she hides in the curtains or freezes or whatever. And for what?"

I turn my back to him and shove the fabric and ribbon into my sewing work bag. I snap the cover on my machine as loudly as possible.

"I'm just saying, it's reasonable to consider quitting," he says. "Unless a miracle happens and she doesn't have stage fright anymore."

I look up at him, stick my tongue out, and clamp my teeth down on it. He throws his hands in the air.

"Very mature, Charlotte."

"I'm biting my tongue," I say, picking up my sewing machine.

"And biting my head off every chance you get."

"Maybe stop being so negative," I hiss.

"Then you stop making excuses for her and homework," David says, pointing at Rylie's backpack on the floor.

"Excuse me?"

"Am I the only one in this house who reads her report card?" David throws his hands in the air.

"She has all As and Bs."

"It could be all As if you would push her more."

"It's first grade," I say, setting the sewing machine back on the table a little too loudly.

"Yes, but she needs to learn discipline early!" he says. "Do you know how hard I had to work to get my scholarships? I want her to work hard from the beginning, not have to make up for lost time later."

I cross my arms and sniff. "She is six, David. *Six*."

"Daddy?"

Rylie stands in the living room doorway, purple T-shirt slightly askew around her neck. Her shoulders are slumped. David's ears turn red. Good. I hope he feels horrible.

"Yes, Rylie?" he says, squatting down to her eye level.

"Did I make you mad?" she asks, lip quivering.

"No! No, honey. I'm..."

He looks to me for help. I smile, showing my tongue firmly between my teeth again. He glares at me and clears his throat. Let Mr. Perfect Grades deal with the pain he inflicted.

A flash of blue catches my eye behind Rylie, and I suck in a breath. The woman is standing behind her in the darkness of the hallway. She almost looks like light on fog, and she is crying. She won't stop looking at me. I swallow a scream and steady myself against my sewing table, pretending to tidy it again.

"Rylie, I just want you to do your best on your homework," David is saying. He's looking at me for backup, but he's not getting any.

"I'm sorry," Rylie says, her lower lip quivering. "I'm a bad kid."

"No, you are not," I say firmly.

"No, you're a wonderful kid," David says, pulling her into a hug. "You're my daughter, Rylie. It's just that your mama and I want the best for you, and school is important, honey."

"I'm sorry, Daddy." Rylie bursts into tears. As I turn away to let him deal with the damage he's done, a cold spot makes my skin prickle. I force myself to walk slowly past a blue shadow in the kitchen doorway.

She's not real. She's not.

EIGHTEEN

"MAMA, IS GRANDMA WATCHING?" My little girl is dressed in a soft purple princess dress that puffs out into a fluffy tutu above her knees. Her crown has been pinned on with every bobby pin in the universe. I feel a rush of freezing air as someone opens an outside door. I hope we get snow instead of sleet.

"Yes, she's all ready to watch. She's out there with G-Pa and Nana and Daddy. Go stand with your teacher."

"I'm going to do the best ever!"

"You're going to listen to Miss Colleen, right?" Every nerve tingles from head to toe.

"Yes ma'am," she says.

"And follow all instructions?"

"Yes, Mommy."

"Pinkie square?"

"Pinkie square," she says, crooking her pinkie and smiling. She runs into the group of princesses about to walk down the hall to the stage. I'll never know how Colleen keeps them in line, but I know I'd better duck out now between performances. David and our parents have saved me a seat that I manage to find in the dark theater. I slide in next to David and lean on my dad's shoulder on the other side.

"Is she behaving?" David whispers.

"She's fine."

"Can't wait! Is she next?" Nana Tanya asks.

"No, one more."

"Did you get her crown to stay?" my mom asks.

"I sure hope so."

We're paying for the professional video by the dance studio's team. David wasn't happy about the expense, but I told him to pay it or buy a nicer camera.

"Did you see Tori and Greg came?" David whispers. He points behind us a few rows. I can't believe they're sitting through the whole recital for Rylie. Tori waves and grins like a little kid, and Greg gives us a thumbs-up. I wave back and settle in to watch the side of the stage for Rylie. If she can just be brave. Colleen hasn't given up on her yet, but I don't know how long that will last.

I finally relax when the lights dim as Rylie's class takes the stage. She walks on a little slower than the rest of her class and stands perfectly in line. As the lights come back up, I see that old face of stage fright and wince. I lean forward in my seat, willing her to be brave. She can do this. My heart thunders in my chest, my hands are cold, and I tap my heel against the floor, waiting with her. Her eyes are wide, and I can see her hands shaking even from this far away. She swallows as she searches the crowd for us.

David waves, and Rylie draws a breath. She sees us. What is taking so long to get the music going? The longer we wait, the more likely it is that she'll run. My dad squeezes my hand, and I can sense all five of us fidgeting in our chairs.

The music chimes.

Her eyes light up. Immediately she's spinning around the stage, a whirl of purple. Her feet are perfectly pointed. Her arms snap in perfect time with the staccato notes of the music. She bows an elegant curtsy at the front of the stage, and I hear someone near the front "aww" with delight.

But most of all, she is smiling. The joy on her face steals everyone's eyes as she moves from element to element. This is the beautiful ballerina I've seen in class every week, not the scared little girl terrified at a parent-only showcase.

"Is that the pas-de-chat you were talking about?" my dad whispers. Mom elbows him to hush.

My bouncing knees shake our whole row. The big jump is coming. She's landed it every week in the studio, but she fell in both dress rehearsals. The music crescendoes, and she steps to the center of the stage. I hold my breath.

She lands it. I thought her smile was huge before, but she lights up the whole stage. I can barely sit still. She dips into the last bow, and I'm on my feet before the music can end.

She finally showed everyone what she can do. I look back at Tori, who is standing along with me. The tears streaming down her face reflect the stage lights. She puts a hand over her heart and smiles. Greg stands and claps with her and nods at me.

I can't wait to see Rylie's face when she realizes Aunt Tori and Greg watched her dance, too.

"Charlotte, she was perfect!" my mom whispers.

"She was!"

"That's my girl," David says next to me. "I told her she could do it."

I close my eyes and bite my tongue. *He* told her she could do it?

The grandparents whisper among themselves. I know my mom understands how amazing this truly is. They have to sit through three more dances before her tap routine.

"She did great, Charlie," David whispers in my ear and squeezes my shoulder as I stand up to sneak out to help Rylie with her costume in the green room.

I pretend to be a dignified human being until I hit the doors to the backstage hallway, and then I run full tilt. Rylie pops up from the floor as I push the door open and runs to me, arms outstretched.

"Mommy! Did you see me?"

I can't keep the tears from falling. My little six-year-old is getting heavy, but I pick her up and spin around anyway.

"You were perfect. My perfectly perfect purple princess!" I say as we spin. She giggles and squirms.

"I did it! I did it, and I didn't get scared!"

I set her down again and hug her tight.

"I am so proud of you. So, so proud."

"I didn't trip! Did Daddy see?"

"Yes, and he's so proud of you," I say. The words taste like soap, but I know they are what she needs to hear. "He had such a big smile."

"Rylie Madsen, that was a spectacular performance!" Miss Colleen says, running up to us and hugging Rylie. "Super, stupendous, spectacular, splendiferous, all the S's!"

Rylie giggles and bounces with her. "I did it!"

"You turned that Stage Fright Monster into a cute little puppy, didn't you?" Miss Colleen's lips and cheeks are all sparkly with glitter, making her smile look even bigger.

"No, I turned him into a guinea pig!" Rylie says. Miss Colleen and I both snort.

"A guinea pig? Well, whatever works," she says, hugging Rylie again. "You're a ballerina now."

"No more Stage Fright Monster!" Rylie yells.

"That's right!" Miss Colleen says. "You better get changed for tap. Go get your bag, baby girl."

Rylie runs to her dance bag in the corner.

"I knew she had it in her," Miss Colleen says. I think there might be a tear in her eye. "I am so proud when one of my kids beats the Stage Fright Monster."

"And turns him into a guinea pig, apparently." I laugh.

"Don't knock it if it works, Mama," she says. "She's a real ballerina, Mrs. Madsen. Nothing will stop her now. Okay, peacock costumes on! You have ten minutes, everyone!"

David will have to let her keep dancing after tonight. There's no way he can deny her talent and beauty. I'm so proud of my sweet girl that I feel like I might burst.

I remove the five million bobby pins holding the tiara on her head and help her into the ridiculous blue tulle costume that David hates. It is a little silly, but I won't admit it. Rylie is all wiggle and bounce, and I barely get her settled before callbacks.

My family is so excited they can't sit still when I find my seat again.

"Is this the peacock one?" David asks.

"Yes, and it's adorable. Hush," I tell him as the lights come up.

Rylie is in front, looking even happier than before. She flaps and jumps around the stage, her shoes tapping in nearly perfect time to the music. She shuffles, jumps, and taps from side to side.

If there's one thing she loves about tap, it is being allowed to make as much noise as possible. The silly birds peck each other, pull each other's tail feathers, and end with a final loud squawk and stomp. It's what Miss Colleen calls a "crowd pleaser."

We have to endure a few other dances before the end of the show, but Rylie gets one final bow with the entire studio. I run to the green room.

"Rylie, get your tennis shoes on so we can go see Daddy and Grandma and G-Pa and Nana," I say, hugging her one more time. "And someone else special is here!"

"I see a real ballerina over here," Miss Colleen says behind me.

"Thank you for believing in her," I say.

"I always have. From that very first class." She watches Rylie put her ballet shoes away and lowers her voice. "If she keeps going like this, she has a career ahead of her, Mrs. Madsen."

"You think so?"

"I wouldn't say it if I didn't mean it. Competition season starts soon. Now that she isn't afraid, she'd be perfect for the team. I'd even give her a solo."

The competition team? And a solo? I can't process the words. I stammer a "thank you" and usher Rylie, now in her tennis shoes, out into the lobby.

"There's my ballerina!" David hollers and wraps her into a hug.

"For my pretty purple princess!" Nana says as she hands her a small bouquet of purple carnations.

Rylie bounces and pirouettes with the flowers. My mom hands her a tiny purple gift bag with sparkly paper inside while my dad hugs her and tickles her cheek with his mustache.

"Rylie-Girl, you were awesome!" Tori says, pushing through the crowd in the lobby with Greg following close behind.

Rylie's eyes light up and she jumps in the air.

"Aunt Tori! Did you see me dance?"

"I did, and you were amazing!" she says, hugging her tight. "The most beautiful thing I've ever seen."

"I turned my monster into a guinea pig!" Rylie says.

Tori gives me a confused look, but she knows by now to roll with it.

"Then you are a wizard!" Greg says, giving her a high five. "Good job."

It's a blur of laughter, pictures, flowers, and hugs before we bundle up against the winter cold to go to the car.

"Thank you for inviting us so we could see Miss Rylie bring the house down!" Tori says.

"She's very talented," Greg says, giving Rylie a goofy grin. "Although it's pretty silly they made you wear a boy peacock costume."

"See, I'm not the only one!" David says triumphantly.

Tori punches him in the shoulder.

"Thank you, Aunt Tori!" Rylie yells from her car seat as David buckles her in. I'm so glad Tori and Greg could come. It means the world to Rylie.

David leans over to me as I'm settling into my seat.

"Greg is going back to school!"

I lean back, sure I couldn't have heard him right. "I'm sorry, what?"

"He's starting a master's," David says, eyebrows raised. "In education administration."

"Education?" Greg never struck me as a teacher type. "What would he teach?"

"He wants to be an administrator for a STEM program," David says.

I chew on my lower lip for a moment. "That makes no sense."

"No kidding. I thought he wanted less work, not more."

"Tori is never going to see him."

"Maybe she won't mind," David says, his voice low so Rylie doesn't hear.

I snort. For a moment we're back on the same side, but it feels wrong. I'm also a little annoyed. Why didn't Tori tell me herself?

Instead of answering, I ask Rylie about her favorite part of the recital. My little chatterbox never stops talking for a moment of the drive home, saving me from having to discuss Greg's grad school further. She keeps it up into the house and through her ice cream treat with her grandparents until I finally say, "Time for bed."

"Mama, I want a guinea pig," she says as I tuck her into bed.

"Of course you do," I laugh. "We'll talk about it tomorrow."

"Ok."

"You get some good sleep so we can have fun with Grandma and G-Pa tomorrow, okay?"

"Mama?" she says, her face suddenly serious.

"What is it, sweetie?"

"Can I keep dancing?"

"Of course, you can. Why wouldn't you?"

"Does Daddy want me to?"

My stomach lurches. "Of course he does. Daddy loves your dancing."

"Pinkie square?"

I crook my pinkie and kiss her on the forehead.

"Pinkie square."

"Ok," she says, pulling the covers up to her neck. "I'm going to name my guinea pig Walter."

I laugh and tuck her in. The ballerina lamp glows a soft pink on her smiling face as I shut the door.

NINETEEN

"SHE WANTS A GUINEA PIG," I say as I walk into the living room. "Named Walter." David is turning up the gas fireplace while my parents lounge on the couch.

My dad laughs. "Why Walter?"

"Who knows?"

"Where'd she see a guinea pig?" David asks.

"Renee got one for Liana and Gabby."

"That explains it all," David complains. "Renee needs to stop buying pets!"

"I am so proud of her, Charlotte," Dad says.

"She finally did it!" Mom says, fists in the air. "Finally! I knew she could."

"Her teacher told me she could have a career in dance if she keeps going," I whisper. Rylie doesn't need to hear that yet. "She asked us to join the competition team. They'd do a contest tour in the spring. She even offered Rylie a solo!"

"When did she say that?" David asks.

"Tonight in the green room."

"That's tremendous!" Dad says. "Prima ballerina in the making."

"Sounds expensive," David says.

"I don't know," I say. The competition team is such an honor, I almost don't care about the cost. Why does David have to bring it up? "It would be worth it for the experience."

"You know, I had a thought the other day," David says. "If Rylie had a loft bed in her room, she'd have space for a ballet barre against the back wall."

"Oh, that's a wonderful idea!" my mother says, patting the arm of the couch.

"We could put her desk underneath the bed and put a barre along the wall where her desk is now. You know, opposite the window?"

"That sounds like a lot of work," I say, my voice a warning that I hope my parents don't notice.

"I think it could take a couple long weekends. Less if Casey wants to help me. We might as well do things to make the house fit us since we aren't moving."

I grit my teeth.

"Absolutely," my dad says. "It's your house. Do what you want!"

"It will be a mess in the meantime," I say. "Where will she sleep?"

"Guest room. But I should be able to get her bed back to normal in a day."

It's a fun thought, but all I can see is dollar signs.

"I don't know."

"Oh, come on, Charlotte," Mom says, "She could practice at home! I fully support this, David."

"I'm just concerned," I say, raising one eyebrow.

"I won't let it balloon," David says, and my parents laugh. They know he can't help it when he gets projects going.

"Would you make it a Christmas gift?" I ask.

David better not complain about the cost of competitions if he's going to the trouble of building her a dance floor.

"Or birthday!" David says. "We could do it over spring break!"

"That's perfect! That's when we were going to invite you to the beach! We could go for the week, and she'll come home to a brand new room!" Mom says, clapping her hands. "Oh, you have to do it, Charlotte."

I suppose we do since Mom and Dad are backing David.

My dad wants to talk about the plans for the room, but my mom has been yawning for an hour. I head to our room, so she has an excuse to go to bed. David follows me, and the more he talks, the more I want to put in earplugs.

"She really is talented, isn't she?" he says as he changes into pajamas.

"I've told you that for four years."

"That was a pretty hard dance, wasn't it? It looked hard."

"Yes, and she nailed it like she's done in practice every week for a month," I say, pulling my hair back into a ponytail.

"I'm proud of her."

"Finally."

"Finally? Charlotte, what is your problem?"

"You acting it like it's this huge revelation that she's talented when it's been obvious from day one if you were paying attention."

David tosses his keys on his bedside table. "Are you serious?" he says. "Every other recital, she has barely made it through or runs off the stage."

"Because she had stage fright."

"Or maybe she was disobeying and ignoring the teachers like always."

"So that means she's not talented?" I say.

"That's not the same thing."

"Sounds like it to me."

"I just said I'm going to build her a dance floor, so clearly I think she's talented!" David says, jerking his shirt off.

I look at him, eyebrows raised, and turn away to find my painting shirt.

"Charlotte, I'm being supportive! You want supportive. I'm supportive!"

I finally find my shirt where it was hiding at the back of the closet and yank it out.

"I'm going to work on my painting."

"Now? Your parents are here!" he says.

"They're in bed. I'm not being rude." I pull the shirt on over my pajamas and walk toward the door.

"You're running away."

"I'll be in the garage. Don't bother waiting up."

I retreat to the smells of grease, metal, and paint in my corner, flipping on the bright lights I've rigged up. The car engine clicks as it cools. My current painting is Rylie at dance class. She's standing at the barre in a graceful arabesque, fine blonde hair falling out of its ballet bun and curling around her face in a halo. I miss those fine blonde curls. Her hair is almost as dark as mine now. I prefer her in her simple black leotard and pink skirt to the overly made-up face and glittery performance costumes. Her natural beauty shines, and she smiles bigger than she ever does in recitals.

At least until tonight. Tonight she knew she'd stolen the whole show. She knew she was the star on that stage, and now that she has succeeded once, I don't think she'll ever settle for anything else. As I work on the hands, I wonder if I should be worried that it will go to her head. I want her to be confident, but I also don't want to set her up for disappointment. Competitions are hard. It's not like reality TV, where the cast seems to win every time. She has the talent, but I don't know if she has the discipline.

There's a flash of *that* blue in my peripheral vision. My chest constricts, and I count to ten, swirling the paint on my palette slowly and deliberately.

"Charlotte." David is standing in the doorway. He opened it so quietly that I didn't hear him.

"What?"

"I wanted to say I'm sorry."

I say nothing and keep swirling the brush.

"I'm very proud of Rylie," he says, running one hand through his hair. "This is the first time I've ever seen her finish a dance. And the competition team sounds like a great opportunity if—"

"It is," I cut him off before he can qualify the statement.

He sighs and shrugs. The door shuts behind him. I stare at the canvas, unable to touch it. The blue shadow is still lingering by the car. I don't want to, but I finally force myself to shift my eyes from the paint to the ghost in front of me.

Her shape is muddy and smudged, but I think she's wearing a blue blouse. Her hair is dark like mine. Her face is hard to make out in the darkness, but I can see her eyes. I swallow and try to breathe.

An idea oozes into my mind. It's horrible, but I have to do something. I need another canvas. There's an extra one in the corner. I slowly reach for it and a sketch pencil. I'll start with her eyes. If she won't leave, then I won't look away.

TWENTY

"I REMEMBER this little girl's birth," Pastor Ryan says. "Almost seven years ago. She was born a few weeks early and scared all of us pretty good. In fact, her birthday is coming up in a few days."

The congregation murmurs out in the sanctuary. Rylie peers out into the pews from the baptistry. She leans against the glass edge and waves, probably at her grandparents. Laughter ripples through the room.

"But she came out fighting, and she hasn't stopped. And seeing how God has touched her heart has been a blessing to all of us. Rylie, who do you belong to?"

"Jesus!" She throws a hand in the air, and I hear laughter out in the sanctuary.

"Amen!" Pastor Ryan says, laughing and squeezing her shoulder with a smile. "On your testimony of your faith in Christ, I baptize you, my new little sister, in the name of the Father, Son, and Holy Spirit."

Rylie goes under the water, pinching her nose and blowing her cheeks large like a chipmunk.

"Buried with Him in likeness of His death."

Pastor Ryan pulls her back up with a huge smile, and I snap a photo as her head breaks the water.

"Raised to walk with Him in newness of life. All God's people said?"

"Amen."

The ancient blessing echoes back into the baptistry along with loud applause, and tears sneak down my cheeks. Rylie smiles up at me, pushing her wet hair back from her face.

"Amen!" she says. I hear more laughter, and Pastor John chuckles as he guides her toward the stairs out of the water. The white robe sends rivulets of water all over the floor as she bounds out of the baptistry and hugs me tight. Her dripping baptismal gown soaks my dress pants and blouse. I don't care. I hug my sweet baby girl right back.

A few weeks ago, when she told me she wanted to pray, I thought she meant for something she wanted, like a toy or a movie. Her words echo in my head as she jumps up and down in the changing room.

"I'm bad a lot, Mommy. And I don't want to be. I want Jesus to fix it. I want Him to fix it all the time, not just when I try really hard. He takes all the bad away forever, right?"

Such a depth of understanding under simple words. I knew she meant every word of her prayer. David and I cried as she sat on the couch between us. The next day she asked for a new Bible. She'll get one today with her baptism letter.

What on earth? Barely visible from the baptistry is a woman kneeling near the altar. Her head is touching the floor, and her shoulders are shaking. What on earth is she doing?

"I love you, Mommy!" Rylie says. I tear my gaze from the woman and look down at my daughter. "You're my sister now, too!"

"Yes, I am, sweetie. Your sister in Christ."

Pastor Ryan prays, and we stand together, listening to the words. Rylie's eyes are shut tight. The woman looks up at me.

It's *Her*. The baptistry curtains close. Rylie skips back into her dressing room to change out of her wet clothes, but I'm glued to the spot. I can't move. I can barely breathe.

"Not at church," I whisper to the walls. "Please, not at church."

"Mama?" Rylie pulls on my arm.

I apologize and braid her wet hair into two French braids. This won't ruin my day. I won't let it. I'll block it out, no matter what.

We hurry out into the church to find David and the rest of the family as the congregation sings a hymn. David looks at me with a strange face.

"Are you okay?" he whispers.

I shrug him off and try to join in singing. The words catch in my throat, and I have to mouth them. Every nerve is on edge as the song ends, and I sit down. Church was my one safe place. Now nowhere is safe.

"Look at her," Mom whispers in my ear, making me jump. She points to Rylie.

Rylie has a pen and paper and is writing down the Bible verses from the sermon. I have to smile in spite of my pounding heart. If Mom only knew how she has changed, even in dance. The other day she ran into the living room and showed me a dance she'd made up for a worship song. She spun and jumped and bowed through the verses, ending on her knees in a prayer pose. I'd never seen worship look so beautiful. I couldn't wait for her to show her grandparents.

The service closes, and it takes every ounce of self-control not to run to the car. Tori catches up with us as we reach the back of the sanctuary.

"I have a present for you, Rylie," she says. Rylie tears open the wrapping and squeals. It's a Bible study for girls, and there is a ballerina on the cover. I smile and thank her too, but I have to get out of this church. Now.

Rylie dances to the parking lot, yelling to all her friends on their way to Sunday school, "We're going to swim in the ocean! And we're going to eat watermelon!"

I try to calm down in my seat in the car by reviewing the plan. After a little party and swimming at Nana's house, I'll follow my parents to their new beach condo. We'll stay until Friday. The car is packed and ready. The weather is warm enough for swimming. Everything is going to be fine.

"Can we have watermelon every day?" Rylie asks.

My mother laughs as she gets into the seat next to her.

"You can have all the watermelon you can eat."

"Let's go to the beach right now!"

"We have to go swimming at Nana's first!"

"Does Nana have watermelon?"

"I'm pretty sure she does. She knows no party is complete without it," David laughs.

Rylie is a fish from the moment she sees the pool, and it's only watermelon that draws her out of the water. My mother-in-law knows her granddaughter. David borrows his mom's truck after lunch. He told me Casey is meeting him at the house after Sunday school. At least we weren't arguing today.

I have tried so hard to keep the peace no matter what. At least David is staying behind to work on Rylie's surprise. I don't think I could tolerate two four-hour drives trapped in the car with him.

TWENTY-ONE

THE WAVES ARE LARGER than usual, and Rylie screams with delight. She runs headlong into the water and splashes against the waves.

"Mommy, come on!"

I don't want to get in the water, but I promised myself I would. The water slaps my feet with prickly cold. I hate being in a bathing suit, and I really hate the thought of fish swimming next to me in the water.

"Mommy, you said you would swim with me!"

"I'm coming, sweetie."

I force myself to wade in until the water is over my knees.

"Mommy, here it comes! Jump!" And we jump over the wave together, laughing. The water hits at my knees and hips and nearly knocks me over. Rylie grabs my hand.

"Here we go!" With a leap, we're over another wall of water, hand in hand.

Rylie screams with laughter. She is a beacon of pure joy. I didn't know she could smile this big. It's so infectious that I can't stop smiling myself. Wave after wave, we jump until my legs are aching. A larger one knocks her off her feet and she slips away for a second.

She stands up, sputtering and laughing. "It got me!"

"Are you okay?"

"It got me, Mommy!" She reaches for my hand again and jumps over the next wave, sneezing water through raucous laughter. "This is so fun!"

I look back on the beach to see my parents relaxing under their umbrella. Dad is snapping photos with his camera, and my mom is laughing behind her book.

"Here comes another one, Rylie! Ready?" We jump and the wave pushes us toward the beach again.

"Can we stay here always?"

I wish we could. The salt on my skin and the sound of the ocean waves makes me feel lighter than I have in years. I can't remember the last time Rylie and I played together like this.

She finally tires, and we run back to my parents' umbrella.

"My goodness, are you going to collapse, honey!" my mom asks me, brushing the brim of her floppy sun hat up from her face.

"Probably." I flop onto my beach towel and groan.

"I love the beach!" Rylie hollers between chugs of water from her sand-encrusted water bottle.

"I can tell." My dad chuckles, setting his camera back in its bag. "What do you say we get something to eat?"

"That is an excellent idea," I say.

Rylie nods. She's chugging more water.

"I vote for burgers," my dad says with a grin. "There's a spot up the beach that has really good ones. And fish and chips for your mother."

"Yuck," Rylie says.

"Not for you, silly," my dad says. "For your grandma!"

We finally agree that food is necessary and pack up to find the restaurant. It's too beautiful to eat inside, so we sit at a table on the pier and watch the gulls begging and diving for leftovers. Rylie is too hungry to talk.

"Your mother and I are going to get a special treat," Dad whispers to me as he stands up and winks conspiratorially. "There's a place that sells fried ice cream. We'll be back in a minute."

Rylie watches them go, focused on inhaling as many fries as her mouth can fit. She's almost to the bottom of the basket. I look out over the blue waves and let them lull me into a trance as I chew my burger.

"Mama, are Miss Renee and Mr. Casey going to get a divorce?"

I practically choke on my bite of hamburger. I swallow it slowly and look at my little seven-year-old cherub, picking at her burger and chips.

"What makes you think that, sweetie?" I ask, trying to sound calm.

I've wondered how they had been doing. Renee picks on him so much in Sunday school.

"Because Miss Renee yells a lot."

"She does?"

"Yeah, whenever I go to their house, she yells."

"At you?"

"No, at Mr. Casey. And Gabby and Missile. Everybody else but me."

"I see."

I can easily see Renee yelling at everyone. She yells at her kids at church, so I'm sure it's worse at home. But I doubt they're in that much trouble.

"Missile said she thinks they're going to get a divorce, and then she'll live in two houses."

"Missile thinks that?"

"Yeah." Rylie crunches a fry and looks back at the ocean. "She was sad."

"I would be sad, too," I say. That's when I notice Rylie's quivering lip.

"Mama," she asks, turning back to me. "You and Daddy don't yell. But you're still mad, right?"

"Sometimes we get mad, yes."

"You're not going to get a divorce, are you?"

"Oh, sweetie, no!" I scoot over on the bench to hug her. My heart is crushed. She is trying so hard not to cry. "Mama and Daddy fight sometimes, but that's never going to happen, I promise." I can't even bring myself to say the word "divorce."

She sniffs and takes another bite of a chip.

"I love your daddy," I whisper, but it feels like a lie. I haven't been acting like I love him. I'm just so angry with him. Why doesn't he see it isn't worth the risk for more kids? I keep hoping he'll realize I'm not going to change my mind and accept it. But holding my sniffling daughter here on the pier, shame pours over me. I thought we had hidden it from her, but she sees we're struggling. I don't know what to do. She scrubs the tears away with her fists and hugs me.

The waves crash against the pier, and we sit for a long moment. I have to reassure her, even if I can't reassure myself.

"Rylie, thank you for talking to me about this," I say, raising her chin and brushing her salty hair out off her forehead. "I'm sorry that Missile is worried, but your daddy and I love each other even when we're mad. And Miss Renee and Mr. Casey do, too."

"But what if they do get a divorce?"

My sweet girl is worried for her best friend. And now I'm wondering if I should let them play so often.

"I don't think they will, Rylie." I don't want to be dishonest, though. Renee has been angry ever since Noah's birth. At Bible study, I heard someone tell her she shouldn't be so hard on Casey, and Renee actually responded, "Shut up." She played it off as sarcasm, but we all knew it wasn't.

"We'll pray for them, okay? We'll pray that God helps Miss Renee and Mr. Casey not to yell so much."

"Okay."

As I whisper a prayer, I worry about what to do next. Should I keep Rylie from playing at their house for awhile? Should I talk to Renee? Maybe David could talk to Casey. Or maybe I could ask Grace to talk to Renee.

"Amen. Can we go play in the ocean again?"

"We'd better wait for Grandma and Grandpa and their surprise."

"Ok. I hope it's a guinea pig."

I snort. "It's not that. But you'll still like it."

TWENTY-TWO

"RYLIE, drop your suitcase in the laundry room so we can wash your clothes."

"Mama, it smells funny."

"What smells funny?"

"The house."

"Hmm. I wonder why?"

"It smells like wood or something."

"Why don't you find Daddy?" I muse nonchalantly from the back of the car. "Maybe he'll know why it smells weird."

"Daddy!" Rylie hollers into the house. She disappears around the corner, and I sneak into the house behind her. "Daddy, where are you?"

She sheds her jacket on the couch and follows David's voice to her room. The door is shut.

"Who is that out there?" David teases.

"Daddy, what are you doing in my room?" she says, hands on her hips. I stay hidden behind the edge of the hallway entrance.

"Open the door and see."

She turns the doorknob and squeals as she sees inside.

"My bed!"

"I made something for you, Rylie-Girl!"

"It's ballet! It's a ballet room!" she shrieks with delight. "Mama, my room!"

"What do you think?" David asks me.

The room is completely transformed. He chose a clean, modern design for her new loft bed, but he painted it ballet pink. He's even hung her tutu on one corner. Her desk is lit by rope lights that encircle the underside of the bed. But the main attraction is the barre.

Not only is there a barre, but David has installed a proper wooden dance floor, filling half the room and a full-wall mirror. He has also added can lights above the floor. Her ballet shoes are waiting for her on the floor.

"Wow, your daddy is pretty amazing, isn't he?" I pat her shoulder and smile at David. "Good job."

"I got a good deal on the mirror," he says. "Casey found it through a friend at work."

"I can dance in my room! I can dance, Mama! Watch!"

She tosses her shoes off, and I wince.

"Is that glass safe?"

"It's from a yoga studio that closed, so it's specifically designed for gyms," David says. "Even if she hits it, it won't shatter." The engineer thinks of everything. I should have known. "But we're also going to lay some ground rules," he winks at me. "Rylie, you have to be careful with your new special mirror and barre. That is glass, and it can break. So can the barre."

"Okay, Daddy."

"No throwing toys, especially hard ones, okay?"

"Okay."

"And no hanging on the barre like a monkey."

"Okay." She is only half-listening. She is too busy putting on her ballet shoes. "Watch me!"

She steps to the barre and stands in first position, left arm on the barre and right arm outstretched.

"And plié!" she says and bends her knees. She snaps back up and grins. "And grand plié!" She bends her knees deeper this time and laughs. "And relevé!" She lifts up onto her tiptoes and raises her arm above her head.

"Such a beautiful little ballerina!" I say.

"Okay, come here and let me show you your bed!" David tickles her and puts her over his shoulders. "See this right here? It's a little tiny table for your water bottle. And if you don't need it, you can swing it out and away, like this!"

The triangular platform glides up, over, and out of sight behind the head of the bed.

"Nice, Daddy," I say.

"Same as our desks in Raymond Hall, remember? Same principle anyway," he reminds me. I nod and grin, remembering those funny small desks.

"And under here is your desk for doing your home-work," he continues. "See this button? That's for the rope lights. Push it."

She jabs the large white button, and the lights blink out. She turns them back on and giggles.

"I want to do my ballet now," she says, wiggling out of his arms and running back to the barre.

"Okay, but what are the rules?" David asks her.

"No throwing hard things and no...um..." she frowns and taps her finger on her cheek pensively. "No hanging! No hanging on the barre."

"Good girl."

I watch her bounce up and down. David turns off the

overhead light, so the room is lit only by her new rope lights. The room is cozy and inviting, perfect for my little girl.

Eyes. It looks like there are eyes peering out at me from the bed. I'm frozen in place. I'm not seeing this. It's an after-image from the bright lights a few moments ago. It must be. I slowly turn away to watch Rylie in the mirror. There are no eyes in the mirror. Just the glow from the porch light peeking through the blinds.

"I'm going to finish unloading the car," I say, leaving David and Rylie in the room. I flip the porch light off as I step through the hallway to the living room and roll my eyes at myself. This is getting ridiculous. I don't know what She wants, but I wish She'd just tell me. These images simply interrupt my day, but I have no idea what they mean. I'm tired of trying to figure out the message behind them.

Maybe there is no message.

TWENTY-THREE

"HI, LADIES," I say as Renee troops through our front door with Liana and Gabby. She told me she was leaving Noah home with Casey for "man time."

"Show me this ballet room I've heard so much about!" Renee says to Rylie.

Rylie grabs Liana's hand and leads everyone to her room. She's made it her own over the last two weeks. Liana and Gabby ooh and ahh.

"Take your shoes off!" Rylie commands. "No shoes on my dance floor. Only socks or ballet shoes."

"And what are the other rules, sweetie?" I ask her.

"No hanging on the barre and no throwing toys. You could break the mirror!" she says, shaking a finger at Gabby, who is too busy taking off her shoes to care.

"It's even fancier than Casey said," Renee says. "This is like a real studio!"

"Thanks for letting David borrow him for the week."

"Got him out of my hair, so thank you!" She laughs.

Rylie steps to the barre and begins a basic warmup routine. After watching, Liana and Gabby follow her lead for a few minutes. We leave the girls to play and fill our coffee mugs in the kitchen. Renee tells me about Liana's gymnastics class, and I nod while I try to figure out how to bring up what Rylie told me at the beach. Maybe I shouldn't worry so much. Kids can assume a lot from small things. I also don't want to upset Renee.

But I can't help but remember her tone in Bible study. I trace the handle of my mug with my finger to focus my nerves. It's not like I have anything to really offer her in the way of advice. Sometimes I can barely be in the same room with David.

"So I have to tell you what happened at the softball game the other night," Renee says, voice low. She glances over her shoulder toward the hallway to Rylie's room. "If David hadn't abandoned the team this year, you would have been there to see Greg blow his stack. Got in the umpire's face and yelled at him right in the middle of the game. It was crazy, Charlotte. He hadn't got a hit all night, then the umpire calls his third out, and he just loses it." She's waiting for my reaction, but I'm so stunned I don't know what to say.

"Wow."

"Casey and Reuben had to pull him back to the bench. Like physically separate him."

I'm at a loss for words. That sounds so unlike Greg.

"Tori just sat there in the bleachers." Renee rolls her eyes. "I mean, come on. Tell him to chill. He was being ridiculous."

"She was probably embarrassed." My stomach clenches. I don't feel good about this conversation at all, but I can't think of anything else to talk about.

"Then she should be embarrassed all the time," she says, sipping her coffee with a smirk. "Yvonne told me Greg didn't apologize until Reuben told him he'd be ejected from the game if he didn't."

"Really?"

"She said he was bright red the whole conversation."

"But he did apologize," I say. It's the only positive thing I can think of.

"It wasn't sincere. He just didn't want to get kicked out."

I say nothing. Renee tends to be dramatic. I don't know Yvonne very well outside of school meetings, but her husband Reuben seems nice. I don't know how much I should believe this story. Greg is opinionated and blunt, but I can't imagine him actually yelling at anyone.

"Don't you think it's messed up, Charlotte?"

"Yes!" I stammer. "I'm just..."

"The whole team looked like jerks in front of Grace Presbyterian. One of the girls I used to work with goes there!" Renee complains.

I don't answer. No matter what I say, I could hurt Tori if Renee repeats it later. I wish I could think of a way to change the subject. Why am I so bad at this?

"So she hasn't told you anything?" Renee asks, leaning her chin on her hand.

"Who?"

"Tori!"

"No."

Renee sips her coffee and peers at me over her mug. "I heard someone say she and Greg were in counseling. If not, they should be. Or at least anger management for him."

I don't know if Tori is still seeing Darren. Our schedules changed years ago, and I ended my visits when Rylie started school. I can't decide if saying nothing is better or worse than trying to come up with something to say.

"Has she mentioned counseling?" Renee says. The

directness of the question shakes me out of my worrying. Suddenly I'm angry. It's wrong of her to ask. Their daughter is terrified they will divorce, and she's poking her nose into Tori's marriage. Of all people!

"No." The word is flat on my tongue, but I try to put a finality in it that will shut Renee down. "And I'm sure Greg was just having a bad day. We all have bad days."

"Yeah, he has a lot of bad softball days." She gives me a look and sips her coffee.

"They have a lot on their plate right now," I falter. "Has he finished installing the new sound system in the youth room?"

"I don't know, probably," Renee says. "He's doing it for free, so he's been kind of slow about it."

I shift in my seat and try to think of some way to change the conversation. I keep thinking about Rylie crying on the beach. I have to change the subject. I can't sit through more questions about my best friend from someone who is supposedly her friend, too.

Renee purses her lips, and I want to tell her not to say whatever she's thinking. Whenever she makes that face, she ends up saying something she shouldn't.

"I also heard he applied to FCS for the high school admin job," she says.

"What?" I say. "Who told you that?"

"Somebody in the office."

"I hadn't heard anything about it from Tori." My voice is more defensive than I mean it to be. Why didn't Tori tell me?

"You don't have to get all mad at me, Charlotte," Renee says, rolling her eyes.

"I'm not mad." I step away from the kitchen counter.

"Come on, let's sit in the living room. The couch is more comfortable."

It's also closer to our children, which means Renee won't be able to say as much. I hope.

"What's with Tori's dresses and stuff lately?" Renee says, settling in on the couch with her legs criss-cross underneath her.

"What do you mean?" I say, shifting uncomfortably in my seat.

"Oh, come on. You know," Renee says. "Her hair. It's always up in a bun or a braid now. And those long skirts."

"They're trendy," I say.

"Uh, no," Renee says. "Not *that* kind. It's just weird. I mean, she still looks cute, but it's weird."

I look down at my hands and wish I had never invited Renee over. I shouldn't have to defend one of my friend's reputation to another. I shiver and notice Her watching me from the kitchen, shimmering like a mirage. What I can make out of Her face looks familiar, but I can't figure out why. It's difficult to make out Her whole face at once, but She shakes Her head slowly, and I can see Her mouth is set in a thin line. I feel a flicker of defiance kindle in my chest.

"You okay, Charlotte? Did you hear me?"

I look back to Renee and sit straighter. "I heard you," I say, my voice crisp. "I like Tori's clothes. Why don't we go check on the girls?"

Renee's cheeks turn pink. In the doorway, a smile flickers across Her face before She fades to nothing.

TWENTY-FOUR

"SO RYLIE TOLD me something at the beach," I say. I slip the fuchsia thread into the bobbin of the sewing machine and start winding slowly.

"You mean over spring break?" David answers from the couch behind me. "That was months ago, Charlotte."

"Sorry. We've been so busy." I watch the thread wind evenly so I don't have to look at David. "It was about Liana. And Renee and Casey."

"Oh?" David turns off the news and puts his phone on the coffee table.

For the first time this evening, I look him in the eye. "She said that Liana was worried they're going to get a divorce." He doesn't seem surprised.

"What did you say?"

"I told her I didn't think they were."

"I don't think they are either," he says, but he doesn't sound convinced.

"But you don't seem too surprised. Did Casey say something?"

"Just bits and pieces." He looks me straight in the eye. "Renee is pretty difficult to live with."

"Oh." I frown and fiddle with the bobbin. "What do you think is the problem?"

"They've always fought a lot. At least that's what Casey said."

"Renee isn't shy about that either," I say with a hollow laugh. She has complained so much about Casey this spring that I'm actually glad Bible study is almost over.

"I don't know what they're working through, but they always have fireworks getting there," David says.

"But they're not splitting up, are they?"

"No way. They're both too stubborn for that." David snorts. "And they don't believe in divorce." He breathes in and waits until I look at him. "Like us. Not on the table."

"Right." I clear my throat. This is why I haven't said anything for months. The other part of what Rylie said is much harder to even admit out loud, much less discuss with David.

I watch him for a moment, and take a deep breath. "Rylie said something else, David."

"What?" I can see tension in every muscle of his body.

"She asked if we were going to...well, you know."

David's face falls. "No. She did?" He sits back against the couch and looks at the ceiling. There are tears in the corners of his eyes as he breathes slowly, his jaw working back and forth. "Okay, that's it. That's the end of this."

"Excuse me?"

"We have to deal with this." He rubs his eyes and sighs. "We have to talk about it."

"Oh, come on."

"We have to," David says.

"It never does any good. Nothing changes."

He looks away for a moment and rubs his hands together in front of his chin. "You mean I never change," he says.

I shrug and go back to my sewing.

"No, you're not going to do that," he says. "Our daughter is worried her parents may split up, and that is our fault. Ours, Charlotte."

"You think this isn't killing me, too?" I say. "I've been miserable since spring break!"

"So we have to talk about it. For her sake, we have to."

I swallow and stare at my sewing machine. I don't see how it's going to help, but maybe Rylie being upset matters enough that he might change. "Fine." I turn the machine off, put away my pins and seam ripper, and cover the sewing table with the dust cloth. I spin in the chair and face him, arms folded. He sighs and folds his hands in front of him.

"I want to know what really scares you about having another child," he says. It's the same question as always. But I can't answer it honestly without saying things that don't make sense. Instead, I have to say the only other plausible answer.

"I do not want to leave Rylie without a mom. Period."

"Of course not." He says his line in our own personal tragedy play. How many times will we have this same conversation? Isn't repeating something and expecting a different result the definition of insanity?

"But there's more you're not saying," he says, frustration hardening his voice.

"That's it. I'm not risking it again."

"I understand that. I promise, I do."

"Then why do you keep asking?" I say. I can't keep the edge out of my voice.

"Because something about it is just off, Charlotte. I know you."

"You *think* you do," I say. This is more insanity. He knows what I'm going to say. "That's the whole problem. You think you know me, but you just don't."

"Okay, fine. I'll give you that."

I stare. This is a new scene in our little play.

"I know you *before* it happened," he says. "But I admit I'm missing something now." He looks me in the eyes until I have to look away. "You know what it feels like to me, Charlotte? It feels like I lost you in that hospital room. You went in one person and came out another."

My mouth is going dry. The old ugly panic clutches me. "I really don't want to talk about that."

"I think that's the problem. We've never talked about it. Ever. Rylie is seven, and we've never talked about what happened."

"Because it was horrible."

"Do you know what I remember most? I remember the nurse. She heard what you said to me."

"What are you talking about?"

"You said, 'Take care of her for me. I love you.' You went completely white." Tears fall silently down his cheeks. He can't look at me. "And then you passed out."

"I don't want to talk about this." My memory of that moment is fuzzy and only comes back in my nightmares. Until David said it, I wasn't sure if it really happened.

"She was scared. I knew I could lose you."

The air turns hot and thick, like trying to breathe through peanut butter. He reaches for my hand, but I move away.

"I told you I don't want to talk about it," I manage to say.

"And then the doctor came in and had me leave. This

other nurse walked me down to the nursery, and I just kept thinking..." He coughs and rubs his eyes. "I didn't know how I was supposed to take care of Rylie alone. She was crying, and the nurse wanted me to hold her. I just couldn't." He stares at his empty hands and takes a deep breath. "I just sat there looking at her. Because it wasn't fair."

"What are you talking about?"

"She was supposed to be with her mama," he says, tracing the edge of the couch cushion with one finger. "It wasn't fair for it to be me holding her first. I held her hand. I patted her. But I couldn't hold her. Not until they told me you were going to be okay." His chest shudders, and he shifts against the couch pillows. "Then we sat there and snuggled, with that oxygen mask and everything. And I told her that her mama was going to hold her as soon as she could."

His voice breaks, and he wipes away the tears that are soaking his shirt. He stares at the floor.

"I've never been that scared before," he says.

"And you want to risk that happening again?" I hiss. "Imagine how I felt!"

He says nothing for several moments, his eyes on his hands. I pick at the edge of my sewing table and wait. Let him stew in his selfishness. I'm tired of this conversation.

He looks up, and something has changed in his face.

"I think that's the problem," he says.

"What?"

"I just realized something," he says. "You know me and statistics." His voice sounds as if he is trying to make sense of a hard math problem like when we studied together in college. He looks me in the eye, carefully watching my response.

"When you were in the hospital, I sat down and

researched placental abruption. I read all kinds of stuff. I knew the stats backwards and forwards because I wanted to know if you'd be okay." He folds his hands in front of his face and looks up at the ceiling fan. "The chances of abruption are pretty low to begin with, and they are still low after you've had one case."

I sniff and turn away from him. "I don't care about the numbers."

"But that's exactly what I'm saying," he says quickly. "I know it doesn't help *you* feel better! Those stats make *me* feel safe, but that's not enough for you. I should know that. I've been married to you long enough that I should know that." His shoulders drop. "I'm an idiot, Charlotte."

"I didn't say it," I say.

"No, really," he says, "I was being an engineer, calculating odds and risk. But you can't see what's going on in my head." David covers his mouth with his hands. "And I'm sorry. I'm mad at myself right now, not you." He reaches for my hand, and I reluctantly let him take it.

"I thought I could make you feel safe. We had this plan, you know? I thought if I helped you see it was safe, we could get back to the plan and keep going." He gives me a sad smile.

My guts are twisting. I count to ten slowly and try to breathe.

"Do you know what I see when I look at you?" David says. "I see a woman who is absolutely terrified. You jump at shadows. You cry in the bathroom when you think I'm not listening. And your nightmares wake me up, too."

I can't look at him. My face will betray me. I don't know what he's trying to say, but I don't think I'm going to like it.

"I'm just realizing that I've been trying to 'logic' you out of being scared, but all you've heard from me is that I care more about a plan than my *wife*," he says slowly. He looks at the ceiling. "You must think I'm so selfish. And you're right. I am."

"So, what are you saying?" I say.

"I'm saying forget the plan for three kids!" he says. "Forget all of it. We're one and done."

If I wasn't so shocked, I might laugh. I don't know how to take this after so much time at odds. My heart pounds in my chest. He's finally apologizing. He's doing everything I've wanted him to do for the last three years. I want to put away all the anger and go back to how we were before, but I don't think I can.

"I'm sorry," he says, squeezing my hand. "I'm trying to pull my head out of...wherever it's been."

"I'm sorry, too," I whisper. I don't feel it, but something tells me I need to say it.

He gently squeezes my hand and offers a hug. I don't know if I want to hug him, but I do anyway. He kisses the top of my head.

"No more kids." He strokes my hair and takes a shaky breath. "We're done. I just want you back."

I don't know how to tell him that the woman who went into that hospital is never coming back. He's finally agreeing and coming to my side, but it's hollow. I pull away, but he doesn't let me go.

"I'm sorry," he whispers into my ear.

Why does it feel like I've lost the battle?

"I love you, Charlie."

My old nickname makes my heart ache. I lean my head on his shoulder.

"I love you, too." It's been so long since I actually wanted to be here. So long since I felt safe with him. I don't fit the way I used to.

"Nice to hug you without you cringing," he whispers. His words catch in his throat. I don't have to look up to know he's crying. He has no idea how messed up everything is, but maybe now things will get better if I give it time.

"Do you think you should talk to Darren again?" he asks after a few moments.

"No." I haven't been in his office in years. Going back feels like admitting defeat.

"I'll go with you if you want. Maybe he could help us both."

"I don't want to see him."

David nods and kisses the top of my head. "If you change your mind, I'll go with you."

"Ok."

We part after an awkward pause, and he squeezes my hand. Over his shoulder, I see a blue shadow walking through the living room.

TWENTY-FIVE

"GOOD MORNING, CHARLOTTE!" Greg's voice startles me in the school hallway. I didn't expect to see him in the elementary school since he's over the high school STEM program. It's Rylie's first day of second grade, and I was hoping to get to her room early to talk to her teacher one more time. He rushes up to me, his hands in constant motion. I've never seen him so energetic.

Rylie grabs my knee and buries her head in my jacket as if she's much younger than eight.

"Hi!" I smile. "Congratulations! Is this your first day?"

"No, I came in last week. Meetings with the faculty and such." He kneels down next to me and grins at Rylie. "Hey there. You ready for school today?"

Rylie buries her face again, and I pat her back. "I think she's a little nervous."

"Nothing to be nervous about, missy. You're a smart girl, and you listen to your teachers, right?" he says.

She nods.

"Of course that's right," Greg says, standing tall again

and putting his fists on his hips like a superhero. "You'll be a model student."

I snort at that phrase. I'm not under any illusions about my daughter. Greg pats her on the shoulder and turns to face me.

"I can walk with you to her class," he says. "It's on the way to my office."

"Thanks. She's in Miss Preston's class." I appreciate the gesture, but I wish he wouldn't. Rylie is nervous enough already.

"I know you will learn a lot from Miss Preston, Rylie." He strides ahead of us and opens the door to the classroom.

The room is covered in a jungle theme. There's even a bookshelf in the corner transformed into a tree. Only two other kids are here so far and both are sitting in bean bag chairs with books. Rylie's teacher has added some extra touches since "Meet the Teacher" Day.

"Hi!" Greg says to the short, slim blonde arranging chairs. "This is Rylie Madsen and her mother, Mrs. Madsen."

"We've met, but it's Charlotte, please," I say. I'm sure she remembers me after Rylie pirouetting around the room last week. Miss Preston shakes my hand again and leans down to see my daughter where she's hiding behind my leg.

"Hi, Rylie! I have a brand new book about ballerinas to show you. Do you want to hang up your backpack and help me find it?"

Rylie nods but doesn't answer.

"Say 'Yes, ma'am,' Rylie," Greg prompts. I kneel down next to her and tip her chin up to look me in the eyes. She doesn't resist, but she looks angry. She frowns at Greg and looks back to me. I wink. It's all I can do without making Greg look bad.

"You're going to have a great day, honey." I put all the cheer I can muster into that sentence, and she tries to smile back at me.

"Here, let's find your name." Miss Preston offers her hand with a smile that is pure sunshine. "I like your backpack. Purple is my favorite color. Is it yours, too?"

Rylie takes her hand and follows her to the row of cubbies. Greg nods his approval.

"I have to get back to the office," he says. "Let me know if you ever need anything. Oh, and have a lovely lunch with my wife this afternoon! Are you going to Padre's? You should go there. Great lunch deals."

Greg lingers in the doorway and salutes Rylie before he leaves. I wish he'd gotten the job at the other school, even though I know the commute will be easier on him this way.

I turn back to see Rylie in a perfect arabesque next to the bookshelf and explaining the proper terminology to her teacher. Miss Preston mimics her with a smile and asks if her form is correct. My daughter tells her to fix her floppy left arm, and I try not to laugh too loudly.

"Mama, Mama!" Rylie runs to me with a grin and points at her teacher. "She took ballet when she was little!"

"I told Rylie she'll have to show me one of her routines at recess today," the teacher says.

I lean down and pull Rylie into a big hug. "Love you, big girl. You have a wonderful day, and I'll meet you on the front steps at three."

"Love you, Mama," she says. She wriggles out of my arms and skips back to the book corner.

I head from the school to the grocery store and fumble through my list with a few tears in my eyes. I still dread homework time this evening. Second grade is going to be a lot of work. I've heard about the workload from the other ladies in Sunday school. Rylie can handle it, but she prefers dancing to studying. Maybe I can figure out a way to work dancing into her homework.

I drive home and put the food away. The doorbell rings as I'm putting pasta in the cupboard.

"I hope you don't mind that I'm early," Tori says, standing at my front door with a big smile. "I had a client cancel their appointment, so I thought we'd take the extra time." She looks elegant in her crisp navy blazer and flowy tangerine dress with an empire waist. Her hair is pulled up into a French twist. The to-do list of chores I'd planned to finish before she got here nags me, but I grab my purse anyway. I'll finish it all somehow.

We decide on a European-style cafe, and Tori lets me drive. She seems a little quieter than normal, like she's thinking. Whatever has her so preoccupied must be good because she's grinning even more than usual.

"I'm so glad you didn't want to go to Padre's," Tori says as she holds the door to the cafe for me. "We've been eating Mexican food all week. I want pasta salad!" The restaurant is busy, but they take our orders in a flash. I must look grungy in my jeans and T-shirt sitting next to Tori in her business clothes. Next time I'll change into a nicer blouse. The room smells like a mix of pepperoni, pickles, and chocolate, but it's delicious instead of disgusting. I think I'll bring Rylie here sometime.

"I saw your hubby when I dropped Rylie off this morning," I say.

"Oh, good! He's so happy! He's building the STEM department from the ground up, so he's getting to be creative. And they asked him to start a robotics club."

"If he ever needs ideas, I'm sure David would love to help," I say. I immediately regret saying it. David doesn't get along with Greg sometimes. Hopefully, Greg won't need help.

"So I was going to tell you..." Tori trails off. "I mean, I was wondering. Goodness, I can't talk today!" She brushes an errant hair behind her ear and shrugs. "I don't know..."

"Spit it out, Vix!" I say, mimicking the joking tone I've heard from Greg so many times. Tori jumps as if I'd touched her with a static shock. She shakes her head and pats my hand hard.

"No, it's Tori. I'm always Tori." She wipes her mouth on a napkin.

I frown. "But doesn't Greg—"

"I'm *always* Tori." She's hiding behind her drink, fiddling with her straw and trying to avoid my eyes. "He knows I don't like Vix. " She grimaces and takes another bite of pasta.

I chew my sandwich and try to think of a way to change the subject.

"I thought it was like David calling me Charlie," I say. "I'm sorry, Tori."

"No, it's his little joke from our honeymoon." She picks up her iced tea and stirs it with a straw. "But it's not funny. I wish he would forget about it."

"I'll never call you that again, promise," I say over my sandwich.

"I'm not mad at you, girl," she says and shrugs. "I got sick the weekend of our wedding. The worst cold I've ever had! I ended up with bronchitis for like a month after we got back. Antibiotics and an inhaler. I look so bad in our wedding photos."

"You looked lovely," I protest.

"You can see my red nose in every picture. I had to carry tissues in my bouquet. My nose dripped during the prayer!

It just got worse on our honeymoon. I was coughing like crazy, stuck on this cruise ship."

"You poor thing!"

"I got it in my head that I would feel so much better if I could get some Vicks Vaporub."

"Oh, *that* Vicks." Her face makes my stomach curdle. She's miserable just talking about this. I wish I hadn't brought it up.

"Greg found me some in town on our second stop. It sort of helped." She shakes her head and spears a piece of apple with her fork. "I ended up spending the whole trip either in our cabin or on a chair on deck so I could at least see the ocean."

"That's so bad! It didn't help at all?"

"Greg said the whole cabin smelled like menthol. We both hate that smell now."

I want to laugh, but she's not laughing, so I just say, "Yuck."

"The last night of the cruise, I made myself go to the big fancy dinner and coughed through the whole thing. Greg said the table behind us were whispering about something, and the only thing he could make out was 'Vicks.'" She raises one eyebrow at me, and her forehead is turning red through her makeup. "They could smell me. The whole dining room could smell me."

She stabs a bit of pasta with her fork. I can't help it. I reach over and squeeze her hand.

"Oh, Tori."

"He thought it was hilarious. He made jokes about it for weeks."

My cheeks burn. "That's not funny."

"Yeah, Greg can be..." She chews on the thought for a few moments and seems to decide not to finish it. "Anyway, that's why he calls me Vicks sometimes." She inhales more pasta.

"I'm so sorry! When you told me you were sick, I thought it was a mild cold."

"It's okay. It was the worst honeymoon ever. For me at least," she says. Her mouth twists into a smile. "He did some snorkeling on his own and said he had fun."

"Oh." The thought is so unfair. "Maybe you can go on another cruise and make up for it sometime."

"I'd rather go skiing or something," she says. "We're supposed to go to Colorado over Christmas and ski."

I ask her about the new home design business she's running. It's still new and fun, and it's a safer topic. We reluctantly put our dishes in the bin and head out to the car.

"I like being my own boss. I keep my own schedule and hand Stacy a report at the end of the week. She lets me handle everything the way I want."

The trip back to my house is too short.

"I'm praying Greg has a great first week," I say as we hug goodbye.

"Oh, please do," she whispers. "And keep praying. Things are going so well right now. I just want it all to keep going."

"It will, Tori," I say as she opens the car door.

"I hope."

TWENTY-SIX

"RYLIE," I whisper to the back seat. She's fast asleep in her booster chair. My sweet eight-year-old has almost outgrown it, but part of me can't bear to let her out of it. I can't believe it has been a whole year since the beach trip with my parents. This year's regional competition was close enough to their house that we didn't have to pay for an expensive hotel. Mom made sure Rylie ate her weight in watermelon and ice cream all week between competition times, and her leotard collection has doubled. By the time we wrapped up regionals, Rylie and Grandma both declared we should make "Spring Break With Grandma" a tradition.

The garage door closes behind our car, and David appears in the door in a dirty shirt and old frayed jeans. I put a finger to my lips and point to Rylie behind me.

"Still has her medal on," I whisper.

"Mommy?" Rylie says, her voice thick with sleep.

"We're home, honey."

"Daddy, I won!" She hurries out of her booster to show him her medal. "And Ellie won for her solo!"

"Who is Ellie?" David asks.

"She's in the preteen group," I explain. "Miss Colleen has the older girls mentor the younger ones. She helped Rylie do her performance makeup."

I'm grateful Rylie took the blush and mascara lessons from Ellie much better than she did from me.

"Yeah, she does ballet and tap *and* jazz!" Rylie says. "She's awesome."

David whispers something in her ear, and she grins wide.

"Mommy, you need to go inside now," she commands.

"Oh, I do, do I?"

"Yes. Daddy said so."

Now I'm suspicious. "Why do I need to go inside?"

"Don't freak out," David says. "I have a surprise for you. It's almost done." He winks at Rylie.

"Did Daddy tell you what the surprise is?" I ask her.

"Yes, he did." She giggles and bounces on her heels.

"Come inside, Charlie," David says, sweeping a giggling Rylie onto his back and galloping past me into the house.

I open the trunk and pull our suitcases into the laundry room. The house smells like sawdust and paint. What on earth has he been doing? We just remodeled Rylie's room last spring. I leave everything on the floor to follow the sound of whirring fans.

Our house has a door where it didn't before. Next to the fireplace in the living room where we used to put a bookcase, there is an elegant French door. It leads out into a room where part of our porch used to be. I can't seem to move forward to look inside, so I stand in the kitchen doorway staring.

"The paint isn't dry yet. Took longer than I expected," David appears in the doorway to the front room.

"Where's Rylie?"

"Getting dressed for bed." He shifts uncomfortably and gestures a hand toward the room. "It's your painting studio."

"My what?"

"Want to see?" He guides me through the living room to the door and stands, watching me.

Track lighting, huge windows, and concrete floor come together before me like one of those weird three-dimensional pictures, and I blink, half expecting it to vanish. Have I stepped into an alternate universe?

"*My* studio?"

"You said painting helps you," David says. He rubs the back of his head with his hand and shrugs. "Now you have someplace to paint that isn't the garage. Somewhere that's yours."

"How did you get this done so fast?"

"Larry, Casey, and Jim from work came over. I had the wood ordered ahead of time."

I feel his eyes on me, but I don't know what to say. I don't know why he has done this. I never said I needed or even wanted a studio.

"It's not huge, but it should be big enough. I hope."

"Why?" My heart pounds in my ears. I'm scared to let myself be happy.

"Why what?"

"Why did you do all this?"

He shrugs and waits for me to step inside. The floor is gritty under my shoes. Wide windows fill the top half of the wall, and I can see my shadow on the grass outside.

"I have my space at my office. Rylie has her dance floor. This is yours."

"I can't believe you did this."

"I can pour more concrete for the porch if we need it," he says. He points to the concrete floor. "It looks weird because

I coated it with graffiti repellent. If you drop a brush or something, the paint won't stick. Easy cleanup."

"Are you kidding?" I can't believe what I'm seeing. This space is perfect. I want to jump around like a little girl, but I'm so scared I'll wake up tomorrow to find I dreamed this. I could never have imagined David would make something like this for me. How do I thank him?

"The lights all move so you can get the right angles," he says. His hands are shaking, and he shifts from right to left.

"I love you." I say that sentence all the time, but I know from his eyes that this time he believes me again. My heart almost hurts looking at this room. "It's amazing. It is absolutely amazing."

"Sorry that it isn't quite finished."

"David, you built a room! A whole, entire room!"

I wrap my arms around his neck and kiss him. He pulls back a little.

"I stink."

"I don't care," I say, kissing him again.

He kisses me back hard and rubs the back of my neck with his thumb like he used to do when we were first married. I had forgotten how safe his arms can feel. He's still here, even after I thought I hated him. He smells like paint and sawdust and hard work. I can feel how much he missed me in his touch and his kisses.

"You like it?" he whispers, pressing his forehead to mine.

"The first thing I'm going to paint is another Starship Enterprise," I say, kissing his stubbly cheek.

"Mommy! You have a studio!" Rylie jumps up and down the doorway and cheers.

"Did you know about this?" I ask her, tickling her arms.

"I kept the surprise! I only told Grandma and Grandpa."

"Your daddy is pretty amazing, isn't he, sweetie?"

"Are you going to paint something tonight?" Rylie asks.

David laughs. "Mama needs to get to bed, and so do you, young lady."

"I have to brush my teeth!"

"Go on, then," I say. She disappears back to the bathroom. "Let me grab my suitcase, and we can go take a shower. I'm a mess, too."

"I'll get the lights," he says, but first, he kisses me one more time, gently pulling me tight against him until I can almost feel his heart beating in his chest.

He turns off the lights and adjusts the fan at the door. I follow him down the hall with my suitcase. We both kiss Rylie goodnight and tuck her in, and I hold his hand as we walk to our bedroom. He turns on the bathroom light and gently brushes my hair back from my face.

"Charlie," he whispers.

I drop my bag, wrap my arms around his neck, and kiss him with all the desire I've held back for so long.

TWENTY-SEVEN

THE SUN STREAMS onto my back from the window of the fellowship hall. Bible study gives me a moment of peace and calm, even after my morning began with Rylie freaking out over lost homework, barely making it to school before the tardy bell, and then discovering the lost homework was in the car. Fourth grade has been miserable so far.

"Beckett is giving up his nap," Morgan whines. "I'm even more tired thinking about it."

"How old is he now? Four?" Debbie asks, raising one thickly drawn eyebrow. "My Jack had colic and then he stopped napping when he was two, so consider yourself lucky."

"But I'm used to a nap now," Morgan says. "I need it!"

"That's why I love the nursery," Tori says with a laugh. "I get to snuggle all the babies and then go home and take a nap." She crunches a carrot while the other ladies work on their own plates.

"Did I tell you about the shaving cream incident?" Renee says.

"I saw the pictures," Grace says over a bite of quiche. I

wish she would sit with us more often, but she has to make the rounds of the other tables.

"Casey's mom will never let me hear the end of it," Renee groans. "Ten minutes before we were supposed to leave for the airport, and I had this pile of shaving cream on my living room floor. I had to scoop it up with a towel and dump the towel in the washer."

"See, that's what I'm talking about," Tori laughs. "I don't know how you do it!"

"Motherhood is work," Debbie says in an unmistakably disgusted tone, her eyes sending daggers toward Tori.

The table grows silent. I hate that I never know when the snippy side of Debbie will come out. She's switched back and forth between groups at Bible study, but she always seems to come back to Renee, Tori, Morgan, and me even though she's Grace's age.

"It doesn't matter how long you wait to become a mother," Debbie says. "It's always going to be work."

Tori's eyes drop to her empty plate, and she coughs. Renee rolls her eyes and twists her mouth over words that I'm sure will come out later to someone who doesn't need to hear them. Morgan buries her head in her phone. But I'm transfixed by Grace. She had been laughing along with the rest of us, but now she is staring Debbie down, arms folded over her chest. She shakes her head and leans back in her chair. I can almost see the wheels turning in Grace's head.

"Life is work," Grace says. "No matter what, it's going to be hard work. And we all have different callings, Debbie."

"Why do girls get so picky about having everything ready before they have babies?" Debbie says. "It's silly."

Tori stands with a timid smile and picks up her plate.

"I'm going to get more quiche," she says. "Anyone need anything?"

She flees the table without waiting for an answer. Renee watches her go and pantomimes whistling. Morgan elbows her and frowns.

"Being ready doesn't always mean you bring home a baby," Grace says. The sentence is deliberate and pointed, and her hands are folded primly behind her plate.

"These young girls worry too much," Debbie says, her tone careless. I cover my mouth with my fist. I can't believe she is still talking. She's clearly not paying attention to the rest of us.

"Deb," Grace says, her voice a warning that Debbie ignores.

"Waiting for the perfect time," she says between sips of coffee. "There isn't one."

"You clearly don't remember how we were at their age, Deb."

This is the closest thing to anger I've ever seen in Grace, and it feels like the Earth is off its axis. Renee and Morgan's eyes are wide.

"Everything has to be set up and ready," Debbie says. She's still not listening to Grace at all. "Paul and I were poor as dirt when we had Jack. He was still in med school."

"I remember," Grace says. "I worked the nursery back then. That was right before Kelly was born."

Debbie's face turns scarlet. She sets her coffee cup down and looks away.

Grace takes a deep breath and answers our unasked question. "Kelly was my daughter. She was stillborn."

My tongue is glued to my teeth, and Renee sips her coffee without looking up.

"Her birthday is next week, actually." Grace's voice trembles slightly.

"I'm so sorry," I say. What else is there to say?

The air has been sucked away from the room. Debbie stares at her coffee. Tori returns, carrying more food, and she frowns at our table, sensing the tension.

"I was just saying Kelly's birthday is next week," Grace says.

Tori nods and hugs her without a word. Did she know about this? I didn't know this about Grace. Had she mentioned it in a testimony? Every conversation we've had replays in my head as I wonder if I've ever said something insensitive.

Grace looks me in the eye and shakes her head, as if answering the worries in my head. "I don't talk about her very often. She would be turning twenty-seven."

Renee squirms, and I get the feeling she'd hide under the table if she could. Debbie excuses herself from the table to go to the bathroom. Good. I hope she feels terrible.

"Nothing can prepare you for that," Grace says. "It's a spiritual battle, and it is exhausting. Sometimes we older gals have selective amnesia. We remember all the times we won and forget how many times we lost."

"I feel like I'm fighting demons with Missile and Gabby every day," Renee says, laughter dripping with sarcasm. It's her defense mechanism, but it still annoys me.

"You are," Grace says with unsettling seriousness.

"Oh, I don't know about all that," Renee says.

"Spiritual warfare is real," Grace says. "Believe me, I had to fight hard when Tony was little. That boy had a head harder than granite. And with Kelly, I had to fight for my own faith. Those days after she died were some of the darkest of my life."

"I'm so sorry," I say.

"He brought me through," Grace says, patting my hand. "I just don't believe in pretending it was easy. It wasn't. It was the worst thing that has ever happened to me. I felt like demons were circling me every morning."

"I don't like thinking about that," Renee says with a shudder, picking up her phone.

"So don't think. Pray. That's how you fight." Grace sets both hands on her Bible and looks me straight in the eyes in a way that makes me feel unsettled.

"It's so weird to talk about," Renee says. She looks like she wants to run away.

"It's really a matter of whether you want to fight with them yourself or do your fighting on your knees," Grace says with a small smile. "Larry will tell you I took a while to learn that."

"You obviously figured it out," Tori says.

"God's grace," she replies. "When you get to be my age, you'll look back over all the ways you messed up your kid, and it's painful, but it's humbling. I made so many mistakes with Tony. But our God is sovereign." She takes a sip of coffee. "I'm going to run to the ladies' room before we start. Can you tell Janet where I'm going?"

"Of course," Tori says. We all watch her walk to the back of the fellowship hall.

Renee puts her hands to her cheeks. "Oh my gosh, please tell me I didn't say anything rude!"

"She knows people don't know what to say," Tori says.

"How did you know about it?" Renee demands. "I've never heard anything about this."

I have a suspicion there's a reason Grace hadn't told Renee, but I bite my tongue.

"I saw her picture in their bedroom," Tori says simply. "It's on the wall next to Tony's newborn photo. You should ask her about it, Charlotte. It's a powerful testimony."

"I'd be so worried I'd say something wrong," I say.

"Debbie's the one who should be worried about that," Renee mutters.

Tori holds her head up a little higher. "I don't think we need to go there, Renee."

"Grace was mad, girl," Renee says. "I've never seen her mad! That was scary!"

"If she was upset, I'm sure Grace will handle it," Tori answers, her tone a gentle reprimand. "She's been friends with Debbie for a long time."

"They're coming back from the bathroom," I interrupt with a cough. In the back of the fellowship hall, Debbie and Grace enter together. Debbie's eyes are red, but she's holding Grace's hand. Grace says something to her, and they both laugh. I watch them both walking back to the front of the room.

Grace grabs her Bible and materials from our table and squeezes Tori's shoulder gently before going to the stage. I wonder what that is about. Tori won't meet my eyes as she opens her Bible. Debbie sits and hides behind her Bible and notebook.

Morgan purses her lips, taps on her phone, and puts it away slowly. I feel my own phone vibrate and see a message from Morgan.

That was weird. Is Tori ok?

I look up and shake my head to show Morgan that I'm as confused as she is. Her mouth twitches to the side, and she watches Tori flipping through her Bible.

"Ladies, open your Bibles to Ephesians 4," Grace says from behind the little podium. "If you missed last week, we're starting with verse 25. Let's pray."

TWENTY-EIGHT

MORGAN PICKS at her plate of fruit and gives me an uneasy smile. I realize I haven't talked to her without Tori being part of the conversation in months, but Tori is late for Bible study this morning. I check my phone, but she hasn't replied to my message.

"How did Rylie's competition go?" Morgan asks.

"She got first in ballet and lyrical. Second in tap." I suppose a different mom would show her one of the dozens of competition videos currently on my phone.

"She's in fifth grade now, right?" Morgan asks

"Yes." I'll be glad when this year is over. Fifth grade has been miserable, mostly because Rylie's teacher should have retired years ago.

"I am absolutely loving my new shift at the hospital," Yvonne says with a smile. "It's so nice to be off on Tuesdays, so I can come to Bible study with you girls."

"Finally!" Renee says.

I'm still not used to seeing Yvonne sitting across the table from me next to Renee. I barely remember when they came over for Fourth of July when Rylie was little. I've avoided hosting big groups in our house ever since. That was the year I thought I would solve all my problems if we moved to a new house. Then I had a panic attack when I saw my ghost at Tori's house.

Their whispered conversations make my stomach churn. Everything I don't like about Renee is amplified when she hangs out with Yvonne. Renee is only too happy to share every secret. It's made Bible study feel unsafe ever since Yvonne started coming. It's like a mid-week reminder of how miserable Hannah and Liana are making Rylie in Sunday school. At least Hannah isn't in Rylie's class at Fellowship Christian School. Debbie has found a different table this semester so I don't have her to worry about either.

Tori walks in, smoothing wisps of hair behind her ears. Her mouth smiles, but her eyes don't match them, and Morgan visibly relaxes. Tori's hands are shaking as she gets settled.

"Prayer requests?" Renee asks, pen ready on her bright-purple notebook.

"My cousin has some lab tests coming up," Morgan says.

"Which ones?" Nurse Yvonne asks.

Why did Morgan have to get her started? I wish I could stop my ears while they talk about medical stuff. I bury my head in my phone until they finish.

"How is Rylie doing this week, Charlie?" Renee asks abruptly. "Is she done with detention?"

The sentence feels like I've stuck my hand in a mouse-trap. I want to glare at Renee, but I drop my gaze to the table and mumble that she's fine.

"My goodness, what happened?" Yvonne asks.

"She built up too many demerits," I say. "It was only a half-day. It's fine."

Yvonne frowns. "What did she get so many demerits for?"

"It's lots of little things," I say. I can't look at Tori. If her husband wasn't so critical, Rylie wouldn't have any demerits at all. She's only eleven. "She had a growth spurt, and her skirts were a tiny bit short until I could go shopping for new ones. And she lingered too long in the hallway one day. They've been pickier about some of the rules lately."

"I hadn't noticed any changes," Yvonne says. Of course she wouldn't notice. The rules aren't enforced on her kids. I want to point out this hypocrisy, but I don't want to hurt Tori's feelings. Even her picky husband treats the Baileys like they are untouchable.

"Well, it wouldn't matter if she didn't sass her teacher..." Renee mutters.

Tori coughs and gives her a look.

"What?" Renee says. "Liana told me!"

Right. Blame your daughter. I'm so angry I could scream, but I keep my face a mask of calm.

"What happened?" Yvonne says to me, pouncing like a cat on yarn. But I can tell she already knows.

"I'd rather not discuss it," I say.

I want to run away from the table, but who knows what they will say if I leave.

Renee wouldn't know about any of it if Liana wasn't in the same class. Liana seems to enjoy telling her mama about every naughty thing Rylie ever does. And then Renee asks me if *I* know about it. It's become a weekly question: did you know about this incident caused by your disrespectful, unmanageable child, Charlotte?

I may talk privately to the scheduler about not putting Liana and Rylie in the same class next year. Hopefully the scheduler will give her a nicer teacher next year, too. My daughter has a knack for getting adults to like her, except Greg and her teacher, Mrs. Morgan. I know Rylie has to learn to listen and respect her teacher, but it's not easy when she's a crabby old lady with a voice like fingernails on a chalkboard.

I shake myself out of my thoughts and realize Yvonne is in the middle of her own prayer requests.

"Hannah got a solo in the choir, and it looks like she may play her violin in the winter concert, too. Oh, and pray for her with the scripture contest coming up. She's finishing up 2 Timothy."

"The whole thing? Hannah is a machine!" Renee exclaims.

Tori is staring at her Bible, unnaturally quiet. I squeeze her hand under the table, and she gives me a sad smile.

"Tor, what's up with you lately?" Renee says. "I heard Greg's engineering presentation went great with the elementary school. Liana said he built an impossible bridge!" She stops when she sees Tori's face fall.

"I was cleaning up a big mess just before I left, so I'm sorry I'm late." Tori's lower lip quivers. "My china cabinet fell over. My grandmother's china is gone."

"I'm so sorry, Tori," Yvonne says. "Can any of it be salvaged?"

"No, it's all gone." She's tearing up, and I give her a soft hug. "It's all I had of hers," she whispers.

"How did it fall?" Renee says, her mouth wide.

"I'm not sure," Tori answers. She purses her lips and looks at her Bible. "It's an antique, and I guess one of the legs was cracked and just gave way."

The other ladies are talking at once, asking how it happened, where it was, and if there is anything they can do. I keep hugging her.

"It was Grandma Patty's, right?" I say. She nods. I'm heartbroken for her. Her grandmother passed before she went to college and didn't leave much behind. She's treasured those dishes. I know exactly which piece of furniture she means. It's a tall white wooden cabinet against the wall in her front room.

All I can think about through class is that china cabinet. I'm so worried about Tori. I can hardly even take notes. Finally it ends, and I tap her arm.

"You want to see Rylie's new costume?" I ask her. "It's in my car."

"Oh, yes, please!" Tori grabs her purse and is ready to leave even before I am.

"I hope Rylie's week gets better," Yvonne says a little too loudly as Tori and I leave the table.

"I'm sure it will," I say, smiling a smile that I'm sure looks as fake as Monopoly money.

We walk to the car without speaking. I'm glad I parked so far out for extra exercise. No one will see us on the back row. I open the trunk to show her the new red leotard.

"It's really pretty, Charlotte," she says, her smile anemic.

"What happened, Tori? Please tell me."

Her eyes fill with tears, and she sits on the edge of the car trunk. "Can you..." She shudders and sobs, unable to speak for a few minutes. I sit next to her and hug her tight. "Can you keep a secret?"

"Of course I can!" I say, squeezing her shoulder. "You know I can. Please tell me."

She nods and takes a deep breath. "Greg doesn't want me telling anybody, but I have to tell you. I had...I got pregnant last year, but I lost it. I lost the baby, Charlotte."

I have no words for her. Instead, I hug her tight and cry.

"We were so happy. I was going to make a blanket from

that yarn, remember?" she asks. I nod, remembering his proposal. "I started making it, and I had everything bought for this cute announcement about God starting a new knitting project. But I started bleeding." She chokes on her tears and buries her head in her hands.

"I'm so sorry. I'm just so sorry." I say. I'm desperate for better words, but I have none.

"It got worse, and I had these horrible cramps. And when I went in, the doctor told me there was no..." She covers her mouth with one hand.

"No heartbeat." I finish for her. "When did this happen?" How did I not see Tori's pain sooner?

"In August, right after school started," she says. "Remember that day we went to lunch?"

"At the café?" That was over a year ago. My heart hurts knowing how long she has kept this to herself.

"I started bleeding that afternoon," Tori says. "You were the first one I was going to tell besides our parents. I had my ultrasound to show you, but I just didn't feel right about it. And then..."

No wonder Greg seemed so excited about me going to lunch with Tori.

"I still have it," she whispers. "I keep it in my purse."

She rummages in her purse and carefully removes a piece of paper from a zipped pocket. She hands it to me, and I unfold it to see a fuzzy outline of a head and hands. I search for words that aren't platitudes, but I can't find any. Instead, I hug Tori and cry.

"I wanted to tell you, Charlotte," Tori says. "Grace told me I should, but Greg was so private about it."

"You told Grace?" I say. Then my heart aches in my chest. "Is that why she got so mad at Debbie?"

"I was helping her redesign her bedroom and saw her

picture of Kelly." She digs through her purse for a tissue and wipes her eyes. "I lost it crying and had to tell her. Greg didn't want me to tell anyone, but I had to."

We sit on the edge of the trunk and let the tears fall. I don't understand why Greg wouldn't want anyone to know, but maybe he's private about grief. Suddenly I remember the china cabinet.

"But what about the cabinet?"

"Oh, that," Tori groans. Anger flashes through her for a moment, and she cries into her hands. "It must have been a crack in the leg. It just fell over."

She looks me in the eyes and breathes in a slow deep breath. She wants to tell me more. I can see it. I squeeze her shoulder, and she jumps a little, shifting on the trunk. She shakes her head.

"It just got me so upset. I had all these plans in my head, you know? Tea parties with a daughter, like you do with Rylie. But the china is gone, and my baby is..."

Gone.

The word left unsaid becomes a lump in both our throats, and neither of us can swallow it down. I know there is more to this. I can feel it, but I can't make her tell me.

"You have to act like you don't know if Greg ever says anything, okay?" Tori says.

"But why?"

"He just..." Tori's eyes are anguished. "Please pretend you don't know."

I promise to keep quiet, but I can't understand why Greg is so embarrassed. I watch her walk to her car, winding her hair into a practiced bun and fastening it with bobby pins. I get in my car and check my makeup in the mirror. I see Tori's car leave the parking lot in the rearview mirror and shudder.

TWENTY-NINE

"CHARLOTTE, I think you should read this book I just finished," Greg says as we file out of Sunday school. Tori follows behind him. "I think it might help you deal with Rylie's attitude."

"I'm sorry?" I'm dumbfounded. I haven't said a word about Rylie in Sunday school in years.

"I know she's been having a hard year so far," he says. "It's a really helpful book! I don't know why it isn't more well-known." He continues with the name of a book and an author I've never heard of, but I'm wondering how he knows she's having a hard time with sixth grade. Did Tori say something? Is he allowed to access student records for sixth graders? I suppose anyone in the school administration can access discipline records, but he should stick to his STEM students.

"I'll make sure to send the book with Tori to Bible study this week," he says.

I grit my teeth. "Thank you."

"That's a great book, Charlotte," Yvonne says behind me. "I was going to recommend it to you last week."

"It really is!" Greg says, nodding to Yvonne. "It's given me some great insights into how to get the students to pay attention. I hope it helps."

"Don't forget it's our turn for snacks on Tuesday," Tori says. "I'll see you then."

I forgot the last time it was our turn, so the comment stings. David finally catches up to me as Greg and Tori head to the parking lot.

"What's the matter?" he asks, seeing my face. I just shake my head. I'm too embarrassed to speak, so I fake a smile as Reuben and Yvonne walk past. Yvonne says something about seeing me this afternoon. I start to ask her what she's talking about, but I need to find Rylie first.

"Let's go home. I need a nap," I say to David with false cheeriness.

When we find Rylie, she's sitting with Ellie in the hallway outside her classroom. The rest of the girls in her sixth-grade class are giggling together, including Hannah and Liana.

"Hi, Mrs. Madsen," Ellie says. She keeps her back to the other girls in Rylie's class and looks angry. "I told Rylie she should come with me to the mall this afternoon. I have to get a dress for the winter formal."

Rylie shakes her head and won't look at me or Ellie. Ellie gives the other girls a look that could melt cast iron. She's so protective of Rylie. I'm glad her family started coming to our church so Rylie has someone to watch out for her in the youth group next year.

"If you change your mind, have your mom text me, and my mom and I will pick you up," Ellie says. She stalks past the other sixth graders with all the superiority a gorgeous blonde sixteen-year-old can muster.

Rylie won't say a word as we walk to the car and stares

out of the window without speaking the whole ride home. David doesn't notice for the first few minutes and raises an eyebrow when I stop him from asking her questions with a hand on his arm. I keep our adult conversation going until we pull into the garage. Rylie is lost in her thoughts. I head into the kitchen and check the baked potatoes I put in the slow cooker before church. David hangs his jacket in the laundry room and takes Rylie's coat for her as she follows him in.

"Rylie, when you get changed, come in here and grate some cheese for me, okay?" I ask.

"Yes, ma'am." She trudges through the living room to her bedroom.

"What happened?" David asks after her bedroom door clicks shut.

"I don't know, but I think it has to do with Hannah Bailey."

David frowns. "I don't follow."

"I think there was a girls Sunday school party today after church," I keep my voice low, and he leans in across the kitchen counter. "And I think Rylie is the only one who didn't get invited."

"What?" David's eyes widen.

"You saw how she was all alone outside her class," I say. "Ellie was trying to cheer her up."

"What about Liana? Wouldn't she make sure Rylie came?"

"Are you kidding me?" I say as I set the sour cream on the kitchen table.

"I thought Liana and Rylie were best friends," David says.

"Liana is one of the worst ones! She's Hannah's minion." I'm furious. I slice the green onions with quick but deliberate strokes so I won't cut myself. "Diana doesn't do anything about it either, and she should."

"Diana..." David looks puzzled for a moment. "Oh, wait. Short blonde hair?"

"Rylie's Sunday school teacher, yes. She lets Hannah and Liana do whatever they want. I saw it at the sixth-grade pool party."

"Girl drama. I do not get it." David drops some ice cubes into his glass and fills it with water from the refrigerator. "And Hannah started it all?"

"Yes!" I am spitting mad. I dump the onions into a bowl and set the knife in the sink. "And whatever happened today, it was deliberate, David. I know it was."

"Are you sure they didn't tell Rylie about this party or whatever it is? Maybe she was invited and forgot about it."

I set the onions on the counter. It's true Rylie has forgotten to tell me about events before, but not for church. I can't deny that's a possibility, even if it's an unlikely one.

"It's possible, but I think it's more likely that Hannah's a brat." I've thought it a hundred times but never said it out loud. David snorts and smirks over his water glass.

"You mean the kid who has the entire book of 2 Timothy memorized?" he says, his voice dripping with sarcasm. "How could *she* be a brat?"

I pull out the plates for lunch and put a finger to my lips when I hear Rylie emerging from her room. She slumps into the kitchen and grates the cheese with a vengeance. She's a bundle of anger and hurt, writhing and struggling beneath the surface. Why are girls so cruel?

In the doorway to the living room, She materializes like light on fog. Her blue blouse is stained with tears. She watches me and clasps Her hands in front of Her like She is pleading with me. I look at Rylie and back to Her. She nods and pantomimes hugging.

She's trying to help. I slowly inhale with my eyes closed, and when I open them, she's gone.

"Honey, come here," I say to Rylie.

"What." Her voice is flat. I fold her into a hug and squeeze her tight. She puts her head on my shoulder and sags against me. We stand in the kitchen that way for a long moment. David sets down his water and comes over to wrap us both in a hug. He plants kisses on Rylie's forehead and my cheek.

"What happened, Rylie?" I say as gently as possible.

"I don't want to go to church tonight," she says into my shoulder.

"Want to talk about it?"

"No," Rylie says.

David watches her turn away to grate the rest of the cheese and frowns.

"I was thinking we could go walk by the lake this afternoon," David says.

Rylie whirls around to face him. "And feed the ducks?"

"Naturally," he says. "What do you think, Mom?"

"Fine by me," I say. "Unless Rylie has changed her mind about going shopping with Ellie."

Rylie opens her mouth to say something and stops herself.

"How about we eat while you decide?" I ask her.

Eating first is a good plan. Rylie globs her potato with butter and cheese. She finally decides on doing both: first the lake to feed the ducks, then on to the mall to shop with Ellie. After lots of texting back and forth, we arrange to meet Ellie in one of the department stores. David and I will walk around on our own while the girls shop.

We finish lunch and change into comfortable clothes for the lake.

"I have to show you how I skip rocks!" Rylie says to David as we climb in the car.

"You can skip rocks?" I say.

"I learned at dance camp last summer," Rylie says. "Sofia showed me how. I'm really good at it!"

I bite back tears. She grabs hold of life with both hands and expects everyone else to do the same. And Hannah...I shouldn't hate a child, but I do. I hate that girl right now. And I hate Yvonne for creating that brat.

Rylie spends the ride to the lake talking about a new worship dance she wants to choreograph with Ellie.

"You know what's not fair?" she says after a dramatic sigh. "Hannah texts in class all the time, but Mrs. Black never takes her phone. She takes everybody else's phone."

"Maybe Hannah is better at hiding it," I say.

"No." She squints at her fingernails. "I think Mrs. Black doesn't want to get in trouble with Hannah's mom. Ellie says everyone is afraid of Mrs. Bailey."

I don't dare respond to her because that's exactly what I think. It's ridiculous, but even I have to admit I'm afraid to cross Yvonne.

David pulls the car into the parking lot at the lake. The sun is hot, but the wind from the lake is cool and gentle this afternoon. Rylie skips from the car to the trail. I close my eyes and let the sun warm my cheeks. Rylie sings and dances her way toward the lake while we follow.

"Mom, look! A rabbit!" The tiny gray bunny hops away under a cedar tree. The grass has turned brown from the hot summer, but a few patches of green have managed to hold on under the trees.

Rylie grabs the bag of birdseed and runs full tilt toward

the rocky outcrop where the ducks like to gather. A few fly away, squawking in protest, but one large goose honks at her and stands his ground.

"Here, fatty!" she says, tossing a handful of seeds at the goose's head.

It squawks again and picks at the seeds on the ground while glaring at us. I sit on a bench and watch her toss seeds up into the sky to challenge the seagulls. Her jumps are elegant and fluid. They morph into arabesques and plies as she spins around the flock of birds. Then she adds in chicken arms and quacking.

"Hey Mom, I'm the Duck Princess!" she shouts and leaps to music I imagine must be playing in her head. She is beautiful and ridiculous all at the same time.

"Rylie, watch out! You're almost in the water!" She skips a few steps back onto the beach and laughs, then quacks and flaps at a nearby mallard who is giving her the side-eye.

"M'lady, I am in awe of your superior dancing skills." David bows low.

Rylie giggles and races toward the beach. "Watch, Dad!"

She is so much younger today than she has been in years. I miss this little girl. I follow her down to the water and try to skip rocks. Mine thump into the water and disappear without the slightest bounce, but she and David get into a competition. David sets the record with ten skips.

I wonder how anyone could want to hurt someone so full of life. These girls must be jealous. I wish I could shake them out of it. Or give their mothers a good shaking. They are crushing my girl's spirit.

"Glad to see you smile, Rylie-Girl," I say as she comes back up from the sand to get a drink of water. "You looked pretty mad this morning."

The storm clouds instantly return to her face.

"Are you sure you don't want to talk about it?" I ask as gently as possible.

Rylie bites her lip and folds her arms, trying her very hardest not to cry. "They all went to Hannah's house after church."

"Who did?"

"Liana and everybody." She sits down on the bench at the edge of the beach and pulls her knees up to her chest. "But not me."

"Oh, honey." I sit beside her and wrap my arm around her shoulders. David stands next to us without saying anything.

"They were going to tie-dye T-shirts," she says, sniffing but stubbornly refusing to cry. "I wanted to go, but Hannah said I had to bring a T-shirt. She said I was supposed to bring one, and if I didn't bring one, I couldn't go. She said everyone knew last week, but I didn't! Nobody told me!"

"I'm so sorry, honey," David says. He swallows and turns away to look at the lake. I recognize that face. He's fighting tears, too.

"Hannah is so stupid. Everybody says she's nice, but she's not."

"Not everybody," I say and hug my daughter like I'm shielding her from the world.

THIRTY

YVONNE AND RENEE have been talking from the moment they sat down at the table at Bible study. Morgan is distracted with her phone. I thought we were sharing prayer requests, but only Tori is listening. It's me, Tori, and Morgan on one side of the round table and Renee and Yvonne on the other.

"David's mom has been sick all week," I say. "She always gets bronchitis in the winter." Morgan nods without looking up, but the other two are flat-out ignoring me. I decide not to finish my thought and give Tori a shrug.

"You okay, Charlotte?" Yvonne says.

I purse my lips, then try to smile. "Yep, just fine," I tell her. "Anyone else have a prayer request?"

"Pray for my friend's daughter, Danielle," Yvonne says. "She was diagnosed with leukemia."

I shamelessly bury my head in my phone. I can't listen to medical details and treatments I should never type into a search engine if I want to sleep soundly. It's a constant temptation to compare my own headaches, nausea, and whatever else shows up to whatever diagnosis Yvonne brings up every week. If she could turn off the nurse-speak for ten minutes, prayer time would be a lot shorter at our table. Maybe I should skip Bible study next year.

"I have one," Tori says. Yvonne is still talking about leukemia, so I clear my throat.

"What, Tori?" I prod. The table falls silent, and Morgan looks up from her phone for the first time.

"It's been a rough few months for me. For us both," she says, her voice uneven. "And I'd appreciate some prayer. I need wisdom."

"Anything specific, honey?" Yvonne asks.

Tori picks at the edge of her Bible. "I have to make some decisions this year that I'm not sure about. Greg, too."

I wonder what prompted this. Tori has been distant for months now. She hasn't mentioned her mom recently, so I doubt that's the problem. I search her face for a hint. Why don't I know what's going on? I should know. She always seems to know what is bothering me even though I stopped requesting prayer months ago. I shouldn't care what Yvonne thinks, but I do. I care what she says about me and about Rylie when I'm not there.

Renee gives me a look and nods ever so slightly toward Tori. I shake my head slightly. I don't know what's wrong, but Renee would be the last person I would tell if I did.

Tori and Greg have been married for eleven years now. I wonder if they're looking into adopting. I write a smiley face and praying hands on my notepaper and gently get Tori's attention. She smiles, but she looks tired.

Would it be prying to ask what was wrong? Tori is my best friend, but sometimes I feel like there are questions I'm not allowed to ask. This might be one of them.

As we pack up at the end of Bible study, I decide I should take her to lunch sometime. We haven't been anywhere for a girl's date in months. I mention it as we walk out to the parking lot, and she nods reluctantly.

"Not this week," she says. "Let me get home and check Greg's school schedule."

"Well, we're going to go sometime," I say. "We haven't gotten to talk in a long time."

"You're right, and I'm sorry, Charlotte. I will make the time."

"You know I'll be praying for you," I say, my voice tentative. "Can you tell me what I'm praying for?"

"Of course I can tell *you*," she says with a sad smile. "I'm thinking about quitting my job."

I realize my mouth has dropped open and snap it shut again. "I thought you liked consulting. What happened?"

"Nothing happened at work. Greg and I have been talking a lot about priorities, and I don't know if working at the firm fits with..." She hesitates, fumbling for words. "I may need to do something with more flexibility."

"Are you..." I don't even know how to ask if she's pregnant, but I can't contain my excitement.

"No." The word is cold, and my smile wilts. She won't look at me.

"I'm sorry, Tori. I didn't mean—"

"Don't worry about it. I'm not pregnant."

"Oh." I don't know what else to say.

"I'd better go. I need to get back home to finish some things."

"I'm sorry."

"Please don't be," she says, brushing the apology away. "I appreciate you praying for me. And for Greg."

"Always."

The drive home feels longer than usual. I'm dreading walking in the door, but maybe She won't be there today. I haven't seen Her all week. I want to work on my painting again.

The house is still and quiet. Rylie will be home from school later, so I tidy the kitchen and head out to the studio.

The familiar pungent smell of oil paints wraps around me like a sweater. I've found the right shade of blue. Deep blue hollow eyes glare at me from behind chin-length face-framing layers of brown hair. The blue shirt hangs about Her shoulders like a death shroud, but I've been careful to make Her fingers grip the arms with the white knuckles I've memorized. She is holding onto her death shroud for dear life. Seeing Her frozen on a canvas seems to make the fear fade. She's harmless there. She can't follow me or scream at me soundlessly or try to touch me and send shivers down my back. The painting pleads with me, tears of agony etching canyons into Her face.

She looks so familiar, like a younger version of my mother. I only catch Her face in snatches and side glances, but I know I've captured it. And that blue shirt makes me shudder.

"I didn't know you were painting a self-portrait."

The words are an electric shock. Every hair on my neck stands on end. I whirl to face David, home early.

"What did you say?"

"It's you, isn't it?"

I look back at the painting, and my breath catches in my throat.

"No..." I try to choke out. But the words die in my throat. She's standing next to me with tears in her eyes, screaming something at me. I refuse to look at Her. I fix my eyes on the painting and swallow.

"No, that's not me." She jumps in front of the painting,

now reaching toward my face, making me flinch. The words on Her lips are unmistakable: *Yes, I am!*

"Oh, sorry, honey. It looks a lot like you."

"I don't even know Her." The words are flat, but they seem to stab Her to the heart. She crumples to the floor and melts into mist.

"I'm sorry. Are you mad at me?"

"No."

"You look mad, Charlie."

"No, it's fine. It's a portrait study. Nothing important."

David raises an eyebrow at me.

"You've been in here working on it every day."

"Just practice. I'm working on eyes and hands."

"It's beautiful, Charlie." He rubs my shoulder and pulls me to him in a tight hug. "She looks sad, though."

"I'm trying to capture hard emotions."

He peers at the canvas with a curious eye and frowns in thought. "Well, she's making me depressed to look at her. She looks so sad."

"Why are you home early?" I interrupt him.

"Client meeting was canceled. I decided not to stick around doing paperwork."

"Oh." I need him to leave. I turn back to the painting and try to pretend I don't see it.

"What's for dinner?"

"Spaghetti." Why won't he leave?

"With meatballs?" he asks.

"Sure."

"Yum. Love you." He finally walks away to the bedroom, leaving me alone with the painting.

That's not me. That's impossible. I peer around the edge of the doorway into the living room, looking for Her. I don't really look like Her.

Do I?

The hair, the eyes, the jawline...it's all identical. But I don't wear blue, and the haircut isn't the same.

The ghost appears in the living room, lying on the couch in the blue silk shirt, mascara running down Her cheeks. She is solid and clear, and Her face is unmistakable.

For a moment, it's as if I've had the wind knocked out of me. When I get my breath back, I start to hyperventilate. I pant and grab the frame of the doorway as the room spins.

She's *me*.

My stomach churns, and I run to the hall bathroom to throw up.

THIRTY-ONE

I DON'T KNOW how this discussion got started, but it wasn't what I was expecting in Sunday school this morning.

"I said I'm surprised you're still allowing her to dance," Greg says, his voice thick with disgust.

"I'm sorry?" I have no idea how to respond or why he's saying this in the first place.

"After all, dance is so sensual, and she's getting to the age that it's going to become a problem."

David and I look at each other. I'm sure Yvonne's eyes are drilling holes in the back of my head.

"Greg, you do know Rylie does ballet?" David says. "Not pole-dancing or whatever you're thinking."

"I don't see that the type of dance makes a difference. I would never allow a child of mine to participate," he says. "There are plenty of creative outlets that are more modest, like music."

"Or stamp collecting," David says, rolling his eyes. "Or baking. Or sitting quietly in a corner like a mindless drone."

"David," I whisper and nudge him. I don't want a fight in the middle of church.

"I think you should consider that she's getting older, and certain things are no longer—"

"I think you should keep your opinions about raising kids to yourself," David interrupts him. "Especially since you don't *have* any, Greg,"

The whole Sunday school room has gone silent. Larry leans his head on his hand, covering his eyes. Grace stares at the floor next to him. Renee, Yvonne, and their husbands are studying their coffee cups. Morgan looks at me and then eyes the door like she wants to run out of the room.

"Rylie is *my* daughter," David says. His voice sounds as if he is building a brick wall with each word, locking Greg behind it. "She is one of the best dancers in her class, and I would be the proudest father in the world if she went on to dance professionally."

"But skin-tight leotards and short skirts?" Greg says. "How is that modest?"

The sentence is almost a slap to my face. As if my beautiful butterfly of a girl could ever be anything other than elegant and graceful. How can he talk this way when he has been to several of Rylie's recitals?

"Okay, guys, hold on," Larry holds up his hands. "Let's all step back a minute."

"I'm not the only one who thinks it's inappropriate," Greg says in a tone of finality. "We can all agree modesty is in short supply in our world. We're supposed to be in, not of, right?"

He keeps going, quoting a book I've never heard of, but I see a few people nodding, including Yvonne. I'm sure she's probably read it.

I want to slap half of the class. What is wrong with them? They have all complimented the worship dances Rylie has choreographed and performed. She danced for our Christmas cantata, and the pastor praised her from the stage. Why are they agreeing with Greg?

"I don't care what random book you found on the Internet to back you up." David's voice sounds dangerous.

"Let's all take a step back, please," Larry says. "We don't have to agree on this."

Tori sits stiff and quiet in her front-row chair. She's looking at the floor. Crimson waves sweep over her cheeks and ears, and her knuckles are white. Why won't she say something? Why doesn't she stop him? She loves to watch Rylie dance.

"I think it goes to the heart of modesty," Greg says. "And that is extremely important for girls."

"Last time I checked, Greg, I am her father, and that means she's under my authority. Especially under your school of thought, right? God put her under my care," David says. I have never seen him this angry. "And since I'm ultimately under the authority of our pastor who came to see Rylie's recital last year and is planning to come again this year, I don't think you have a leg to stand on." David tosses his full cup of coffee into the trash and draws himself up in front of Greg. Greg sets his coffee cup on the floor and stands up to face David. I feel Morgan put her shaking hand on my shoulder from the row behind me.

"I don't feel well," Tori says suddenly. She picks up her purse and stumbles to the door. She won't look at anyone. Greg gives David a disgusted glare and follows her, and Larry runs after them both.

The room is uncomfortably quiet. Grace clears her throat but doesn't say anything. I put my head in my hands and bite my tongue.

"Since I have everyone's attention, Rylie's dance recital is coming up," David says. "I know she'd love for any of you to come. She's doing ballet, tap, and lyrical."

"I'd love to come," Morgan says and leans forward to catch my eyes. I muster a passable smile.

"I'll get you the address," I say. I'm so embarrassed. What do we do from here?

"Tell the whole class, Charlotte," Grace says, her voice a little shaky. "I think Ellie Piper is in it, too, right?" I fumble for the recital paper in my purse and let David give everyone the information. I can see Yvonne and Renee writing notes to each other. I'm tempted to throw a paperwad at them since they're acting like they're in middle school.

Larry returns and says Tori thinks she's getting a migraine. David leans forward, elbows on his knees, like an athlete waiting for the coach to call him. I chew my tongue and gently pat his arm.

"I'm going to acknowledge the elephant," Larry says as everyone quiets down. "As believers in Christ, we have got to give each other grace. And we also have to remember that there are disputable matters in scripture. We have to be careful not to try to bind someone else's conscience in an area that's not clear."

"Amen," Morgan says quietly.

"I don't know a good analogy here. Meat sacrificed to idols isn't quite right." He stares at a spot above the doorway for a moment and bites his lip. "It comes down to the fact that you are responsible to God for your life and your family. The Holy Spirit is who will bring conviction if necessary." Larry sighs and holds his hands out, palms up like a prayer. "I feel like I need to say this as clearly as I can. Don't try to be the Holy Spirit. You'll do a terrible job."

There is a murmur of uncomfortable laughter.

"Let's all take a minute to reset and pray, okay? One minute of silent prayer, and I'll open us up."

David says nothing. He glares at the floor, still furious. I'm furious, but it makes me want to shrink and disappear. The lesson is a blur, and no one is in a talking mood. We all want it to end. Larry closes early, and David and I leave to find Rylie in Sunday school. At first, no one follows us down the empty hallway.

"David, can I talk to you a minute?" Larry says, rushing to catch up.

"Guess I'm in trouble?"

"I tried to calm Greg down," Larry says. "I don't know why he was so—"

"I've had it with him," David says. "He cannot talk about my daughter like that, Larry."

Larry raises both hands in defeat and nods. "I definitely understand. I think you were right to confront the legalism, but got a little heated—"

"Heated? Are you kidding me?"

"I don't agree with him, David," Larry says, "but this is complicated—"

I leave David to talk it out. I don't want to hear about it anymore. I want to go home and hide in our bedroom and take a nap. I want to finish Rylie's costume for the recital and forget any of this ever happened. I wait for him in the car with Rylie, and we ride home in a tense quiet. Even Rylie seems to feel it and says very little at lunch before retreating to her room. At the sound of Rylie's bedroom door shutting, David can't contain himself.

"Larry said he was going to talk to the pastor about Greg. If he doesn't, I will." He leans against the counter and sighs. "I thought he wanted to switch classes. If he's going to, he should just do it."

"I think he wants to lead a class," I say, putting the last dish in the dishwasher.

David stares at me, eyes wide. "You're kidding."

"That's what Tori said last summer," I say. "Let's go change."

"You know, Greg was weird when he worked at RHL," David says as I pull our bedroom door closed. "I worked with his department several times, but he wouldn't ever talk to me." He yanks off his blue polo shirt and sits on the edge of our bed, picking at the pills on the collar. "I tried to get to know him, but it was like he was hiding."

"Maybe he was."

"Something bugs me about this whole mess." David straightens the collar of his shirt and holds his mouth to one side in thought. "He was always working weekends, but no one else on his team ever needed to. What was he doing all day? Watching YouTube?"

"Maybe he wasn't very good at that job," I say.

"Maybe," David says. "But I've seen his STEM magic show. He's smart."

"Who knows."

"Just bugs me." David hangs his shirt in the closet and stands, looking at his shirts. "Remember when we saw Tori that one time at Darren's office before we went in together? Did Greg ever go to counseling with her?"

"I don't think so," I say. I sit on the bed and hug myself, ignoring a wispy barely-there Other Charlotte in the bathroom doorway.

David looks at me, chewing on his lower lip. "I'm going to call Larry and make sure he talked to Pastor Ryan."

THIRTY-TWO

THE TALL BRADFORD pear tree in Tori's front yard is finally blooming. Tori jumps in the passenger seat and squeals with delight. Her long hair is wrapped in a thick bun at the nape of her neck. After the argument at church, I thought she might cancel our girls' day, but she's almost giddy as she buckles her seatbelt.

"I needed this shopping trip so much!" she says. "I've been so busy painting the house. I need a break."

"Your mission is to help me find some new clothes." Even though her clothes are much different than they used to be, Tori still manages to look beautiful. Hopefully her fashionista side will come out to help me today.

"So, where are we going?" she asks, adjusting her sunglasses.

"I thought I'd let you pick."

"Dangerous to let me pick, hon. Are you sure?"

I follow her directions as we cruise through town. She is bouncing a little in her seat. She jumps out as soon as I park the car in front of the consignment store she's mentioned so many times.

"You need that dress in the window, Charlotte," she says. She pushes open the thick wooden door and waves a hand through. The shop has exposed brick walls and an industrial-style ceiling with drop lighting. A long green counter runs along one wall. The shop is quiet, and the woman behind the counter waves to Tori with a grin.

"To the scarf bar!" Tori says. I follow her to another counter at the back of the store. It is covered with dozens of racks, boxes, and piles of scarves. I'm overwhelmed by all the choices, but Tori curates her selection in minutes. As we move through the store, she convinces me to try half a dozen outfits and plants herself outside my dressing room.

"You should wear more green. It's a great color on you," she says as I look over the green skirt I'm trying on. I know she's trying to make me feel good, but being treated like a fashion model makes me self-conscious.

"How is freelance going?" I ask, trying to get the focus off of me.

"It's fine."

"Are you getting new clients?"

"A few. Mostly it has helped Greg. It made a big difference to him."

Greg. I was really hoping to not talk about Greg at all today. "That's nice."

"He loves having me home. He usually comes to eat lunch with me, and he can have me bring things from home if he forgets something."

I shut the dressing room door behind me. I rehang and sort the clothes and frown at my reflection.

"Charlotte, is something wrong?" Tori's voice echoes off the ceiling. I make a lame excuse, but I'm lost in thought. What is it that worries me? I must be overthinking this.

David's stories about Greg's weird behavior are making me look for signs of...signs of what? I don't know. I don't want to actually think what I'm thinking. I shake my head to clear these anxious thoughts and follow my best friend to another boutique a few doors down. This one isn't consignment, and we split up to explore the whole store.

"I'll yell 'Marco' if I can't find you," she says.

"Polo!" I laugh as I head toward a rack of jeans.

This feels normal. This is how we usually get along, laughing at inside jokes. I haven't seen Her all morning. I've been painting and sewing and trying to do anything that makes Her disappear. I wish I knew what would make Her disappear forever.

"Charlotte, I found the perfect blouse for you!" Tori calls from across the little shop. I push around a clothing rack to find her.

Every muscle and nerve in my body freezes in terror. Tori is holding *Her* blouse. I recognize every detail of the shirt's buttons and collar.

"No, no, no, no, no..." The words are choking out of me unbidden. I bite down hard on my tongue and spin away from this nightmare. Tori is saying something, but I can't respond. I can't think. I can't even breathe. I dump the clothes I'd been holding on the closest rack and run for the door. I have to get out of here. I have to get away.

I crash into the door and run to my car. The sunlight is too bright in my eyes, and I can't find my keys to open the door. I fall to my knees and dig for them, shaking my purse hard to hear the jingle. Where are they? I suck in a breath when my fingers close around them and fumble with the unlock button.

Inside the car, I lean over the steering wheel and try to

breathe. I can't stop shivering despite the heat. I can't think about anything but the blue blouse. I never thought it was real. It couldn't be real. All that was missing was tear stains. When I close my eyes, I can still see it.

A knock on the passenger window makes me jolt upright.

"Charlotte, it's me." Tori is standing at the door, her hand on the handle. I'm unable to force my mouth to form words. "Can you unlock the door?" she asks.

I nod and claw for the lock button. She opens the door a crack.

"Can I get you a drink?"

A drink? Yes, I want a drink. I nod.

"I'll be right back. Can you turn on the air conditioner, hon? You're going to get overheated in there. And breathe into your stomach, real slow. Know what I mean?"

My breath comes in shuddering gasps, but I manage to nod and mouth "thank you" before she disappears into the bright sunlight. I fumble the key into the ignition and turn the air conditioner on. Cool air blasts my face.

My nightmares are coming to life.

"God, help me," I whisper. The rumble of the engine vibrates through the steering wheel. The passenger door opens, and Tori sits next to me.

"I brought water and crackers."

"You didn't have to do that."

"Take it, hon." She unscrews the cap on the bottle of water, adds a straw, and hands me the bottle, making sure I have it securely in my hand. "Is there anything else you need? They told me I can have some ice if you want an ice pack on your neck or something."

"I think I'm having a panic attack." I wipe away tears from my cheeks and sniff. "I'm sorry. I'm so sorry!"

"You have nothing to be sorry for."

"You have wonderful taste. It wasn't—"

"It wasn't about the blouse," she interrupts. "I understand. I promise you didn't hurt my feelings. Believe me?"

I look up from my lap and try to smile. "Thank you." It's all I can muster.

"I've never told you about my mom," she says. She squeezes my hand and swallows. "I keep it to myself because she's pretty embarrassed about it even now. She had panic attacks all the time when I was little. Still gets them sometimes. Got to be second nature taking care of her. I saw your face, and..." She waves her other hand toward her forehead. "I knew."

"She has panic attacks on top of her heart and everything else?"

"She jokes her whole body is waging a civil war," Tori says, her face grim. "Dad didn't know how to handle it, so I sort of figured out what helped. Here, eat a cracker. It helps her sometimes."

I crunch the cracker between my teeth. For a moment, I enjoy the buttery crispness and sips of cold water. It almost blocks out the panic that has every nerve on edge. Almost.

"You should ask Darren for a recommendation for a psychiatrist. They might be able to help you figure out your triggers and stuff."

"I don't want to take drugs. I usually have them under control."

"No shame in it, Charlotte. My mom needs them."

"I don't like them." The thought makes my stomach curdle. "There are so many side effects."

"There're lots of things a psychiatrist can do to help you besides meds, you know. There are techniques to calm down, relax, knowing your triggers, lots of things. And honey, Darren isn't qualified for that kind of thing."

"I guess you're right."

"I remember the one you had at my house."

I shudder. The first time She appeared somewhere outside of my house. The first time I knew She was a she and couldn't escape Her. Tori clasps her hands in her lap and waits until I look her in the eye.

"That was a long time ago. But you're having them more often, aren't you?"

"Always seems like you're around to see them."

"Hey, better me than anyone else, right?" she says, raising an eyebrow. "I love you, and I know what's what."

I try to stop the tears, but they are as inevitable as a thunderstorm. Tori wraps an arm around my shoulders and leans her head on mine.

"Girl, I would do anything to take this away from you," she says. Her voice is thick with tears. "Anything."

I think back to that moment where the Other Charlotte stood there weeping in front of the painting. She's not a ghost, and she's not a hallucination. If I hadn't seen that blue blouse in Tori's hand, I might be able to make myself believe I'm crazy. But I'm not.

"I think David thinks I'm crazy," I whisper.

"I'm sure he's worried about you. Has he seen you have one?"

"Not like this."

"You must be really good at hiding them. You shouldn't do that, honey."

"I don't want him to worry."

"If you get a doctor to help you, he'll understand," she says, squeezing my shoulder. "You have a wonderful husband, Charlotte. He'll support you."

"I hope so." Everything is blurred and foggy when I think about David. I don't know how to talk to him. I've been lying to him for so long that everything tangles in my head. How many excuses and lies does he hear from me every day?

"Don't you say that. He loves you more than Star Trek."

I can't help but laugh through my tears. Tori squeezes my shoulder and laughs with me.

"I'm sorry we haven't gotten to do this in so long," I say. "With dance class and school and everything, we're so busy. And then I ruin it by freaking out."

"When is Rylie's next recital? I want to go again."

"Really?" I can't believe she wants to come. My stomach turns sour as I think of Greg's rude comments just a few weeks ago. Tori takes a deep breath.

"I don't think there is anything wrong with ballet, Charlotte." The sentence spills out of her like it took all of her energy. "I don't...Greg is..." She can't seem to get the words to form. She shakes her head slightly and smiles at me. It's a genuine smile. I feel like I see a glint of defiance in her eyes. "I would really love to see her recital."

"I think there's a card in my purse." I fumble through my bag, vision still a little blurry from tears, but I find one of the cards. Tori carefully places it in her wallet.

"You tell her I'm planning to come. She has a duet this time, right?"

"And two ballet pieces. And a tap piece. She didn't want to do that one, but they made her. She's all about ballet and lyrical now."

"I can't wait! Will she be doing pointe soon?"

"They'll decide after the recital. I know they wanted to check her ankle stability first."

"Rylie-Girl has a gift," Tori says with pride.

"Dance is all she wants to do," I murmur.

Tori pats my shoulder and smiles. "Feel like you can walk? We need to get you something to eat."

I know I should eat. I know I should do a hundred things that will help me feel better. How am I supposed to function like this?

"Let me guide you, hon. We'll be okay."

THIRTY-THREE

SHE IS MULTIPLYING. This morning as I prepped for Rylie's twelfth birthday party, She cried on the couch while I hung the '90s-themed decorations. She appeared again in the living room on the couch when the guests began to arrive, mascara-smeared eyes staring into space. I ignored Her until I realized that there was another Charlotte, standing at the kitchen sink, washing invisible dishes. The one at the sink wasn't wearing the blue blouse.

As soon as we sang and blew out birthday candles, I told my parents and David that I was getting a migraine.

Now I'm hiding in our bedroom with my head underneath my pillow because I know if I lift my head, She'll be there. I curl my knees to my chest and block out every sound and bit of light. If I can't see Her, She isn't there. I'm so thankful no one from church came. It's just Rylie's classmates from dance and a few from school.

How can there be two Other Mes? My heart almost hurts from pounding so hard. I try to count and breathe.

One...

How can there be more than one?

Two...

Wild explanations from all the sci-fi movies I've ever seen are jumping through my mind. Multiple universes? An alternate reality? What is this monster who looks like another version of me?

Three...

Why, God, why? Why me? Why do I see Her?

Four...

I'm losing my mind.

Five...

She is taking me somewhere, kicking and screaming. Where is She taking me? She's changing me, turning me into Her.

Six...

If there's more than one, is that a sign that I'm about to snap? Does this mean I'm going to end up drugged, halfway to a coma after a psychotic break? What will David do? What will happen to Rylie?

Seven...

Why God? Why are you letting this happen? What did I do?

Eight...

Who is she?

Nine...

Who is she?

Ten...

"WHO ARE YOU?" I scream into the pillow.

I keep screaming it over and over into the cotton fabric until my throat is raw. I'm terrified to uncover my head. If there were two of them, how many will there be now? I would rather smother myself under this pillow than lift my face and find Her looking at me again.

THIRTY-FOUR

I'VE BEEN FUSSING with this blue ribbon for hours. The other costumes for Rylie's recital were ready to wear, but her teacher left the duet costumes up to Sophia's mom and me. Mostly me, since Sophia's mom doesn't know how to sew. I can hear the duet music playing in Rylie's room. She's practicing again.

Sewing calms me. I never see Her when I sew. I rarely see Her when I paint too. Both activities seem to scare Her away. Occasionally I see Her in glances, but She doesn't seem to want to stay.

"Mom?"

"Sewing."

Rylie walks in, out of breath.

"Can you watch for a minute?"

"Which part?"

"Just watch."

She pushes the play button on the old school MP3 player we gave her a few years ago, which starts the duet music near the end and marks the routine for a few steps. Then she jumps, chassées, and glides around the room like a bird. The music flows like water. She slips slightly at the end on a jump, but other than that, it is perfect.

"Lovely," I say as the music fades. "Watch that last jump."

"I know. I keep slipping." Rylie sinks onto the couch. "I land funny on the turn, and then I slip on the jump."

"Did Miss Colleen notice?"

"No. Sophia still can't get that middle section right, so she was busy with that," Rylie says, stretching her neck.

"Ask her about it at rehearsal tonight."

"Miss Colleen will have to cut one of the turns if Sophia can't get it. And Sophia keeps talking about pointe. Ellie says there's no way she'll move up to pointe if she doesn't fix her turns."

"Don't worry about Sophia. Do your best."

"I guess," she peers at the pile of blue and green on my lap. "Is it done yet?"

"Not quite, but you can try it on."

"I'm all sweaty." She smiles and fingers one of the ribbons.

"I hope you like it," I say.

"Mom, I always like your stuff." She stands up, shoving the player in her pocket. "I'm going to take a shower. Where are we eating?"

"Eating?"

Rylie's jaw drops. "Your birthday dinner!"

"Oh no," I say, covering my mouth with my hand. "Forgot what day it was."

"Good grief, Mom. How do you forget your own birthday?"

I laugh and set the costume on the table. The clock has betrayed me.

"Because I'm old and going senile, and apparently, I can't

read a clock either! Go get cleaned up. Dad should be home in a few minutes."

She chasses out of the room to take a shower, and I gather up my sewing supplies. The Other Charlotte is there again. She sits at the table, eating invisible food and crying. I ignored Her while Rylie danced, but now I glare at Her.

The garage door opens, and David comes in with his coat and laptop.

"Hello, Birthday Girl," he says, kissing my cheek. "Where's Rylie?"

"Shower. She's been practicing her duet all afternoon."

"Come back to the bedroom with me. I want to tell you something."

I follow him back through the house, and he quietly shuts our bedroom door behind us.

"My boss told me about a position in Colorado and said I should apply," he says, watching me carefully. "They would fly me up there if I get an interview."

"Colorado?" My gut clenches, and I try to ignore the shiver starting in the base of my spine. "But we'd have to move."

"Yes, but I wouldn't have to travel as much," he says, pulling off his green polo shirt. "I really want to stop the remote work trips. I'm sick of missing Rylie's stuff. And this would mean I wouldn't lose my seniority."

"We don't know anyone in Colorado." The Other Me appears behind him, yelling at someone unseen. I guess my ghost hates this idea.

"We'd be closer to your parents," David says.

"And farther away from your mom."

"She'll visit," he says with a shrug.

"What about dance?"

"There're dance studios out there. Denver's huge."

I can't bring myself to say anything. I don't want to make any big decisions right now. I just want to keep my head down and survive.

"Do you think I should apply?" he asks, tugging his work shoes off.

It's too much to take in. A different city. A different church. Different everything. My skin pricks with cold as She runs past me, vanishing before She reaches the door. She looks angry. David gently squeezes my hand, and I make myself look at his face.

"Do you think I should apply?" he asks.

"You'd better warn Rylie," I say. "She's supposed to take her pointe prep exam after the recital. She'll be upset about leaving after all that work."

"I'll talk to her if I get an interview."

There is a knock at our bedroom door.

"Speaking of Rylie," I say, nodding toward the door. "Come in!"

"I'm ready!" Rylie bounds into the room, wet hair slicked back into a thick bun. "Are you going to wear that?" she says pointing to my faded T-shirt.

"No, I'm going to change."

"Hello, daughter!" David grabs her around the shoulders and hugs her tight. She wriggles but doesn't push him away.

"I need to get the presents," she says, as if suddenly remembering. "They're in my room."

"I said not to buy me anything," I whine as she leaves to get them.

"And I said too bad," David whines back.

I dress in a daze. I can hear them laughing in the living room, but I can't make myself leave our bedroom. The Other Charlotte is flickering in and out of the room. She's always upset, but this time She is angry. I feel like I might be sick and fill a cup with water in the bathroom.

What does She want? I can't ignore Her all the time. Some days Her presence is like white noise, drifting through the house like a blue shadow I barely see. But right now, She is as solid as me, and I'm terrified to somehow touch Her.

"Charlie, are we going?" David shouts from the living room.

"Coming!" How can I pretend to be happy? I'm so exhausted from this fake joy I have to wear whenever anyone can see me. I want to crawl in bed and sleep, but I edge past the angry ghost in the bedroom doorway and hurry to the car.

David and Rylie laugh and joke all the way to the restaurant. The little Italian bistro used to be one of our go-to date night destinations, but we haven't been in years now.

"Happy birthday, Mom!" Rylie says as the waitress settles us in the booth.

"If it's your birthday, you'll have to save room for dessert. Our tiramisu is wonderful." Our waitress points to the photo on the menu.

"I'll remember that, thank you," I murmur. Rylie begs for soda, but I make her get water.

I order lasagna. Comfort food. Rylie decides on fettuccine Alfredo. David gets a steak with a pasta side. I ask the waitress to leave the dessert menu for later. David pulls the bag out from under the table.

"That's mine! Open it first!" Rylie says.

I recognize the bag from the boutique Tori and I visited, and my heart pounds. Rylie is antsy as I pull out the tissue paper. I reach inside and pull out something in a beautiful blue silk fabric. The color takes my breath away.

It's the blouse. No matter how hard I try, I can't will away the tears in my eyes. Rylie's eyes are on me as I hold the blouse out. It's a beautiful top. It's a beautiful shade of blue. Rylie must have thought a long time about what to get me and carefully selected this shirt, but all I can think about is throwing it in the fireplace when we get home. She has no idea what this blouse means.

"I picked it out myself, Mom! It's just like your painting," Rylie says, her voice unsure. My girl knows something is wrong. She can see I'm not smiling, and I see the hurt crease across her forehead. With acting skills I've so carefully developed after so many years, I smile my happiest smile. I will not break her heart. I may be losing myself, but I will not let the Other Me hurt my daughter, no matter how much She hurts me.

"This is perfect for me, sweetie. Perfect." I pull her tight against me in the booth and kiss her forehead to hide my face. "Thank you so much."

"Are you sure you like it?" She sounds worried.

"I love it." The words taste like soap. "I absolutely love it. How did you know this was the right thing? Look, you made me cry."

"See, I told you she would like it, Dad!" I've convinced her. Rylie grins and puts her folded hands under her chin like a Cheshire cat. "Open Daddy's now!"

I look up at David, and the slightest frown curls the corners of his mouth. I haven't fooled him. I may have convinced Rylie, but he knows I hate the shirt. He knows I'm not happy.

"Happy birthday," he says, holding out a little box. It's obviously jewelry, and I know exactly what it is before I touch it.

"Sapphire earrings," I say. "To match the shirt. Round

ones." The ones that match. The pair the Other Charlotte wears when She's not screaming.

"You peeked!" David says and puts the box behind him playfully. He is acting now, too.

"I didn't peek! I promise. I know you too well."

I do know him. And he knows me. I know that he loves to buy me fine jewelry because he hates the costume stuff I usually wear. I know he's trying so hard to help me, even though I can't be helped. I know he will never understand what is happening to me because I don't understand it myself.

Rylie giggles as he finally gives me the box. The blue jewels sparkle in the light of the chandelier. I kiss him on the cheek. "Thank you," I whisper in his ear.

I look him in the eye, willing him to see that I love him even though I can't trust him. That I will do anything to stay with him and Rylie.

"Of course it's a perfect match. We went shopping together!" he says with a fake smile.

The waitress is back with our food. As I put the blouse back in the bag, something inside me breaks. I'm too tired to fight this anymore. I'm giving up. It is inevitable. I'm becoming Her, whatever that means. Maybe I already am Her. Maybe She won a long time ago, and I'm just too stupid to figure it out until now.

THIRTY-FIVE

I STARE at my hair in our bathroom mirror. I think if I used scissors first, then the razor, I could shave off the monstrosity on my head.

I just needed a haircut. A simple normal trim so I would look nice in pictures for Rylie's recital on Saturday. Then my hairstylist had an emergency and the salon owner handed me to a new stylist. From the moment the lady started cutting, I knew she was doing it wrong. She talked about her sister's new baby and her friend's wedding. She told me half a dozen bits of celebrity gossip. She was talking and not paying attention. I knew her scissors were too close to my ears. I should have stopped her. Why didn't I stop her?

How could I let someone give me *Her* haircut?

I swore I would never get this style in a thousand years. I screamed, and I know the whole salon thinks I'm crazy, but I would rather be bald than look like this. I swore to myself I would never get *Her* haircut.

The Other Charlotte watches me from next to the shower. I can tell She hates this haircut too. I glare back at Her, and for a moment, it's a standoff. I give up and look back at my real face in the mirror. The single difference is in what we're wearing, and it makes me shudder.

What am I going to do? Should I cut in bangs? I've never looked good with bangs, but anything is better than this.

When I look back, the Other Me has faded away again. Good. I hate Her so much. I hate every single hair on my head.

The garage door slams.

David is back with Rylie. I haven't answered his texts, so I know he's wondering where I've been. I hear Rylie calling me, but I don't want to answer.

"Charlie?" David steps into our bedroom, but I can't tear myself away from my reflection. My skin feels like I'm covered with invisible ants.

Rylie dances into the room and bounces up and down behind me. "Mom, you look amazing! I love it! Dad, look!"

"That's a good look on you," David says.

"I hate it."

"What? Why?" Rylie is shocked. Her eyes go wide with disbelief. "It's so cute on you!"

If only she knew how those words cut me to ribbons. "I'm sorry, sweetie, but I don't like it," I say.

"Why not, honey?" David asks.

"I hate this kind of style." I don't ever want to look like the Other Me, the horrible ghost that haunts me every day and wants to destroy my life. But I can't say that. "It was a big mistake."

The story tumbles out of me about how the new girl didn't listen and cut it too short, and now I'm crying again because I would rather be bald than have this haircut. David tries not to laugh at me, but Rylie is horrified.

"But it's so cool!" she says, fluffing the sides with a brush.

"Someone I don't like has this same haircut." It's the

closest I can get to the truth. "I'm going to have Kaci fix it when she feels better."

"But it's perfect! Please don't change it, Mom!" Rylie says.

I bite back the tears and try to smile. And there She is. She's watching my every move in the mirror, shimmering in and out as if She were made of smoke, but Her cold, dead eyes are impossible to miss.

"Charlie? Honey, what is wrong?" David says. I realize Rylie has left the bathroom and is rummaging on my dresser for something.

"I can't look like Her," I whisper. My words are hoarse with panic, and I try to swallow. He looks afraid of me now.

"Like who?"

I can't pull my eyes away from Her, but She fades like mist in the wind. Somehow I think it is inevitable. She's remaking me. She will force me to become Her no matter what.

"Here, Mom. Let me do it," Rylie says, holding out a square scarf with cornflowers and daisies. She folds it into a headband and wraps the silky fabric around my head. "That's how Aunt Tori used to do hers," she says with a smile. I nod.

"I need to take a nap," I hear myself say.

I'm not here. I'm underwater.

"I'll order pizza for dinner," David's voice echoes.

But when I look up to respond, he's not there, and somehow I'm sitting on my bed without knowing how I got there. I lean down until my head touches the pillow. I'm too exhausted to think. I'm too exhausted to breathe.

Somewhere in a dark corner of my mind, a little voice is screaming, "Wake up, Charlotte! You have to figure this out!"

But I can't listen anymore.

And then the alarm clock reads three in the morning. I

slowly become aware of David's even breathing behind me. I haven't moved a muscle since I fell asleep earlier, and my limbs are taut and sore. I struggle against the heaviness and turn over. David has covered me with a blanket.

A sharp pain stabs my neck behind my left ear. I fell asleep with my earrings in. I pull them both off and drop them on the nightstand.

I want to cry, but I have no energy for it. My tears have dried up. Hunger pangs gnaw at my stomach. I slip away to the hallway and out through the dark house to the kitchen.

I can still smell pizza. Rylie and David must have ordered it and eaten while I slept. Guilt claws at me, but I ignore it. The leftover pizza is in a bag in the refrigerator. I turn on the light over the sink and eat a slice cold. I'm thirsty after I finish, so I fill a glass of water and drink it.

And that's when She appears. In the dark it is hard to see her, but She's there on the other side of the counter. Her hand holds an invisible fork, and She eats off of an invisible plate, chewing and staring at me with blank dead eyes. Bite after bite. She jumps as if something has spooked Her from behind and vanishes in a shimmery fog.

"Charlie, you okay?"

David is standing in the doorway from the living room, bleary-eyed.

"I was hungry."

"Oh. I got extra veggies for you."

I hadn't noticed what was on the pizza, but I recognize the flavors of green peppers, onions, and olives in my mouth.

"Thank you."

"Why don't you get your pajamas on and come back to bed?"

"Okay."

His hands clench and unclench several times.

"Charlotte, are you awake?"

"Yes."

"You're not acting awake."

"I'm going to have some more pizza." I open the refrigerator and grab another slice.

He pulls a glass out of the cupboard and fills it with water before sitting down on the barstool where the Other Me had been.

"You're still wearing the thing." He points to my head. I pull the scarf off and set it on the counter. He takes a sip of water and smiles. "It does look nice. The haircut, I mean."

A small voice somewhere deep inside is screaming in terror and demanding I do something. I don't care anymore.

"Why were you so upset about it?"

I shrug. I want to eat my pizza and go back to bed.

"I like what it does for your eyes."

I should say something. I should tell him to shove that comment where the sun doesn't shine. I should tell him I'm going crazy. I should tell him there's a ghost of me with the same haircut. Then he'll call Darren or maybe someone else who can drug me until I don't see Her anymore. But I don't say anything. I take another bite of pizza.

He frowns. "Do you want me to make some tea? Or hot milk or something?"

I shake my head. David finishes the glass of water, but he doesn't move. He watches my every step as I finish the pizza, wash my hands, and fill another glass of water. I down the water in gulps and put the glass in the dish drainer. He hands me his glass across the counter. I look at it for several seconds before realizing he wants me to put it in the drainer with mine.

I follow him back to our room. He turns on the bathroom light so I can find my pajamas. I stumble around, pulling off my blouse and pants, and sit on the bed to steady myself. The T-shirt and shorts are soft pink modal material that brushes against my skin like feathers.

I move into the bathroom and pull out a washcloth to remove the remains of my makeup. My hair startles me every time I catch a glimpse over the washcloth.

"Charlie, did you hear me?"

"No."

"I said, 'Why don't you give it a few days before you change your hair?' You might decide you like it."

The tiny voice inside is hysterical, but I am numb. The washcloth is cold against my eyes and nose. I finish washing my face and brush my teeth. My side of the bed is somehow still a little warm from where I fell asleep on top of the covers.

Every step I take to run away from this thing, every attempt to make Her disappear has shoved me forward to being Her. I am turning into this woman that I don't want to be, and there's nothing I can do about it. She's planned it. The hysterical screaming part of me is running out of breath.

David pulls me close and wraps one arm around my waist. I peer into the darkness at my clock glowing on the nightstand and wonder how long I'll have to let him hug me before he falls asleep and rolls over.

THIRTY-SIX

THE HALLWAYS at Fellowship Christian School are nearly silent as I hurry to Principal Lewis's office. I pray I don't run into any of the teachers I know. We had a flawless dance recital on Saturday, but only two days later, Rylie is in trouble. Why can't we have a whole week without something going wrong for Rylie? I'm barely keeping my sanity right now. Our house was full of Other Charlottes as I left this morning.

My footsteps echo on the ivory tile as I walk this all-too-familiar path to find out what Rylie did and what her punishment will be. I pass the rows of green and sky-blue lockers. Brushing my hair from my face makes me shudder. I can't get used to Her hair.

Morgan, Larry, Grace, and our pastor all came to see Rylie's recital. Tori didn't, which I know shouldn't surprise me. It still stings. After our disastrous shopping trip, I thought that she really meant it when she said she wanted to come.

"Charlotte." David's voice makes me jump as he rushes to catch up with me.

My stomach sinks. If they called David, Rylie must have done something unthinkable. They never call him.

"Do you know what's going on?" he asks, grabbing my hand in the doorway.

I shake my head and let him lead me into the office.

"Please go right in," the secretary says. "She's ready for you."

"What happened?" I ask the principal as apologetically as possible.

"Mr. Madsen. Charlotte. I'm so sorry about this," Mrs. Lewis says. I wish I didn't know her face as well as I do because her seriousness is scaring me.

She gestures for us to sit down and straightens her glasses on her nose.

"Rylie isn't in trouble," she says, obviously choosing her words with care. "She's in the library right now. I wanted to tell you personally what happened and what we have done about it. Rylie told me she got in trouble with you this morning on the way out the door to school?"

"Yes. She didn't finish her homework."

I knew her temper would get her in trouble at school. A bad morning at home always leads to a bad day at school. David sighs and sets his briefcase on the floor.

"She was a little angry when she came into the building this morning, and she told me that she was still angry after her first class," Mrs. Lewis says. "And when Mr. Butler told her in the hallway to correct her posture, she told him to shut up and leave her alone."

"I'm so sorry—" I begin, but David interrupts me.

"Why was Greg even talking to her?" he says, sitting up straight in his chair.

"What happened was absolutely not Rylie's fault," Mrs. Lewis says. "I want you to know I'm so upset and very sorry."

I'm dumbfounded. Rylie sassed Greg, an administrator no less, and this woman is apologizing to us? It's like the Twilight Zone.

The principal interlaces her fingers in front of her. "Mr. Butler lost his temper. Multiple students saw the same incident. He yelled in her face and called her an inappropriate name."

"What?" I can barely process the phrase.

"I am so sorry, Mrs. Madsen. There is no excuse for his behavior."

David puts his hands on his knees as if steadying himself. "What did he call her?" he says through gritted teeth.

The principal looks down at her desk and purses her lips.

"He called her a 'rude little slut.'"

I look at David in horror, and he blows out a loud breath.

"He called Rylie what?" David seethes.

Principal Lewis clasps her hands in front of herself uncomfortably. "Mr. Butler is now on administrative leave until the school board can meet to discuss the incident. Again, I am so sorry. I apologized to Rylie, too."

"Where is he now?" David says. His look is dangerous.

I am nauseated with anger. I want to find Greg and slap him.

"He was asked to leave campus and escorted to his car as soon as I became aware of the incident."

"I want to know exactly what happened after that. What else did he say?" David says, flattening his palms over his knees as if trying to tamp down his fury.

"I'm told he tried to keep yelling at her and followed her

around the hall, but Rylie stayed calm until she found her homeroom teacher."

"How were there no other teachers around?"

"We were changing classes," Mrs. Lewis says, smoothing the sleeves of her magenta cotton blouse. "Rylie went back to her classroom, and her teacher walked with her to my office so I could deal with the situation. He followed them both here, and I called security."

"I don't understand why there wasn't another adult in the hallway," David says.

"He was the hall monitor for that section this morning," the principal says, looking sheepish. "The usual monitor called in sick."

"I want to see my daughter right now," I say.

"I sent her to the library with Mrs. Cates," Mrs. Lewis says.

"Well, we're going home immediately. Honestly, I'm not sure if I want her to come back to school until I know that Greg will not be coming back."

"I completely understand that. I will work with her teachers to make sure she does not fall behind." She walks to the office door and tells the secretary to bring Rylie.

"How long before he is fired?" David says.

"Well, there are some procedures we have to follow. I assure you, I am taking this extremely seriously. I will meet with the school board as soon as possible." She covers her mouth with one hand and looks at me. "Mr. and Mrs. Madsen, above everything, I want my students to feel safe and loved here. I hope you know that."

I stare at the floor, picturing Rylie cowering as an angry Greg calls her a word we don't even allow in our home. I purse my lips to keep them from trembling.

"So you're saying he followed my daughter all the way down that hallway screaming at her and calling her *that*? In front of everyone?" I say.

"Again, it was unconscionable, and I sent him home immediately."

"He needs to be fired," David says. "And I'm keeping Rylie home until he is. I don't want her to be afraid to go to school because he's here."

There is a knock, and Rylie stands in the office doorway.

"Are you okay, honey?" I say, standing to meet her.

She nods, but she shrugs off my hand from her arm and won't look at any of us. David steps around me and puts his arm around her shoulder.

"I've explained everything to your parents," Mrs. Lewis says, trying to smile and failing. "They feel it is better for you to go home. I will talk to your teachers for you."

I pull her chin up to make her eyes meet mine. It doesn't take much anymore. She's getting so tall. Her eyes flash, and I can tell she's about to cry. For Rylie, that is worse than death in front of strangers. I need to get her out of here.

She takes a deep breath and blinks before her "game face" settles over her, hiding all her emotions like she does before competitions. I gently place my hand on her shoulder and guide her out of the office while David thanks the principal. There is only so far she can hold it in, and I can't let her break in front of other people. David stuffs the school charter and the teacher honor code under one arm and puts the other around Rylie's shoulders like a shield. We walk as quietly as we can through the empty hallways and out to the parking lot.

Rylie buckles into the front passenger seat, but she still won't look at us or say anything. David pulls me aside and shuts the driver's side door so she can't hear.

"I'll take the day," he says. "I need to run back to the office and get my laptop. I left without it."

"I'll meet you at home then."

He pulls me into his arms. For a moment, the sun shines on my shoulders, David holds me tight, and I imagine this is all a nightmare and I'll wake up any second.

"Why don't you take her to lunch and get something for me for later?" David asks.

"I don't know if she'll want to go."

"I think she should. Tell her Daddy said so."

He goes to Rylie's side and kisses her on the forehead. He whispers something in her ear, but she stares resolutely at the floor of the car.

"Love you, Charlie," David says. "I'll see you at home in a bit."

"What do you want for lunch?" I ask my daughter.

Rylie looks at me like I've asked her for the code for a nuclear launch.

"There's a cafe that..." I falter. It's the one Tori likes. "There's a new one we could try. Over by the mall. How about that?"

"Whatever." She crosses her arms and shrinks as deep into the seat as possible. I start the car and drive across town in silence. She sniffs over and over, wiping her eyes with the sleeve of her hoodie. There's a package of tissues in my purse. I know she doesn't want to admit she's crying, so I pretend I need a tissue myself and leave the package out on the console between us. Two stoplights later, she decides to take one. I listen to the air conditioner and try to sort my thoughts.

Greg screamed at my daughter in public. He's supposed to be the adult. What is wrong with him? I'm suddenly furious with Tori. I'm furious with everyone at Fellowship, too. How many people have seen this coming and done nothing? Come to think of it, Larry should have done something. We've all been walking on eggshells around Greg for months. David is the only one who has challenged him openly.

"They have croissants," I say. I just want her to talk to me.

Rylie shifts in her seat. "Whatever."

"Rylie, you are not in trouble. Not at all."

"I was already a freak, and this happens."

"You are not a freak!"

"Whatever."

I don't know what to say, so I say nothing.

"Is Mr. Greg going to be fired?"

"Probably."

"Good."

I don't know how to protect her from the storm that is coming. Everyone at church will hear about it. Tori will be so embarrassed. Will she even come to church at all? I wouldn't if I were her.

"Aunt Tori is going to hate me."

The sentence makes my blood freeze.

"Tori would never hate you. Never." Why am I defending Tori?

"She already does. She didn't come to my recital." Her breath hitches. She's crumbling.

"I'm sure she wanted to."

"No, she didn't. Mr. Greg doesn't like me, so she can't like me anymore either. That's how it works when you're married." Rylie scrubs furiously at her eyes to hide the tears. Such adult words from my little girl. Surely she can't think that. I don't think that. David doesn't think that. Is this how she sees our marriage?

"That's not true."

"It is true."

"Rylie, it isn't. Maybe sometimes that is true, but it isn't true of Aunt Tori." I stumble over the word "aunt." I don't know if she deserves the title anymore.

"Yes, it is."

"Honey, she knows her husband..." Her husband what? Has a temper? Is a total jerk with a smug smile that I want to slap off his face nearly every week in church? I let the sentence end. Anything else would make it worse.

"He's the only one who gives me demerits, Mom! I don't get any from anyone else this year."

"Yes, I know."

Rylie looks angry, then sad. "Is that why Aunt Tori doesn't come over anymore? Because I'm a problem?"

"Sweetheart, this is not about you."

But even as I speak the words, I feel a spiderweb of anger wrapping around my heart. All of Greg's comments about my parenting are flooding back to me. The rolling eyes. The scripture quoting. Tori should have stood up to him. She should have told him to back off. Why didn't she do something?

Maybe because she agreed.

The thought is like a slap in the face. She stopped saying I was a wonderful mom a long time ago. All her concerned comments about my anxiety echo in my mind, suddenly hollow. She even wanted me to go on medication. She probably thinks she'd do a better job with Rylie. Aunt Tori would be more patient, more understanding, more dedicated. Aunt Tori doesn't have panic attacks and hallucinations.

"I don't want to go in," Rylie says, jarring me out of my thoughts.

"We can wait until you're ready." I'm being ridiculous.

This whole situation is so unbelievable. How does this happen at a Christian school? I'm sure David is ready to sue everyone by now.

"I want to go home," Rylie mumbles.

"We at least need to get food for your dad."

She stares at the ground and sniffs again. "Nobody did anything, Mom. Not a thing."

"Your teacher did."

"Yeah. But Liana didn't. Nobody from my class would help me," she says, tears falling down her cheeks. "He's so stupid,"

"I agree. He is stupid."

She looks straight at me, shock filling her face.

"Anyone who calls a beautiful, kind, funny, sweet girl like you a name like that is stupid. Stupid and horrible."

Rylie smiles in spite of herself, but only for a flash.

"Why didn't you tell him to leave me alone?"

Why indeed. Why didn't I stand up to him? Why didn't I tell him to leave disciplining her to someone else at school?

"I should have," I say.

Rylie opens her mouth and shuts it again. She stares at me, her eyes hard, then slowly softening.

"I should have told him off, honey. I was a coward. I'm sorry."

She looks away, her face unsure. "I tried to tell you," she whispers.

She did. She told me a hundred times, and I didn't listen. All those demerits, detentions, and countless extra essays. Guilt hangs on me like a lead coat, and I let my tears spill over. My poor baby.

"I'm sorry, honey. I'm so sorry."

She sniffs, and tears roll down her cheeks. I haven't seen

her like this in a long time. We sit and cry together in the heat of the car. She doesn't say anything else, but I can feel a wall falling down.

We grab food and head home, talking about anything but what happened. Instead of lunch, Rylie asked to take a nap for the first time in her entire life.

A text from Renee arrives as I hear the garage door opening.

OMG, what happened?

I mute her number. She can get her news somewhere else.

David drops his bags and hugs me in the dining room. "Is she okay?"

"I don't know," I say.

"I'm going to go over the by-laws tonight, but I'm pretty sure they have to fire him," he says. "And if they don't, they'll have a lawsuit on their hands."

I breathe in slowly. The whole idea of suing makes me sick. "Probably."

"Charlotte, he verbally assaulted our child!" David hisses. "Either they punish him, or we punish them."

Rylie walks in from the living room. He picks her up and hugs her tight. She grunts as if she's being squished.

"I'm hungry," she says.

We sit down at the table to eat. David grabs both our hands to pray, but I don't hear a word he says. Across from my seat next to Rylie another Charlotte materializes and stares at me. I can barely bring my fork to my mouth, and the food tastes like sand. How can I eat with Her staring at me like that?

Other messages are making my phone buzz, all from numbers I don't recognize. Moms I've never talked to want to know what happened. I show one to David, and he shakes his head that I shouldn't answer it. I mute my phone and put it away in a cabinet. I'm so glad we've refused to let Rylie have a cell phone until she turns thirteen.

THIRTY-SEVEN

"WHY DO we have to go to church?" Rylie says, her eyes on the road outside the front passenger window.

"It will be good, sweetie," I say as I turn into the church parking lot. I don't really want to go myself, but I feel obligated to at least attend the worship service.

"No, it won't," Rylie frowns.

"He won't be here," I say.

"It doesn't matter. Everybody else is going to be weird."

"Well, they shouldn't be. You didn't do anything wrong," I say. But I know she's right.

We're late and end up sitting in the very back. I'm glad we missed the greeting time. I still get a few waves from people. I can't get comfortable on the pew, and it seems Rylie can't either. She usually takes notes on the sermon, but today she scribbles and fidgets. I write the bare minimum just to keep my conscience from bothering me.

"See? Not so bad," I say after the benediction. "I see Ellie waiting for you by the door."

"At least she still likes me," Rylie mutters.

Ellie has been so kind. She's sent me messages every day since she heard about the mess to see how Rylie is doing.

"You can come get me if we need to leave early."

"Whatever."

I watch her meet Ellie, who wraps her in a big hug. She keeps Rylie under one arm as they leave through the back doors of the sanctuary toward the youth room. Halfway down the aisle toward our department, I freeze.

Greg is sitting on the front row. He's seen me, so there's no way I can avoid him. I never considered that he would come to church after the mess he caused. The sanctuary is still full of people, and I'm holding up traffic. I have to walk past him. I decide to walk as quickly as possible and try to get around him without speaking. Why did I come without David?

He stands as I come closer and stretches out a hand to me.

"I'm so sorry, Charlotte," Greg says.

"I don't think I should talk to you until the board makes their decision," I say, pushing past him.

"Please, Charlotte! Tori left me." His eyes are wild. "She left me last week, and now I'm going to lose my job on top of everything."

The words do not compute. Greg slumps onto the pew and puts his head in his hands. I'm conscious of so many people around us, listening, and watching. I want to run away, but I can't.

"I lost it. I wasn't mad at Rylie. I wasn't thinking straight because I woke up that morning, and Tori was gone. She was gone!"

My whole face is on fire. I have to get away from him.

"I just lost my temper. Please, Charlotte. They're going to

fire me." He looks up with tears in his eyes. "I just lost my wife, and now I'm losing my job!"

"Tori left you?" I keep my voice low.

"I don't know. I don't know where she is. I don't know anything. She walked out on me."

I should say something. I should tell him to shut up. I should say I hope they do fire him. The words won't come, and I simply stand, watching him cry on the front row of the sanctuary while familiar faces stare at us. Where is our pastor? Where is Darren? Someone has to get me away from here.

"I'm going to lose my wife and my job in the same week. Please tell Rylie I didn't mean it," he wipes tears away with a tissue. "Please, Charlotte. I'm so sorry. I'd give anything to take it all back." He peers at me over the tissue. "I'm losing everything."

"I'll pray for you," I say. It's a lie, but it lets me leave. I finally hear our pastor as I walk away, so I hurry to the only safe place I can think of: the ladies' room. Thankfully it's empty. I stare at my bright pink face in the mirror and try to calm down.

It's too much to fathom. Why would Tori leave? What could have happened? There must be more to this than her picking up and leaving. She would never leave him without reason.

I don't want to go to Sunday school. Rylie was right. This was a bad idea to come to church in the first place. I pull out my cell phone and click on Tori's name. I could send her a message, but this is not a text message conversation. This requires a phone call. Instead I select David's number.

Tori left Greg. I don't know why.

The message scatters into the airwaves, and I fiddle with

my earrings in the mirror. David responds almost immediately.

What?!? When?

Last week. Greg told me. He's here at church.

What is he doing at church? Do not talk to him!

David has been reading up on the legal issues to see
what we need to do to sue. I don't know that I want to drag
Rylie through a lawsuit, but if the school doesn't fire him, we
may have to.

*I got away as quick as I could. I told him I can't talk to him
until the board makes a decision.*

A twinge of guilt gnaws at me. I'm supposed to be forgiv-
ing. I'm supposed to model the right behavior for Rylie.
What is the right behavior here?

"Charlotte! How are you, ma'am?" Yvonne's voice echoes
behind me as she opens the bathroom door.

"Fine," I answer flatly. I put my phone back in my purse
and wash my hands.

"I was worried about you and poor Rylie and David after
this week."

There it is.

"Yes, well—"

"Hannah told me what happened when I picked her up
from school," she says, shifting her purse on her shoulder.

"Hannah was there?" I already know she wasn't. Rylie
told me who was in the hallway. If Yvonne can find a way to
answer my question that doesn't make her daughter sound
like a gossip, I'll be impressed.

"She told me Greg lost his temper." Good job dodging
the question, but I'm not in the mood.

"So she saw it?"

"I...I don't know. It sounded like there were a lot of
people in the hallway that afternoon."

I finish washing my hands without responding.

"I understand Greg may be losing his job?"

"I'm letting the school handle everything. I don't think I should talk about it."

"I heard that Tori left him." I freeze and look at her in the mirror. "Mrs. Black told me when I came in this morning." Rylie's Sunday school teacher. Of course she did. I decide not to say anything. Yvonne fiddles with her purse and finally says, "I certainly hope it isn't true. Have you talked to Tori?"

"It is true."

"She left him?"

"He's in the sanctuary, so you can ask him yourself."

"It's such a terrible situation, especially since his STEM program was going so well at the school."

I feel my jaw actually drop. Is she siding with *Greg*?

"I hope Tori won't walk away from their marriage without trying counseling. I know Renee mentioned she had asked about a counselor a few years ago," Yvonne says, looking at me in the mirror. Now my ears are hot, and I grip my cell phone.

"I'm sure Tori would appreciate that Renee is telling everyone that." It's out there now, and the words might as well have been a slap in Yvonne's face.

"Oh, I don't think she's telling everyone," Yvonne says, sputtering and moving her hands around like she's searching for an excuse. "She mentioned it for prayer. I'm sorry, Charlotte. I thought you might tell me how I could pray."

"No, I can't." Who am I right now? I never snap at people, least of all the mother of the child who is out to make Rylie miserable. "I honestly don't want to talk about this."

"I'm so sorry. Let Rylie know I hope she can get back to school soon."

"We'll see."

"Are you not going to have her come back?"

I look her straight in the eye without saying a word. It only takes a moment for her to drop my gaze.

"Hannah was wondering when she'd be back."

"Hannah was wondering?" I say. I can't believe she's blaming her nosiness on her kid. "I wasn't aware Hannah ever talked to Rylie. *About* her, but not *to* her."

I hurry out of the bathroom, leaving Yvonne staring after me in shock. I regret it. That will make things worse for Rylie. What is wrong with me this morning? We need to go home.

The hallway is thinning out as people head to the classrooms, but I bump into Grace, walking back from the coffee station.

"I'm so surprised to see you, Charlotte!" Her hug feels like a protective wall around me. "How is Rylie?"

"You heard what happened?"

She looks at the floor and smoothes her chin-length gray bob behind her ear. "Renee told me. Is there anything I can do?"

In a flash, I'm so angry I can barely think straight.

"How about banning Renee from making prayer requests for the next few months? I think that would solve half my problems."

Grace's face falls, and she looks at her coffee cup. Guilt floods over me. I have to go home. I'm offending everyone around me, and Grace is the last person I would ever want to hurt.

"I'm sorry, Grace. I didn't mean—"

"No, I'm sorry. I've actually talked to her about it." She

holds onto her cup for dear life and sighs. "She doesn't see it as a problem. But I see it, Charlotte. It's a big problem."

"I'm going to get Rylie."

The hallways are empty as I hurry to the youth room. I spy Rylie at the back of the room between Jerry, the youth pastor, and Ellie. She's hiding. She looks relieved when she sees me, and we run to the car.

"Mom, you look so freaked out. What happened?"

I could lie, but she would know. She always knows. "Mr. Butler was here."

Rylie's eyes widen. She buckles her seatbelt and waits for me to finish.

"Aunt Tori left him."

"Good."

"Well, not *good*, honey. That's not something to rejoice over." My voice is feeble. I agree with her.

"I know. But still," she says, crossing her arms with an angry smile. "Good."

THIRTY-EIGHT

I DON'T THINK David has driven Rylie to school since her first day of kindergarten, but I'm grateful he's here for her first day back. It's been almost two weeks since the incident. The high school principal, Greg's boss, called us on Tuesday with the news that the board made Greg's termination official. We waited another day so Mrs. Lewis could meet with us to discuss changes being made to hall monitoring. I was encouraged by that meeting, but David said he'll wait and see. Our pastor called us the next morning to see how Rylie was doing, and David had a long conversation with him about the relationship between the church and the school, administrative practices, and federal regulations. I was too busy trying to ignore a dozen Other Charlottes in the room to pay attention.

My phone buzzes with a message from Ellie for Rylie.

Don't forget the lock-in on Friday, it reads, followed by a series of goofy emojis. *You have to show me your new dance!*

I hand the phone to Rylie in the back seat. She reads the message, smiles a half smile, and hands it back.

"You ready, Ry?" David asks.

"I don't want to go in," she answers, sinking lower in her seat.

"Just be determined to have a good day," David says, squeezing her hand. Watching her miserable face, I wonder if we should keep her home the rest of the semester and start fresh in the fall.

"Do you want me to come in with you?" I ask.

"No! No, stay in the car! I'm fine!" She scrambles out of the back seat and rushes away from our car without looking at us. Without looking at anyone. I watch her practically run to the front steps, eyes on the ground. She ignores Liana at the door and disappears inside. Liana turns away from the door, rolling her eyes. I wish I could hear what she said to Rylie. Maybe she was trying to be kind, but I don't trust her. Not anymore.

At least Greg won't ever be coming back. Mrs. Lewis's secretary told me he didn't behave very nicely during the disciplinary hearing and destroyed his chances of being reinstated. I probably shouldn't know that, but it doesn't surprise me.

David is saying something. "Charlie, are you there?" he says, gently putting a hand on my shoulder.

I look into his eyes and try to pay attention.

"Sorry, I was in my own world."

"Thinking about what?"

"That I hate Greg." I've never said that out loud before, but now I can't take it back.

"A sentiment a lot of people probably share right now," he says with a dull laugh as he drives out of the school parking lot. "Have you heard from Tori?"

"Not since she left him."

My head is foggy. My ghost has been following me all around the house and outside for the last week. I've never seen Her this much, and it's making me sick to my stomach. I'm exhausted from trying to figure out who She is and what She wants from me. Pretending to have migraines let me hide in my room as much as possible. I was going to call a psychiatrist, but every time I try to pick up the phone, I chicken out. I'm so afraid they'll lock me up so I never see Rylie again.

"Charlie." David is waving his hand in front of my face. We're already home, and I've followed him into the house in a half trance. The room is filled with a half dozen Other Charlottes. One is sitting on the fireplace, staring into space. One is leaning against the doorway to the kitchen. Two others are pacing and trying not to look at me at all.

But none of those scare me as much as the one who is kneeling on the floor in front of me, weeping. I look up at David, and he has been talking again.

"I'm sorry. What?"

"Did you hit your head? You keep staring into space like I'm not even here."

"I'm fine."

"You are not fine!" he says, cupping my face with his hands. "Charlie, you are clearly not okay! You are scaring me!"

Scaring *him*? If I wasn't so distracted by the screaming Other Me throwing things in the studio, I'd tell him to shut up.

"I've hardly slept since this whole mess started," I say. "And all the migraines. I'm just tired."

He stares at me for a moment with the same scared face as the Other Me behind him in the doorway. "Then I'm making you take a nap."

"Okay." Whatever will get him to stop talking to me. "I was going to take a nap anyway."

He doesn't believe me, so I yawn, looking away from the Other Me still weeping on the floor beside him. He leads me to our bedroom and sits next to me on the bed.

"I don't know if we should have let her go back," I say.

David bows his head and folds his hands in his lap. "I don't know either. She's tough, though, Charlotte. Tougher than either of us."

My phone buzzes with a message from Morgan.

Did you know Hannah is telling people Rylie set up Greg to get him fired? I know that's crazy, but I thought you should know. I got asked about it at choir practice last night several times.

I can't process what I'm reading. I hand my phone to David and study the embroidered pattern on the comforter.

"That's..." He stares at my phone and shakes his head. "That's ridiculous."

I take the phone back to write Morgan back. *Who is Hannah telling?*

The response is a list of names from the church youth group and FCS. Morgan promises me she's been shutting down the rumor, but I know it won't matter. David looks over the list. "You have got to be kidding me," he growls. "How can she take his side? Yvonne and Reuben should be ashamed."

Another Charlotte runs through the room, and my gut clenches as I realize that I'm going to make it even worse. Rylie is about to be the kid with the crazy mom looking for attention. They're going to eat her alive. Yvonne is probably writing the prayer list right now, and I'm sure we'll be at the top. I hate that woman. God forgive me, but I hate her and her stupid child.

"Everything we could do will make it worse," I whisper, biting back tears.

"So I guess we pray."

Pray. I'm supposed to remember that. I'm supposed to ask God for help. So why am I the last person in a room to think of it? I nod, but I don't know if I want to pray. If He is there, then what are all these Other Mes? I don't recall seeing clones of yourself that are invisible to everyone else in Psalms or 2 Timothy. I wonder what the Bible says about ghosts. Or being crazy...

"Why don't we? Right now." David takes my hand and bows his head. "Father..."

I don't listen. I nod my head once in a while to keep him from noticing. Shutting my eyes helps, though. My head clears. I can pretend to be alone again.

David finishes his prayer, and I mutter an "Amen."

He tucks the soft throw over my shoulders. "Now, take a nap," he says. "Rylie knows she can call you to come get her anytime. Can you manage without me?"

"I'll be okay," I say, wiping my eyes.

"I'll be back after midnight Friday night."

"Okay. I'll be up. Rylie is going to the lock-in with Ellie."

"Call me if you need me to come home early, Charlie. Mom can come over tonight if you need her." I would rather die than let my mother-in-law see me like this.

"I'll be fine." If the room stays empty after he leaves, I will have told him the truth. "Love you."

For a few moments after he leaves, I'm truly alone. I listen to the sound of his car pulling out of the driveway and look over the list of names Morgan sent again. I could clean the kitchen. I could paint. I could vacuum the living room. I want to get up and move, but everything feels pointless. The feeling weighs me down until I wonder if I will smother myself in our mattress.

I finally sit up and watch the blurry figure rummaging in the closet. She's looking for shoes. I can tell by the way her hands are moving. She fades away as she sits on the end of the bed. The clock tells me I've been in bed for hours, but there are still hours left before Rylie gets home.

Maybe if I get out of the house, I can breathe. I felt a little more normal when we dropped Rylie off this morning. But where can I go?

The lake. At least there I should be able to get away from the others. I've never seen them there. It looks chilly outside. My black hoodie jacket smells like lavender from the closet sachet.

The drive is so familiar that I'm barely aware of it. The live oak tree near the shore is finally losing the last of its leaves. I used to wonder if the tree was sick, but that's its natural pattern. When everything else is green and growing, it stands stark and gray in the spring wind with nothing to lose.

The swift breeze off the lake bites my cheeks and ears and whips my hair into my eyes. I sink against the trunk into the hollow space where I usually sit with Rylie.

I don't know how long I cry into the sleeves of my jacket, but when I look up, a gull is flying overhead. It glides in place on the wind, white wings spread wide to catch the cold gusts.

My phone buzzes with a text message from David.

First flight was fine. Hope you had a good nap.

I follow the path back to my car. It's the lone one in the lot. The unusual chill in the air has driven all the runners to the gym.

It's a short drive to the school where I pull into the

pickup lane. I see Rylie on the stairs, and wave. She runs to the car, jumps in the back seat, and slams the car door. She usually sits in front with me, but she won't even look at me now. She throws her backpack on the floor, and I hear her seatbelt click. My heart pounds in my ears as I think about the text message from Morgan. I know why she slammed that door, but she needs to know she can't do it again.

"Rylie, please don't slam doors," I say, turning the car onto the street toward home.

"Leave me alone!" she says, burying her face in the door.

"You're being very disrespectful. Take a minute and calm down," I say.

"It's all your fault! They all hate me because *you* made this a big thing," she says, hugging herself low in the seat.

"What are you talking about?"

"Everyone says I set him up because you wanted him fired!" Rylie says, her voice rising.

The words knock me speechless. Morgan didn't tell me this part. I blow out a slow breath, trying to think straight.

"You made them, didn't you?"

"They were going to fire him anyway, Rylie." The words are gravel in my mouth. "Mrs. Lewis—"

"You told her she had to, didn't you?"

"He needed to be fired!" I say.

"I hate you! I'm quitting that school forever. Forever!"

My insides curdle and shake.

If Greg had screamed at Hannah or one of Hannah's friends, he would have been the pariah of the whole school. Instead, they're pouncing on Rylie, using the incident as an excuse.

The sound of Rylie crying in the back seat tears holes through me until I am sure I will throw up. I want to strangle Hannah right now. But I have to be a mom.

"Rylie, I am not the enemy," I say, looking at her in my rearview mirror. "I'm trying to do the right thing."

She turns, and the look she gives me cuts my heart into pieces.

"Why didn't you do it sooner?"

THIRTY-NINE

"YOU'RE WEARING IT!" Rylie says with a huge smile as she gets in the car. The silk of the blue blouse is like sandpaper against my skin, but I'm wearing it. It's a peace offering after the long argument in the car yesterday that continued into the house and back out to dance class. I hate this shirt, but I need Rylie to know I'm on her side. I am so glad the school week is over.

"Of course I'm wearing it," I say. "It's beautiful." I will wear it even if I would rather wear a shirt made of barbed wire.

"It looks so good with your eyes, Mom."

"Thank you, sweetie," I say. The words are sour in my mouth. "You have good taste. Was today any better?"

Her expression wilts, and she sinks into the seat.

"I hate this stupid school," she says.

"You don't have much longer. Just a few more weeks. I talked to Mrs. Lewis after I dropped you off, and she's trying to help."

"Mom, I'm really sorry," Rylie says suddenly. "I'm sorry for yelling at you. This whole thing is stupid."

"I forgive you," I say. "I need you to know that I'm trying to make it easier for you, sweetie, not harder."

"I know," she says. "Nothing will fix it."

"Maybe not. But he has to have consequences. You get grounded. Adults get fired."

"Jared said if Mr. Butler didn't get fired, his mom was going to pull him out of school," Rylie says, a smug smile creeping into the corners of her mouth.

"Jared? Is he the one with blond curly hair?"

"Yeah. Mr. Butler said his hair was too long like every week, so he hates him, too," Rylie says. "I like his hair. It's cool."

"Me too. He reminds me of a boy I liked when I was your age."

"Mom..." she groans, and I can see her ears are turning red.

I change the subject so she won't be too embarrassed. "Are you ready for pointe prep?"

She chatters about ballet the whole way home, grateful for something to talk about that isn't school or boys. My phone buzzes with a text message.

"That's probably Ellie," I say.

Rylie picks up the phone and answers the message. "You know..." she says with a sneaky tone in her voice. "If I had my own phone, I wouldn't have to borrow yours all the time."

"Thirteen, punk. One more year."

"I'm just saying, Mom. It would be convenient!" she says, throwing her hands up with mock innocence.

"Thirteen!" I say with a laugh. I can't fault her for trying.

We pull into the garage as she finishes texting Ellie about picking her up for the lock-in. "Hey," I say, grabbing her hand before she can rush out of the car. I wait until she looks me in the eye. "I love you, Rylie."

"Love you, too." She leans her head on my shoulder and hugs me awkwardly over the center console. I bite my lower lip so I won't cry.

My phone buzzes again. It's David this time.

Headed to the airport. Last interview was easy.

"Are we going to move?" Rylie asks, looking over my shoulder.

"We don't know yet. We'll see," I say, putting my phone away. "Better go get your chores done before Ellie gets here."

Rylie races into the house, but I can barely trudge. I know as soon as I step inside, I'll be surrounded. I take a deep breath and step into the laundry room.

Immediately, I see Her in the kitchen. The Other Charlotte is frantic. She paces next to the counter, tears streaming down Her face. I know that look. My heart pounds in my chest. What does She see? I see Her hands frantically moving. I think She is trying to write something. She holds her hands up as if there is something between them, but I see empty air. I look away, only to see another Her standing on the other side of the counter weeping. There are a half dozen in the kitchen. I can't even count how many are in the living room. They are all solid as I am.

One ghost shoves an invisible something in my face now. I close my eyes to get my bearings and when I open them, She is kneeling on the floor, weeping. Her mouth opens in a silent scream, and for the first time, I can read Her lips.

"Don't let her go!"

Don't let who go? And where? I bite back my terror and pray Rylie doesn't walk in on me looking at something that no one else can see. She has been through so much this last week. Rylie doesn't need my fears on top of it all.

The Other Charlotte continues begging me. She mouths, "Please! Don't let her go!" over and over and over.

I finally force myself to mouth, "Who?"

She points to Rylie's room.

The lock-in. She doesn't want me to let Rylie go to the lock-in.

The room becomes a whirlwind of screaming ghosts. My stomach turns, and I run to my room. I heave into the toilet and gag again on the taste of bile. The room is spinning. They haven't followed me yet. I stare at the white porcelain and try to block out the pounding behind my eyes and the nausea that makes my insides churn.

"Mom?" Rylie calls from her room.

I want to reassure her, but I don't have a voice. I can't let her see me like this.

"Mom, where are you?"

I can't move without my stomach wrenching, so I sit paralyzed on the bathroom floor. I wish I hadn't turned on the bathroom light. I hear Her in my room. She's going to find me.

"Where'd you go?" She steps into the bathroom and stumbles on the rug. "Mom! Are you okay?"

She leans down but jerks back when she sees the toilet.

"Oh no, Mom! I'll get a towel." She raids the bathroom closet and hands me one of my older ragged washcloths. "Should I call Dad?" she asks. Her voice is tiny and afraid.

"No, sweetie. I...I got sick."

"Do you want some water or something?"

"Yes, please."

She rushes out of the room. I can't hold back the tears any longer. It hits me like an avalanche. The room is empty, but somehow that's even worse. I can't stop crying. Rylie reappears and hands me a blue plastic cup full of ice water.

"I'm sorry, honey. Sometimes I get vertigo."

"What's that?"

"It means I get dizzy and nauseated," I whisper.

"I'm sorry, Mom."

"I'll feel better in a little bit. Go ahead and finish your chores, okay? Don't worry about me."

"Are you sure I shouldn't call Dad?"

"He can't do anything, honey. He's about to fly home."

"Oh." Her brown ponytail bobs as she nods, but her eyes won't leave mine. "I could call Nana?"

"I'm okay. It's getting better. Thank you for the water."

She leaves reluctantly after I promise her half a dozen times that I will be fine. Thank goodness that Ellie is willing to drive her to and from the lock-in. I don't know if I can move.

I watch the minutes tick by on the bathroom clock. Rylie comes in to check on me several times. Finally she sits on the floor next to me and won't leave.

"Mom, are you sure I shouldn't call Nana?"

"I'm feeling better, I promise," I sit up and sip my ice water.

"When does Dad get home?"

"This evening."

"Okay." She gently hugs me. I must look terrible. I avoid the mirror as I stand up. She seems convinced that I'm okay, so I walk back through the house filled with Other Charlottes.

She is everywhere. It's like walking through one of those mirror mazes in a haunted house, except the reflections have a mind of their own. The laundry room is empty. My head is still spinning, but the slow, methodical chore of moving laundry from dryer to laundry basket, washer to dryer, dirty clothes to washer, grounds me. I will be ok. I will.

"Mom?"

I follow the sound of Rylie's voice, trying not to pay attention to the Other Mes following me in fits and starts.

"Yes?"

"How does this look?" She wears a bright pink T-shirt with a black tank underneath and black skinny jeans. She holds up a black leather boot and a black tennis shoe. "Should I wear the boots or the Converse?"

"Probably Converse. You'll be playing games, right?"

"Yeah." She tosses the boot onto the wild mess on the floor of her closet and laces up the tennis shoes. I freeze in the doorway as the other me sits down on the beanbag next to her.

"Sweetheart, are you sure you want to go tonight?"

Rylie looks up at me, her face a mix of anger and worry.

"You don't want me to?" It's not a question about the party. I'm suddenly furious at the other me. This is the last straw. I will not hurt my daughter any more. I will not let her do this to us.

"Of course I do!" How do I explain this to her? "I was just thinking..." She didn't know I heard about Liana, and I wasn't going to tell her unless she told me first. Rylie looks me straight in the eye, waiting. "I know you'll be with Ellie, but Hannah and Liana will be there, too."

She frowns.

"Stupid Missile."

Ah. Liana's old nickname. Rylie only uses it when she wants to embarrass her. I lean against the doorway of her room.

"She's a big fat liar about everything anyway. I don't need

her. I don't need any of them. I'll hang out with Ellie and the other juniors."

But I can see in my daughter's eyes that their words wounded deeper than any knife. What those girls said to her has burrowed its way into the deepest part of her heart. She is hurt and angry, but she hates showing weakness. She knows weakness gets you picked on even more. I wish she didn't have to know that.

"Liana is weak, honey. She'll regret how she's treated you someday."

"She's stupid." She laces up the black Converse tennis shoes with a furrowed brow and quick angry movements.

I want to wrap her up in a hug and make those girls vanish in a puff of smoke. The hurt in Rylie's eyes stirs up a rabid anger in me that scares me. She sits back in her beanbag chair and the Other Charlotte vanishes like a blown-out candle. Suddenly I don't care about being the mature adult anymore.

"I wish I could hurt them as much as they hurt you, Rylie. Those girls are horrible. Hannah is horrible! It makes me so mad I could scream." Her eyes go wide, and she turns back to me.

"Mom!"

"I won't do anything. That's not what I mean." My voice is small and tight. "It would be pointless to do anything. But I still wish I could." There is venom in my words that stings even me. Rylie rubs her temples with her fingers.

"They didn't like Mr. Greg," she says. "He was always getting everybody in trouble at school. But now they all hate me!" She grits her teeth against her tears. "You know Hannah makes fun of Mr. Greg at church all the time. All the time, Mom! But I didn't."

She cuts herself off and frowns. I know why. Because she loves Aunt Tori and wouldn't want her to be mad.

"It's all stupid," she says. She pulls her knees up and buries her chin in her lap. "Hannah does all this mean stuff. And no one cares."

All the answers are things I can't say. That she's beautiful and talented and intimidating. That she makes them feel less important even though that's never been her intention. Rylie is something they can't categorize because she's so mature but still so young. Young women yearning for adulthood are afraid of things they can't categorize. Adults are, too.

"They're afraid to think for themselves," I hear myself whisper. I sit next to her on the bed and pat her hand gently. I realize she isn't pulling away like she usually does. "That's why. They don't like themselves."

"I don't like them either," she mutters without a hint of irony.

I snort a laugh and sigh.

"I'm supposed to tell you that it will all get better when you're older, but it doesn't," I say, thinking of Renee whispering prayer requests behind my back and Yvonne's backhanded compliments in Sunday school week after week. I wonder if Rylie has heard things from Liana over the years. I hope not.

"Hannah's mom is stupid. That's why Hannah is stupid," Rylie says. She does know. She leans over and hugs me. The tears fall silently down my cheeks. I sense another Charlotte standing in the doorway to Rylie's room, but I ignore Her.

This moment is crisp and bright against the darkness of everything I've been hiding for years. My fear tears at the edges, pushing against razor-sharp corners and leaking out in thin slivers. Rylie shudders on my shoulder, and I pull her tighter.

"Don't ruin your mascara, sweetie," I whisper. I don't want to make her stop. I'm crying, too, but I know that tears will make her even more vulnerable. She looks up, black already smeared under her eyes.

"Can I borrow your makeup remover?" she sniffs. "Mine doesn't work."

"Of course." But I don't move. I kiss the top of her head and hold her because I know this moment will not last. The Other Charlotte is collapsed on the floor in front of us, sobbing and hitting the carpet with a bruised palm.

"At least Ellie still likes me," Rylie whispers.

"Of course she does. Ellie is the best," I say, pulling back to look Rylie in the eyes. "Aren't you lucky? And the other junior girls like you, right?"

She nods.

"You go have fun with Ellie tonight, okay? You hang out with her. And forget the rest of them." Maybe Ellie can change everyone else's mind. Maybe she'll be able to shut Hannah down. "Now let's fix your mascara, ok?"

The doorbell rings, and Rylie looks panicked. I push her toward my bedroom.

"Go get my makeup remover and fix it. I'll talk to Ellie, ok?"

"Can you get my backpack for me?"

I wave her off and walk to the front door to let Ellie in.

"Hi, Mrs. Madsen!" Ellie has her hair pulled up into a messy bun. She's wearing a long tunic top with leggings.

"Don't you look cute!"

"Thank you! Where's Rylie?"

"She needed to fix her makeup. Come on in. I'm going to get her backpack." I try not to flinch as dozens of Other Mes in the kitchen scream at me not to let Rylie go. But I won't let Her tell me what to do. My daughter deserves to have fun with her friends after all the misery of the last weeks.

Rylie bounds into the hallway. Her mascara is back to normal, but her eyes are red.

"You girls have a great time, ok?" I hand her the back-pack, forcing myself to let go of it a little too obviously.

"I'll take good care of her, Mrs. Madsen," Ellie says.

"Love you, Mom," Rylie says and hugs me. I hug her back and kiss the top of her head. Ellie drives them both away while a hundred Other Mes surround me, crying and screaming soundlessly.

FORTY

DAVID CALLED before he boarded the plane and debriefed me on his interviews. He likes Denver. He even drove around a few neighborhoods near the building to get ideas about a new house. I'm doing the same thing, except on my computer because it's the only thing keeping me sane.

The room is so full. There are hundreds now. She has multiplied until She fills the room. Each version wears the same blue shirt that I hate so much. Some have their hair clipped back, while others seem not to care about tangles and knots. One stands at the counter making cutting motions. Another paces back and forth in front of the back door. One weeps, kneeling in the doorway to the living room. Dozens more pantomime chores throughout the room with hollow eyes.

And then there's the one screaming at me. She is right next to me, her mouth open in a silent scream, shaking her fists at my face. She reaches for my shoulder, and I jerk back involuntarily. I thank God there is no one home to see me like this. I have finally gone mad.

I try to shut out the Other Mes and focus. The clock says

11:00. I texted Ellie, but I haven't heard from her. I have forced myself to wait, minute by excruciating minute. What if She was right? What if I shouldn't have let Rylie go tonight?

I close my eyes and shake my head. Ellie and Rylie could be singing karaoke to the radio in the car on the way home and not hear the message. I shouldn't worry. If I thought I could make it without being sick, I would go lie down on the couch, but the whirling of ghostly forms through the room makes me too nauseated to stand.

The phone rings, and I snap it on without looking at the name.

"Hello?"

"Hi, Mrs. Madsen." Ellie's voice sends a chill across my skin. She sounds as if she is about to cry, and I know deep in my gut that something is very wrong.

"Ellie?"

"Um, did you come get Rylie early? Everyone else has gone home, and I can't find her."

"You can't find her?"

"No, ma'am. We played sardines earlier, and I didn't see her after the game. I thought maybe you..." Ellie breaks down in loud tears, and someone else asks for the phone.

"Hi, Charlotte," our youth pastor says. "Rylie isn't with you? We were thinking that maybe she went home early."

"No, I was about to call Ellie to ask where she was."

"Oh."

In the silence, I realize the room around me is growing even more crowded. I flinch as I step through the ghostly figures to the refrigerator. The flyer for the party is stuck to the front with a magnet. All the movement in the room feels like gravity is folding in on itself.

"Charlotte, I'm so sorry. I don't know what happened. All

the sponsors are still here with us, and none of them signed her out to go home."

"So nobody knows where Rylie is? No one?"

I slump against the refrigerator. Cold creeps up from my toes over my body as if I'm being dragged underwater. The icy pinpricks sting across my skin until they reach my neck, and I shiver uncontrollably. I shut my eyes as my vision spins. I'm on the rollercoaster in the dark, but I'm so cold. The fireworks crash around me, and I'm being shoved through an invisible wall of ice. I can't move or speak or even think. Everything is cold and dark.

Then the cold is gone, leaving a dead emptiness in my stomach. I force my eyes open.

I'm still sitting against the refrigerator, but the room is empty. The Other Charlottes have vanished.

"Charlotte, are you there?" I hear Jerry on my phone.

"Yes..." I manage to whisper.

"Are you okay?"

"No, I'm not okay! My daughter is missing!" The room is completely still and silent but for the sound of the air conditioner. There are no Other Charlottes in the room. Nothing at all. Tears blur my vision out of focus. The stillness is suffocating. What happened to them?

"I'm going to make some phone calls to some parents. Is there anyone she might have gone home with? Renee, maybe?"

"I...I don't think so." *My daughter is missing.* The phrase reverberates in my head.

"I did have to step away a few times, but there was always another adult at check out. Diana was with me. And Debbie. I'm sure they saw her. We're going to check the sign-in again. Let me make some phone calls, okay?"

"Jerry, please find her."

"We have twelve adults looking all through the church. I'll find out who she went home with. I'm sorry, Charlotte. We will figure it out." He pauses. "You know, Liana did this same thing after girls' night out. She slipped out with Hannah and didn't sign out. But she called her mom."

Every muscle in my body goes rigid.

"Rylie doesn't have a phone, Jerry."

"Oh." His voice changes. "I'll call you right back, ok?"

I hang up, and the invisible wall of ice knocks my breath from my lungs. I shiver, and the movement stings me from head to toe like the pinpricks when your foot or hand falls asleep. Is this what a seizure feels like? My face stings so much that my eyes water, and I rub my cheeks with the backs of my hands.

I see Her again.

She is sitting at my desk in front of the computer. She is doing exactly what I was doing in the moments before I knew Rylie was missing. She holds an invisible phone and stares into space. There's only one. I look around the room for the others, but this one ghost is enough to suck all the oxygen from my lungs.

I watch Her answering the phone in pantomime. She skips and shimmers and answers the phone again, in exactly the same way. It's like something from a horror movie. The room seems to shrink in around me until I think I may suffocate.

I have to call David.

I dial with shaking hands, but it goes directly to voice-mail. I forgot he's still on the plane. Why does David have to be on a plane right now? Why can't he be home? That stupid interview!

"David, call me as soon as you get this message. It's about Rylie. Call me immediately."

I hang up and stare at my phone, ignoring the stillness around me. Finally, it lights up with Jerry's number.

"Did you find her?"

"No, and we don't think she signed out either."

"What?"

"We're trying to figure out what happened, Charlotte. I'm so sorry."

"How could she leave early without someone noticing?" I say, my voice rising to a shriek. "It's supposed to be a lock-in!"

"I was all over the place with the activities, but I promise we had more than enough leaders. We'll find her."

"I think I'm going to call her grandma."

"Good idea. Maybe she went there instead of home. Is there anywhere else she might have gone?"

The sentence doesn't process at first. Then I realize what he means.

"Jerry, Rylie didn't run away!" I shout. Rylie has too many reasons to come home. Even if she was angry with me, she would never run away from David. The thought is like a razor in my heart.

"No, I'm sure she didn't. Call me back either way."

I hang up and watch Her at the kitchen table, answering the invisible phone and staring into space, like a skipping record. I've never been more afraid of Her.

I dial Nana Tanya's number.

"Hello," she answers, her voice slightly higher-pitched than normal.

"Tanya, it's Charlotte. Please tell me Rylie is with you."

"Rylie? No, she's not here. What happened?"

"She went to the lock-in tonight with Ellie, and now no one knows where she is." I can't sit still. I start to pace back and forth next to the kitchen counter.

"Oh..." Tanya sounds breathless. "Could she be at a friend's house?"

"No. Not after everything with school."

"Are you sure?"

"The youth team is looking for her," I say, my voice breaking. "No one knows who she left with. Tanya, I don't know what to do! David is still on the plane!"

"Okay, deep breath. Press pause for a minute, sweetheart. I'm sure she's being her usual forgetful self."

"What if something happened?"

"They'll find her. Should I come wait at your house so you can go to the church?"

"Could you?"

I hear the television in the background shut off. "Let me get dressed. I'll text before I leave."

I hang up and call my mom's cell phone.

"Hi, honey! A little late to call, huh?"

"Mom..." My voice breaks, and I can't speak again for a long moment. I finally find the words to explain.

"Oh, baby, I'm sure she's with friends," Mom says. "She just forgot to call you. Rylie's being Rylie."

"I just know something bad happened."

"Let's try not to panic yet. I know you want to. I want to. But let's try not to." I hear my dad's voice in the background, and she tells him what happened. I hear the buzzing of the speakerphone as Mom turns it on.

"Honey, she's bad about remembering stuff, right?" Dad says.

"Where's David?" Mom asks.

"He's still on the plane."

"Oh honey, and you all alone," she says. "No wonder you're freaking out."

The sentence sets my teeth on edge.

"I am not freaking out. I am scared for my daughter who is missing!"

"Charlotte, surely it's just a mistake."

I know that I'm usually crazy, but one glance around my completely empty kitchen tells me that I am definitely not losing it right now.

"Rylie is going to have a lot of apologizing to do," my dad says.

I manage to gracefully hang up. My phone vibrates with a text message from my mother-in-law.

Heard anything?

I bite my lip and try not to cry. I don't know if having my mother-in-law here would make things better or worse. David won't be back for another forty-five minutes. But she could be here in thirty.

No, still nothing.

I dial Jerry's number again, praying Ellie has found Rylie.

FORTY-ONE

I PACE AIMLESSLY around our house as I wait for my mother-in-law. Every time I've been unfair or didn't listen to Rylie replays in my mind. My eyes hurt from crying. I am utterly helpless until my mother-in-law arrives so I can go to church. And even then, what can I do? If she's missing, what can I possibly do to find her? Why didn't I let Rylie have a phone so she could call me?

Worst of all, the Other Charlottes are slowly returning. I see them everywhere, but they are dim and hard to see. Some are fully transparent. Most aren't wearing the blue shirt, which terrifies me, but I try to focus on what is real. After I called Jerry, I called everyone from church. Renee told me to text her as soon as I found Rylie. I hung up on her. I hung up on Yvonne, too. I didn't have time for fake platitudes.

I scroll through my phone to my very last possibility. I haven't heard from Tori in two weeks, all my texts in the meantime are still unread. I take a deep breath and call her number, praying she picks up.

It goes immediately to voicemail.

I can't sit still, so I walk through the sea of ghosts until I end up in Rylie's room. I notice her ballerina lamp on the desk and remember when my mother-in-law brought it over. This room was so different then. It was a nursery, full of fuzzy blankets and brightly colored toys. I had set it on the chest of drawers next to the changing table. I'd designed or chosen every detail except that ballerina lamp.

I turn on the lamp and let its warm glow fill the room. I remember rocking Rylie to sleep in that soft pink light. It was the first time she slept more than three hours. I turn toward the window and think of how the trees made patterns on the windows.

The horrible cold pours over me again. The Other Me is here, rocking in the corner in an invisible rocking chair. She is transparent and shimmery like a ghost. Usually, she is as real as me. The longer I look, I realize She looks different. Her hair is long, pulled back in a messy bun, and she's wearing the soft pink pajamas I finally threw away last week. They look brand new. She rocks back and forth, staring down into Her arms cradled around emptiness.

I take a step toward Her to get a better look at Her.

She jumps.

She looks up at me in absolute terror and squeezes Her eyes shut. She keeps rocking with Her eyes shut. I stumble back over a pile of Rylie's clothes and stand against her bed, staring. She keeps rocking with eyes resolutely shut. She's afraid of me. She's never been afraid of me before. I'm always afraid of Her.

I step toward Her again. She keeps rocking, eyes closed. She looks calm, but I can see Her hands are shaking. I reach toward Her.

She vanishes like a blown-out candle, and I'm left alone.

Why is She afraid of me? This is even worse than all the others disappearing in the kitchen.

My body shivers violently. I stumble down the hallway to our room to wash my face. The bathroom light is too bright, like the cold lamp of a surgical unit. I pull my hair back with a headband and splash my face with warm water. The washcloth is rough on my tender eyes as I rinse away the mess of mascara and eyeshadow. I rinse my face and blot it dry. I don't know what else to do. I glance at myself in the mirror and wince at my hollow eyes and messy hair. I miss my long hair.

The cold snakes down my back in pinpricking rivulets.

She's here again. She is so transparent I would miss Her if I didn't know exactly where to look. Her hair is long and falls in waves over Her shoulders. Her eyes are wide in terror, looking straight at me, but She shimmers like She is made of fog. I can barely see sparkly black eye makeup melting down Her face. She is calling for David. I whip around to look for him, but he isn't there.

I back away into the corner next to the shower and hold myself up with the towel bar. I remember the steam of the shower seeming to swirl and move as if a person were walking through it. I told myself it was my imagination. Just the heating fan. The Other Me turns to run out into the bedroom, trailing away like smoke as she goes.

I stumble to the sink and put my hand on the mirror to make sure it is really there. The cold hits me harder than ever.

This time I look Her straight in the eye. She is as real as me. Her hair is newly cut, and She is crying. Her image shudders like a video skipping forward, and She's wearing the scarf Rylie fixed for me. Her eyes are smudged with makeup. She's talking to an invisible Rylie and David, trying to explain. She shudders and skips, and She's back to brushing her hair.

Then She's gone.

I back against the shower and see another flash of Her. The shiver starts at my neck and spreads over me in a flash. She is waiting on a pregnancy test. A loud clatter sends me jumping back from the shower, and I watch my shampoo bottle spin at the bottom of the tub. It comes to a stop next to the drain. When I look up, She is lying on the floor of the bathroom, bleeding.

She looks at me in utter terror, and I sink down onto the floor and cover my face with my arms.

How?

Memories crowd into my mind of Rylie dancing and playing. The fights with David. The time I nearly dropped Rylie from sheer exhaustion when she was six months old. Each brings shocks of ice big and small until I am shivering so hard I can't breathe. The ice keeps hitting me, locking my muscles. It grips me with fingers made of needles. I gasp for air, but breathing hurts.

Is this what it's like to die?

The thought echoes back and forth in my brain, and I'm suddenly plunging into a dark hole. I know this feeling, this rollercoaster in the dark. Is this memory or reality? Am I dying?

The rollercoaster slams through the dark and jerks me through the ice over and over. The question screams through my skull like a hurricane.

Did I die?

Is my whole life an illusion, the last firing of neurons as my brain shuts down in an ugly hospital bed? Is Rylie on her way to the NICU, and I've lived an entire twelve years in those split seconds?

Shouldn't I feel peace?

"Where are you, God?" I whisper.

The tile is cool against my cheek. I use the feeling as my anchor. I count to ten, letting the soft pressure against my cheek guide me back to reality. The smooth cold surface that smells like cleaning supplies suspends me from myself. I float above the fear in a cold dark river. This river is familiar. It has taken me before, after Rylie was born.

Where is it taking me now?

My stomach lurches me back to the bathroom, and I grip for where the toilet should be. Thankfully I find it.

I'm having a panic attack. I must be. I wipe my lips with a piece of toilet paper. I'm just having a panic attack. I will ride it out and find Rylie.

My stomach twists again. I scream into the foul-smelling toilet bowl. I don't know how I have anything to throw up. I've barely been able to eat all day.

I force myself up from the floor even as the world is spinning around me and splash warm water on my hands and face. I am so cold, but the heat stills my chattering teeth. I stumble through the house, looking for the right memory. I have to tell Her. I have to stop Her. She has to listen to me.

She's standing in the kitchen. I'm too dizzy to stand, so I end up on my knees.

"Don't let her go!" I scream, speaking the words as clearly and slowly as I can. "Please! Don't let her go!"

She stares at me, frozen in terror. She mouths, "Who?"

The ice stabs me in the heart as I point back to Rylie's room. She runs past me and disappears.

"Please! You have to listen!" I scream, scrambling for a piece of paper and pen on the counter. I'll try earlier. I have to try!

I write "Don't let Rylie go!" on the sheet and hold it in

Her face as she appears in the laundry room doorway. She ignores me. I pace the room over and over, trying to find a version of Charlotte that will listen to me. One of them has to.

"God, please! Make me listen!" I scream, falling on the cold tile of the kitchen. "Why can't you make me listen?"

The sobs tear through me. I slap the tile with my hand.

"Please! Please listen!" I cry.

I close my eyes and scream into the floor in agony. It's pointless. I know it's pointless because I've already seen myself try it! I won't listen.

My phone lights up with a call, and I see David's number. I have to pull it together. I take a slow deep breath and answer.

"Charlotte? Is everyone okay?"

"Rylie is missing." The wall of ice hits me again, and I can't speak. I stare as She stands in the kitchen, yelling without a sound. She's yelling at David. I turn away and walk into the living room, keeping my eyes on the floor.

"She never..." I swallow the sobs in my throat.

"Charlie, what happened?"

"No one knows where she is."

"Have you called my mom?"

"Yes, she's coming."

"Good." I hear his fast footsteps through the phone. He's probably racing to his car since he didn't check a bag. "Did you call Renee to check?"

"Yes, she hasn't seen her. I've called everyone, David, even Yvonne! No one has seen her. I swallow the bile rising in my throat. "I shouldn't have let her go."

A knock on the front door sends my heart racing, and I stumble through the hallway to open it. My mother-in-law is dressed in an old T-shirt and sweatpants.

"You weren't answering my messages." My mother-in-law shuts the door behind her and hugs me. "Did they find her?" I shake my head and can't stop the tears.

"David's on the phone," I manage to get out between sobs.

"Here, I'll talk to him." I let her take the phone and sit on our couch, unable to stop the sobs. I have to get control of myself. I can't find Rylie if I can't calm down.

"Charlie, do you want to meet him at the church?" she asks. I manage a nod and try to breathe. She finally hangs up and sits next to me, her arms around my shoulders. I wish my mother-in-law could see all these ghosts floating around the room. She'd understand that this is serious. Rylie isn't forgetting to call. Something is horribly wrong.

"Let's get you calmed down and you can meet David at the church," she says gently. "She's going to feel terrible about doing this to you, Charlie. Goodness, one look at you, and that will be punishment enough."

FORTY-TWO

THE DRIVE to our church is short with no traffic on the road. I probably shouldn't be driving at all, but I don't have a choice. I shiver with cold. The church is mostly dark, but the youth building lights are on. Jerry, Ellie, and several other youth sponsors are waiting for me in the front hallway.

"I'm so sorry, Mrs. Madsen," Ellie says. She's crying, and she hugs me hard. "I don't know what happened. I've been here all night! She was here and then she was gone. Stupid sardines!"

"We've gone through the whole church," Jerry says. His eyes are red, but I'm too angry to feel bad for him. "Diana just mentioned that maybe she fell asleep somewhere, so we're going to canvass again and yell louder."

"Rylie wouldn't fall asleep."

"I don't think she would either," Jerry says. "I'm sorry, Charlotte. We are calling all the parents who had kids here tonight to check if she went home with one of them. And I called the police. They're sending someone."

The word *police* makes me sick to my stomach.

"Did you use the sanctuary for worship?"

"Yes."

"We should check the sanctuary again." I don't know why, but I have to go to that stage in the sanctuary. She's spent so much time on that stage for praise dance performances. It's her space.

Jerry hangs his head and nods. "The side door should be open. The lights are off though." He points down the hallway instead of through the atrium. "I'll wait here for the police."

I step into the stillness. I can see streetlights outside through the stained glass.

"Rylie? Are you in here?" My voice echoes off the vaulted ceiling, and the rafters creak from the wind outside. I walk down the aisle, trailing one hand over the arms of the pews. I remember doing this as a child. The hollow tap of my fingers against the cool smooth wood beats a rhythm that reminds me of a heartbeat.

I walk to the table in front of the stage. The simple wood frame is as old as the church itself. The front panel reads, "In Remembrance of Me." I sit on the front row and bow my head. I don't know what I'm looking for. She's not in any of the pews.

This church is full of memories, but which one matters? Which one will bring Rylie back to us? I think of the hollow eyes of the Other Mes over the years. Maybe I *won't* find her. Maybe this is all inevitable and I didn't know how to tell myself the truth.

I finally raise my eyes from the communion table to the baptistry. Someone has left the curtains open. I look at the tall wooden cross that hangs over the water and let myself remember Rylie's baptism. She loved the white robe they gave her to wear. She wanted to keep it, but I told her we could take a picture instead.

The cross blurs through my tears. I need to do something more than remember. I lower myself to my knees on the edge of the stage, but I can think of nothing to say. How can I pray? I have no more words.

As I lay my forehead against the green carpet, the cold hits me. She went under the water, excitement lighting her face like a candle. I can almost hear Pastor John saying, "Buried with Him in the likeness of His death. Raised to walk with Him in newness of life."

I wipe my tears away and peer into the baptistry. I see Her, eyes shining with pride and love. It replays in front of me. I know Rylie is bounding out of the baptistry and soaking my clothes with a hug. But I can't see my little girl. I can only barely see the Other Charlotte, wrapping Her arms around empty air and mouthing words of love. My head is heavy, and I drop it back against the carpet as the memory skips back and forth. I don't need to look up to know that the Other Me panics. Now I'm the weeping one. I don't want to see her fear. I want to remember my daughter.

If I can reach out to the past, if I can see it in front of me like it's real, why can't I change it? Why can't I stop Rylie from disappearing? If these memories can see *me*, why can't I stop myself? Why won't I listen?

Tears gouge down my cheeks and burn the backs of my hands. I lay against the steps and wail. My voice belongs to a wounded animal, and I cannot control it. It comes out of my throat unbidden. The sound scares me. I vaguely remember crying out like this when Rylie came into the world.

"Charlotte?" It is David's voice behind me. I struggle to my feet. It feels like I have been weeping for hours. Days. He gently pulls me into his arms, and we sit together on the front pew.

"Charlotte?" I hear Jerry saying from behind us. "Is this Rylie's?"

I look up to see him standing next to a police officer who is holding a fluorescent pink backpack.

"Yes. That's her ballet shoes." I choke over the sob in my throat. "She wanted to show Ellie a new song."

Jerry can't look at me. The officer sets the bag down on the pew next to us.

"We found it behind the check-in desk," he says. "Does your daughter have a phone?"

"No," David says. "Not until she turns thirteen."

"Can you describe what your daughter was wearing tonight? Hair color and eye color?"

I tell him everything I can remember. David stands up and starts pacing back and forth in front of the altar as the officer talks to Jerry and the dispatcher.

"So what are you doing to find her?" David says, grabbing my hand. "What do we do?"

"We are doing everything we possibly can," the officer says, giving us his full attention. "I have a daughter, and I would be losing my mind if this were my girl. We are using every resource we have."

My phone vibrates in my pocket, and I nearly drop it, trying to get it out. Please let it be Rylie calling. Please God, let it be my daughter.

The screen flashes with a notification for an *Amber Alert*. It's for Rylie.

FORTY-THREE

THE POLICE PROMISED to watch for Rylie on patrols and told us to stay home in case she comes back. Comes back from where? Rylie has been missing for hours. I wander from room to room in the house, staring at her bed, the pile of ballet laundry, her favorite cereal in the pantry. And I watch myself laughing, grinning, then crying, screaming, and always picking up that horrible phone call from Ellie in the chair in the kitchen. The Other Me is everywhere. I conjure Her up with every regretful memory. Even the happy memories sting. It is like walking in the Arctic in summer clothes. I'm assaulted by the cold that precedes and the pinpricks of pain that follow every memory. I wonder if I will ever be warm again.

David stopped following me a long time ago, and my mother-in-law gave up soon after him. He sat on the back porch, staring into the empty yard. Empty to him. It's filled with the fog of broken moments I feel more than remember. All the times I wouldn't cartwheel with her or play with the Frisbee. All the times I was tired and wanted to get dinner finished and Rylie in bed.

There's one room I've avoided. I can't face it. My studio sits cold and dark as I wear a pathway in the carpet with my bare feet.

It's almost five o'clock. David is still sitting on the porch. He hasn't spoken since two.

One of my paintings of Rylie is slightly off-kilter. She sits on a swing, her four-year-old face surrounded by a halo of curls. I straighten it with a finger. It was the first time I tried to paint after Rylie was born. The memory is murky. I turn away from it and watch the Other Me in a blur of searching in a cabinet that is no longer there and pantomiming painting in the kitchen. It was so long ago. Then I realize there is a monster lurking in the cabinet in the studio. It's the painting. Her painting. *My* painting. The room quiets for a moment as I let my mind go blank. I don't want to think anymore. Every moment is another moment without Rylie. Another moment she could be hurt or dying. It hurts to breathe. I would give anything to change what happened.

It's a crazy thought, but it snatches me up in a moment. What if I made Her? What if painting Her somehow made Her real? I spent so many hours trying to get that face right, to find the right shade of blue, the straggly eyebrows.

I have to destroy it. If I destroy the painting, maybe I'll stop this. If I trapped Her in reality by creating the painting, maybe I will destroy Her if I destroy it. And if She is the link between now and my past, maybe if I end Her, I will stop the past from happening.

All I know is I have to try.

The cabinet is a mess, but the canvas is there in the back, wrapped in a paper bag. The image mocks me, captured in painful detail by my own brush before I knew what I was seeing. I need my razor blade.

I pull out the thick blade and set the painting against the

wall where I won't damage the furniture when I smash it. First, I'll break the frame. Then I'll shred the canvas into tiny pieces. If I obliterate Her, maybe I'll reset back to when I can change things. Maybe I'll stop it this time. I slip on the old pair of tennis shoes I use to work in the yard so I won't hurt my feet.

The first kick snaps the side of the cheap frame. The second is harder. With each kick, I get angrier until I'm hurting myself through the shoes. The frame finally gives. I grab the razor and slash it from the top to the bottom right through her face and hands. It feels like blasphemy, like defiance. Cut after cut goes through the paint and the fabric as I will Her into nothingness. It started with the painting, and it will end with it.

"Charlie, what are you doing?"

David looks at me from the doorway in horror.

"I'm going to burn it."

"No, honey, wait!" He moves to stop me, but I push him away and keep slashing. I have to stop it. I hear him begging me to stop, calling my name over and over. I imagine the razor cutting past the paint into something deeper. It looks like I ran the canvas through a shredder.

"Charlie, please stop."

I ignore him and go to the garage to grab the metal bucket I once used for mop water. The matches are still on the top shelf in the kitchen cabinet. I stuff the shredded pieces into the bucket and put it outside on the porch.

"Charlotte, don't," my mother-in-law says from the doorway. I ignore her. David waves her away.

"Put it out further. Acrylic smoke is toxic." He seems to have given up trying to stop me. He unreels the garden hose from the corner of the patio.

I strike the match on the box and drop it into the

bucket. It burns slowly, then all at once. The smell is terrible. I back away and watch as the flames consume the painting.

I close my eyes and stand still, waiting for something to change. To start over. The acrid plastic smell of burning acrylic stings my nostrils and I shiver in the dark, but nothing happens.

"Charlie," David touches my shoulder like I'm made of glass. "Why?"

"I had to. It's all my fault."

"What?"

"I don't know how, but this is all my fault."

"Charlie, I told you to let her go to the lock-in. I agreed."

"It's all my fault! It's me! It's me, David!" I run back into my studio and throw the closest canvas to the floor. "This is all my fault!"

"Stop!"

"I did this!" Every brushstroke seems to be laughing at me. I blindly tear at the canvases and stomp over them, ripping my studio to pieces.

"This isn't your fault! Charlie, your paintings!" David yells. "Please don't!"

"It's me! I did this. I'm to blame!"

"No, you're not!"

I whirl around to him, and the dreaded cold hits me. She materializes in front of me, blocking my view of David. There's my old beautiful long hair, the clean artist's smock, and paint-smudged fingers.

"Yes, I am!" I scream. She flinches and covers Her mouth with her hand. I see the mask fall back over Her face as She turns to respond to David, and I crumple to the floor. It didn't work.

God, why? A moan oozes out of my throat like poison.

David kneels over me and reaches for my arm like he's being forced to pet a rabid dog.

"Charlie, don't."

"She blamed me," I cry. This ache in my heart is like labor pain. It hits in waves with each fresh realization of how much I pushed Rylie away.

"You didn't do this."

"But I did! David, we're never going to find her. God, please kill me. Take me instead, please!"

"Charlotte." His voice is rough with anger, and he grabs me by the shoulders. "Never say that again. Never, you hear me? We are going to find her."

"Why did I let her go? Why?" The question wrenches out of me over and over. I am utterly broken, and I will never be mended. David cannot put this back together. No one can.

I stare at the brick wall of our house and shudder as the ice hits again. Inside, I can barely see Her walking from the kitchen to the living room and diving back behind the kitchen wall. I remember being so terrified of something moving outside. Now I know it was me. Such a strange moment to remember when my child has vanished. What is the point? I can't change anything. I can't stop her from leaving.

Why didn't I listen? Why didn't I keep Rylie safe?

FORTY-FOUR

DAVID ASKED Nana to stay at the house while he goes to the police station with more photos of Rylie. Her picture will be shown on the local morning news. I've let David handle it all. My phone has been blowing up ever since people started waking up. Message after message pings in the car speaker system as I follow the back road around the loop to the lake.

Rylie won't be at the lake. I know she can't be here, but I have to look.

The car bumps the concrete block at the front of the parking space, and I stomp the brake. The park is empty. It's too early for kids to be playing. There are two other cars in the parking lot that probably belong to runners or bikers. I lock the car and zip up my coat against the wind off the lake. It will probably be hot once the sun is fully up. Patches of gray clouds race above me as I force myself down the path we've walked together more times than I can count. I don't want to find her here, but I have to look.

The asphalt path winds through the patches of trees around the lake. I follow it to our usual spot.

I have learned to hate this cold. I shudder as the Other Me appears, sitting against the tree. She is watching the beach below with a soft smile. She hasn't noticed me. I step out of Her line of sight. I remember the way Rylie ran and jumped on the sand. I think of her skipping rocks and throwing bread at seagulls.

I kneel on the pavement and weep. If I can see the past, why can't I change it?

"God, please. Let me fix it!" I shout into the wind. I just need to find the right moment. The right memory that will let me end this. "Please, let me fix it!"

My phone rings. I don't recognize the number.

"Rylie?" I croak as I pick up the call. "Rylie, are you okay?"

"Charlotte? It's Tori."

It takes all my self-control not to throw the phone.

"Oh."

"What's the matter?" Tori asks.

"I'm at the lake looking for Rylie."

"You're looking for Rylie?"

"She disappeared from the lock-in." There's silence on the line, and I almost hang up. "Why are you calling me? I need to keep the line open in case Rylie calls."

The phone is muffled, and I can hear her saying something about Rylie.

"Charlotte, I don't—"

"What?"

"Greg left me a message on my cousin's phone."

A voice I don't recognize says something about calling the police. My stomach fills with lead.

"Tell me."

"He called most of the night," Tori says, her voice breaking. "Ever since about midnight or one. But the last one was just a few minutes ago. He said, 'Come home, or I'll make sure Rylie never wants to see you again.'"

I stare at the old live oak, bare branches stark black against the gray early morning sky as her words sink in.

"Charlotte, I'm so—"

I hang up and run to the car faster than I ever thought I could run. Greg has my daughter. I hit the speakerphone and dial David's number as I pull out of the parking lot. I'm closer to Tori's house than he is.

"Did you find her?" he says.

"David, Greg took Rylie."

"What?"

"Greg took her! I'm going to their house. Get there as soon as you can. Bring the police!"

"Honey, slow down," David says. "I can't understand you."

"Tori called me! I'm going to get her."

"I'm coming!"

"I have to drive. Wherever you are, get to their house."

"What did Tori tell you?"

His tone. It's *that* tone.

"You don't believe me," I spit through gritted teeth.

"I believe you! What did she say so I can tell the police?"

Rage hits me like a brick wall, and I can barely drive. "That he has her!"

"Honey—"

"Listen to me, David!" I scream into my phone. "I'm not crazy! Tori told me Greg has Rylie, and I'm going to get her right now. Meet me there!"

I jab my finger at my phone to hang up and drive as fast as I dare across town to their house. Thank you, God, that traffic is light so early in the morning.

David's number lights up on my phone again. I let it ring as I turn down the street to Tori and Greg's neighborhood.

FORTY-FIVE

MY THROAT HURTS FROM CRYING, and the steering wheel is sticky from my sweaty palms. The cross-shaped air freshener on the rearview mirror sways back and forth. I pull my eyes away from it to peer at the house through the dirty windshield. The house is so perfectly kept. I see the lilac bushes in bloom. The hedges are pruned, and the front walkway is swept. The windows are bright and clean as always, but Tori's bright-green curtains have been replaced with plain white ones. Even with the windows closed, I can sense her absence.

There's something wrong with the lawn. I'm not sure what it is at first. I stare until I figure it out: the grass has been mowed but not edged. Greg always edges the lawn in a very specific way. I follow the edge of the lawn around the front of the house and next to the walkway. He edged the east side, but he stopped halfway through. Greg does not let *anything* interfere with his lawn routine. My stomach fills with lead. I remember the time I visited Tori for lunch so many years ago. I talked to Tori in the living room, and Rylie played in the kitchen. And Greg came home from work early.

I jump out of the car and run to the front door. I know Rylie is in this house. I know it because She knew it. My heart nearly stops as I grasp the doorknob. The door is unlocked and ajar. It is silent in the house as I push it open, but I can see the door to the patio standing open. Maybe he is outside in the backyard.

I stand in the white foyer on the khaki and white patterned rug. All the pictures are missing from the stairway and hallway walls. I peer into the living room. He's taken down every picture in the living room, too. His office looks the same. Then I notice the patches on the walls where the picture frames had hung. There are patches everywhere. One of the bookshelves has a broken shelf. And the chair Tori reupholstered is on its side, the cushion torn and exploding batting onto the rug. Every wall has holes and patches. The stairs are missing balusters and a few are splintered in half.

The house looks like a war zone.

"Charlotte?" Greg is standing on the landing between the two floors. His eyes are wild, and there's a cut on his forehead that has been bandaged.

"Where is she?" My voice is sharp as a knife.

"Charlotte, I didn't hear you knock. I'm so glad to see you."

"Where. Is. She." The words echo off the ceiling. I feel a hundred feet tall. I will destroy him if he lies. If he moves. If he even flinches. I will attack. Everything in me is begging him to give me an excuse.

"Tori still hasn't come home."

"Not Tori! Where is my daughter?" I shout.

He doesn't move. "Charlotte..."

"Where is Rylie?"

"I heard that Rylie ran away. I'm sure you're upset."

For a moment, I waiver. Maybe I'm crazy. I've never liked Greg. Maybe I'm blaming him for something he has nothing to do with. I look him hard in the eye, and the cold hits me again. I'm almost used to the blast of ice, but I still blink. My eye catches something moving in my peripheral vision. I glance at the kitchen through the dining room and see Her. She runs from the kitchen counter, and I see Her scoop up an invisible Rylie.

"She's always been so wild," Greg's voice echoes above me. The Other Charlotte is terrified, but when She looks me in the eye as She flies past me, I know. Something in Greg's voice is wrong. He's pleased with himself.

My palms hurt from my fingernails pinching into my fists. I grind the words out through gritted teeth. "Give me my daughter. Now."

"I don't have her, Charlotte. I know you must be upset. If you were to instill more discipline in your house—"

"Shut up and give me my daughter!" I run up the stairs toward him. He backs away from me, yelling something I can't understand. "Rylie! Rylie, I'm here! Run, Rylie! Run!" I scream as I run up the stairs. My shoe catches on the rug on the landing, and I stumble forward onto the second flight.

"Charlotte, calm down. Think about what you're doing." He backs down the hall.

"Rylie, I'm here! Rylie!" I scream her name over and over as I stumble up the stairs, tears streaming down my face. If he's hurt my baby, I will tear him apart. My muscles are screaming with adrenaline, and time slows down as I claw my way up to the second floor. The walls are pockmarked with holes the size of a fist, and a sickening feeling fills my stomach.

Greg is at the end of the hall, both hands outstretched in front of him. "Charlotte, please calm down!"

"Give me my daughter now!"

He winces and puts an arm up to guard his face. Outlined by the window at the end of the hall, he looks like an animal cowering in a cage. His clothes and hair are disheveled, and he's barefoot. He's so pathetic that I stop and draw back a little, unsure.

What if I'm wrong? What if I've totally lost it, and he has nothing to do with it? What if all the whispered prayer requests and worried comments people make when they think I'm not listening are right? I clear my throat to speak.

Something flies toward my face. I react without thinking and jerk back as Greg's old softball bat whizzes past my nose. He freezes, the bat in both hands. His eyes are almost glowing with hatred.

I jump at him and claw his face with my fingernails as hard as I can. He wasn't expecting me to fight back. He jerks away, leaving his groin unprotected, and I kick him. He doubles over and falls into the wall. I keep kicking and try to knock the bat away. He curls up on the ground, yelling at me but doesn't let go of the bat. I stomp on his hands and arms. I'm scaring myself.

Suddenly he swings the bat, and I feel a sickening crack as it crashes against my shin. The pain sends me to the ground, but I don't stop. I reach for his ear and yank as hard as I can. He screams like a child.

I kick him with my good leg and throw myself on the arm that is holding the bat. I slap and scratch his face and tear at his eyes. He yanks at my hair but can't get a good grip on the short strands. I bite his arm that still holds the bat, and he drops it with a scream.

"Where is my daughter!" I ignore the sharp pain in my

leg and reach for the bat. It rolls away from my hand toward the stairs.

"I don't know! I don't know! Stop, Charlotte! I don't know!"

For a moment, I am frozen, staring at him on the ground, my fingers reaching behind me and finding nothing but air. I realize how vulnerable I really am. I caught him off guard, but he's taller and stronger.

A crash sounds in the bedroom next to us. Rylie *is* here.

His fist shatters against my jaw, and I see stars. I'm too stunned to move. There is blood on my hand. Is it mine or his? He tries to hit me again but misses and grazes my shoulder. The room spins, and I flip over, lunging for the bat. My bad leg is jerked from under me, and I wail from the pain. He grabs my other leg, and I hit the floor hard, knocking the wind from my chest.

My mind flies to when Rylie was born, and the cold pours over me. The pain, the fear, the certainty that I was going to die. The memory is sharp like stepping through broken glass.

"Rylie!" I cannot leave my little girl without a mother and in the hands of a monster. I gasp for air and flail against him. My fingers barely connect with the edge of the bat. I claw at it until I get a good grip, and slam it on his arm with every scrap of rage in my body. I kick away as he curls up against the bannister and stand over him. My bad leg is on fire.

"Never touch her again!" I scream, bringing the bat down on him with each word. "Never!"

I leave Greg whimpering on the floor and grab the doorknob. It's locked, but I hear movement inside the room. There's a muffled cry. I frantically jerk the knob in my panic until I see the lock and twist it. The door pops open.

Rylie is sprawled sideways on the floor, her mouth gagged with a scarf. She knocked over the chair she is tied to. Her arms are bound to the chair arms, her legs to the legs, and she is struggling against the jump rope he used to hold her waist. She's wearing the same outfit she wore to youth group, minus her shoes and jewelry. She screams "Mama" through the gag.

"Baby, I'm here!" I tear at the gag, but it's tied too tight. I set her upright and grab the back of the chair, tipping it toward me. I drag her out of the door and down the hall, hopping on my good foot, the two bottom legs of the chair scraping and gouging the wood floor that Tori refinished by hand. Greg is still next to the wall. I don't know what to do. I have to get something to cut the ropes. I can't break the chair, so I have to cut the ropes somehow. I can't leave Rylie to run to the kitchen for a knife, but I don't know how to get her down the stairs. I keep telling her that it's okay. That I'm here.

"It's okay, baby. It's okay. I'm getting you out of here."

I want to keep hold of the bat, but I can't carry it and Rylie. I throw it down the stairs so he can't reach it. Then I grab Rylie and the chair from behind and lift, praying I can get them all the way down. I lean against the stairwell wall as I scrape the chair down the stairs one excruciating step at a time. Rylie is whimpering, but I can't see her face.

My leg is on fire as we reach the landing. I can't carry her anymore. I let the chair down on the back so she's looking up at me, crying and screaming through her gag. I slide down onto the last flight of stairs below her and pull her toward me on her back, trying to slow the slide with my body. I cry out when the chair leg hits my shin, but I won't stop until I get her down the stairs. The room spins as we both slip and slide down the stairs onto the entryway floor.

"This is all her fault!" Greg roars from the second floor. I hear him stumbling toward the stairs, and I force myself to stand.

"I'm getting you out of here," I whisper in her ear as she whimpers and cries, looking up at me in terror. Where is David with the police? What is taking them so long? What was I thinking? I have nothing to defend myself and Rylie.

I dig for my phone in my pockets, but they are empty. Did the phone fall out, or did I leave it in the car? Do they have a phone in the kitchen?

"All of this is her fault! Tori has ruined me! She leaves, and then that little brat costs me my job!" His voice is almost whining.

I pull Rylie toward the kitchen in the chair, trying to look for anything to cut the rope around her arms. I see rope burns and welts around her wrists. My leg hurts so much that I don't know how I'll keep going. Somehow I pull her around the kitchen island and grope for the knife block on the counter, trying to stay low so he can't see us if he makes it down the stairs. I hope I hurt him so much that he can't walk.

The knife block is empty.

"How many times have I said she needs to be more respectful?" His voice echoes down the stairs. His words are muffled, as if his mouth is full of cotton. Rylie's chest heaves, and she bites down on her gag. I put a finger to my lips and search the drawers as quietly as I can. "None of this would have happened if she had done what I asked of her!"

I find a knife in a drawer. It's small, but it looks strong enough. I show it to Rylie and go to work on the gag in her mouth. The scarf is one of Tori's favorites. It rips and tears easily. I jerk it away from her face and kiss my little girl's cheek.

"Mommy," she whispers. "I love you. I'm sorry!"

"I love you, too, baby," I whisper. "We are getting out of here." She nods despite her tears and pulls against the ropes to give me more space. I saw the thick jump rope-like material. The fibers barely tear with each stroke.

"He said everyone would think I ran away," she whispers. She eyes the doorway behind me.

"You're going to have to run with me, honey," I say, furiously sawing at the ropes.

"I can't walk," she whispers.

I look at her feet. One of her pinkie toes is bent at a sickening angle, and both feet are covered in cuts and bruises.

"What did he do to you?" I gently touch her heel, and she sucks in a breath. Where are the police? Why didn't David listen to me?

"Did Tori tell you how she's been lying to me all these years?" Greg's voice makes me jump and nearly cut Rylie with the knife. "How she's been keeping us from having a child?"

I block out his ranting and go back to sawing, but I taste bile in my throat. I'm halfway through.

"All I've ever wanted was a family. To be a father. To raise children that are respectful and obedient."

It's taking too long. The fingers on Rylie's right hand are slightly purple.

"That woman lied to me for five years!"

The rope snaps, and I hurry to work on the other knots.

"She said she wasn't ready! Then she said there was something wrong with her. That they were trying to figure it out." He's in the living room now, and my hands cramp around the knife. Rylie squeezes her eyes shut. "She told me they had to do tests! That she couldn't have any children. Lies!"

The knot snaps and unravels. Rylie's hands come loose, and I rip at the bonds around the chair legs.

"I would have been the best father to our kids. The best!" He limps around the doorway into the kitchen and leans against the oven, but I can't look at him. "It's all her fault. All *your* fault!"

Ice. Cold pours over me and She's standing in the kitchen doorway, looking into the living room. I know exactly what she's looking at. Seven years ago, I stood in this kitchen and felt like I was too protective, watching my daughter tap dance in the hallway for my best friend's husband.

"Crawl behind me and go out the back," I whisper to Rylie as I stand up straight with the knife in front of me. "Go as fast as you can and scream for help."

I don't look back, but I hear her shimmy for the door as I look Greg straight in the eye.

"You actually think you'd be a good father?" The words come out like cement blocks. "What kind of father beats a child?" Weight after weight, I imagine the words tied around his neck and dragging him to the floor. "You kidnap an innocent girl and hurt her, and you actually think you would be a good dad. Are you insane?"

"It was for her own good," he seethes. "You and David disgust me."

"How dare you," I hiss. I never thought I could kill someone before, but right now, I know I can.

"I told your precious little brat that she could go home when *my wife* came home!" Blood drips from his nose onto the white tile floor. He cradles his jaw in his right hand and steadies himself against the door. I hear Rylie screaming outside. I know she's looking for the neighbors.

"Tori is never coming back! Never!" I scream to distract him.

He lunges for me. Everything is a blur of arms and legs and the flash of the knife blade. He hurls Tori's owl cookie jar at me as I duck around the counter. The bottom smashes into tiny shards, but the head bounces down beside me intact, black eyes staring at me. I shove away from the counter and lurch into the main room toward the television. There's nothing left to throw. The lamps are gone, the bookshelves are empty, and even the throw pillows are missing from the couch. My leg is on fire.

"You call yourself a Christian?" I scream at him. He's limping behind me. I push over the antique hall table behind me as I round the corner into the hall. The effort sends me crumpling to the floor on my bad leg. I hear him scraping across the floor. I try to crawl away, still watching the doorway to the living room. If I can just get outside, I can make it to my car.

He stands over the table, eyes wide. There is blood trickling down his face from his hair, and his cheek is red and puffy. He leans one arm against the doorway.

"Like anyone would believe you. Look at you." He spits blood on the table and coughs. "They all think you're crazy. Everyone."

He leers at me, smiling despite the cut on his lip.

"Poor Charlotte. She's so anxious. So protective. So *paranoid*," he says with a low chuckle. "I guess she finally snapped. She lost her mind. Rylie running away was too much."

I keep the knife pointed at him and push myself away with my other hand.

"Tori will tell them, you know," he says. "She'll tell them

how you're broken. How pathetic you are. How you've been hiding panic attacks."

My throat closes.

"She'll tell them your pathetic, delusional mind blamed me, and that it breaks her heart to see you so broken."

"Shut up!"

"And they'll lock you up, Charlotte! They'll lock you up and drug you so high you can't see straight."

"Shut up!"

"Because that's what they do to crazy people, right? Poor, crazy Charlotte! We all knew she'd have a breakdown!" he yells, stepping over the table and picking up something off the floor.

It's the bat.

I fight against the pain to crawl toward the front door, still holding the knife. It's mere feet, but it seems like a mile.

"If I go down, I'm taking you down with me," Greg says, spitting blood on the rug. "Self defense," he says, his voice as dark as tar.

I claw away from him, ducking and scrambling until my leg gives way underneath me. Blood drips off his chin as he raises the bat over my legs.

The door flies open.

"Drop it! Get down on the ground!"

A black figure is standing in the doorway, and I see others outside. For a moment, time freezes as I look down the barrel of a gun. The ice hits me again, and the Other Me bounds through the hallway ahead of me. I watch Her hug an invisible Tori for a second and flee into the sunshine. Then I see the gun again. I drop the knife on the floor and slowly kneel.

"Get down on the ground right now, man!"

I hear Greg saying something behind me and a heavy

noise of something hitting the floor.

"Ma'am, come over behind me. Can you come over here?"

I realize that he's talking to me. I scramble toward the door on my knees and behind him, out into the sunshine.

"Mom! Mom!" Rylie is across the street in a police car.

"Charlotte!" David runs to me and picks me up, nearly knocking the breath out of me. "Are you crazy? He could have killed you!"

"I had to get her," I say, my voice breaking. I lean on his chest and weep. "Is she okay?"

"Ma'am, let me help you away from the house, please," a police officer says. He and David practically carry me across the lawn to the police car on the other side.

A tall, imposing officer is standing guard next to Rylie, offering her water. The older couple who lives across the street is standing on their front lawn. The wife is crying. My leg is on fire, but I drag myself to Rylie.

Another police officer rushes to help me across the street. "We have backup coming right now, ma'am, and the ambulance is around the corner."

"Can we help?" The neighbor asks the officer.

"We'll take your statement in a moment."

I kneel in front of Rylie and kiss her poor bloodied feet. She puts her head on my shoulder and cries. The pain in my leg is unbearable, but I have to hold my baby. David sits next to us, tears streaming down his face.

"Mom, I want to go home," Rylie says. Her chest shudders against mine. I will never let my daughter go again. Never.

An ambulance siren screams and then dies as it reaches our street. They pull up in front of the police car and two paramedics jump out.

"Please, he hurt my daughter." I show them Rylie's feet.

"We'll help you, honey," the woman says to Rylie. "Are you hurt anywhere else?"

"I hit my head," Rylie says. "I fell when I tried to get out of the chair and hit my head."

I try to follow the paramedics as they carry Rylie to the ambulance, but the injury in my leg is too painful.

"Ma'am, let us get your daughter to the ambulance, and I'll help you next," the paramedic says.

My body aches in every joint and my throat is dry as if I'd finished a marathon without a single drink of water. The first paramedic carefully snaps a brace around Rylie's neck while the other one helps me get into the ambulance and straps my leg into a splint.

I'm deflating like a balloon. Normally I'd be shrinking into a puddle of embarrassment, knowing the neighbors are watching. Let them look. Let them see what kind of monster they lived next to.

"Sir, you'll have to meet us at the hospital," the paramedic tells David. He gives him directions to the hospital. David kisses us both and steps out of the ambulance.

"I will see you at the hospital," he says. "And Nana will be there with me, Rylie." The doors close, and Rylie covers her face with her arm and sobs as the ambulance flies down the road.

"I'm so sorry, Mom," she says. "I was mad. Stupid Hannah was mean, and Liana was mean, and I went outside so I wouldn't cry. And he grabbed me. He grabbed me and put me in the car."

She shudders and can't seem to breathe for a moment.

"My poor girl!"

"He said I ruined his life."

"He ruined his own life, Rylie. He did everything to

himself. You had nothing to do with it."

"Mom, what happened to Aunt Tori? The house was so messed up."

I remember the holes in the walls and shudder.

"Did he hurt her?"

"I don't know, baby."

"Mommy," Rylie falters. "What if I can't dance anymore? My feet hurt so much."

I squeeze her hand and kiss her on the forehead.

"You will dance," I tell Rylie fiercely. "I promise, you will dance. We'll get the best people in the world to fix everything. I promise." I kiss her hand and look up at the paramedic. "This girl is one of the most amazing ballerinas you've ever seen."

"That's wonderful, honey. I love ballet."

The paramedic gets Rylie talking about ballet and her favorite music, winking at me when Rylie's not looking.

As the adrenaline wears off, I realize the full destruction I saw in Tori and Greg's house. How much of her redecorating was to cover up damage? Did she come home every week from church, worrying that the Sunday school teacher had made him angry? I used to admire her style that seemed straight from the pages of a magazine, but I can't unsee the holes in the walls and the torn chair.

A few years ago, when she started wearing her hair up all the time, did he make her do that? Did he make her change her clothing too? A horrifying thought tears through me: what if he was hitting Tori, and not just the walls?

"I think I'm going to throw up," I tell the EMT. She grabs a blue bag and makes me hold it over my mouth.

Tori and I became friends in Darren's office, bonding over brokenness, but she never let me see hers.

FORTY-SIX

ANOTHER DOCTOR VISIT DOWN. I slump onto our couch and put my leg up on the opposite arm as David carries Rylie into her bedroom to rest. My mother-in-law is in the kitchen making lunch. She almost lives with us now. The small, partial fracture in my fibula still aches even though it has healed. Hopefully, once I get the boot off tomorrow I will be more useful.

I've lost count of how many hours we've spent in doctor's offices over the last six weeks. We've seen surgeons, specialists, physical therapists, and sports medicine doctors.

Or rather, David has seen them. He handled everything for the first few weeks until my doctor cleared me for more activity. Even today, I was playing catch-up to understand the sports medicine specialist that David and Rylie know all too well.

It was so hard to let him do everything. I felt like a failure, stuck at home for weeks. I still feel guilty about resting when I should be packing boxes.

"So she'll dance again?" Nana says from the kitchen doorway.

"Her toes are healing, and her arch looks great," I answer. "All the important tendons and ligaments are fine. He failed."

The thought gives me grim comfort. Greg thought he could punish Tori by making sure Rylie couldn't dance anymore, but he only succeeded in giving her ugly bruises and sprains and breaking two of her toes. I stopped him before he hurt her ankles or legs.

"When is the grand jury thing?" Nana asks me.

"They finally gave him a public defender, so soon, hopefully," I answer. I had no idea how slowly the justice system moves. We've had dozens of meetings with the police department and various investigators, as well as the prosecutor.

I still can't understand why he hurt my daughter. Based on what the police have told us, he was stalking the church, looking for Tori at the lock-in and grabbed Rylie instead. I've heard him called a nutcase, a narcissist, and a half dozen other names I can't repeat. But I just think of him as the dictionary definition of "miserable failure."

I survey the front room from my seat on the couch. It's lined with boxes in a semi-organized jumble. I still need to pack my sewing machine and supplies. I wonder if I'll have to alter Rylie's costumes in Colorado myself or if they'll have someone to do that. Hopefully, Rylie will be up for the surprise going-away party at her dance studio tonight. Colleen cried when I let her know we were moving.

David walks into the living room, reading from his phone. "Casey says Jerry might step down from the youth ministry."

"Really?" I don't know how to feel. "Do you think he should?"

David clenches his jaw and says nothing, heading into

the kitchen to talk to his mom. He's still furious with Jerry and blames him for what happened. I'm not as angry. I hold Jerry responsible for Rylie being missed, but I don't blame him for what Greg did. Jerry has to be held accountable, but I don't know that he deserves to lose his job.

I don't know what justice would be for Jerry or any of the volunteers who weren't paying attention when she slipped out the side door. I think their guilt is probably more than enough punishment.

Pastor Ryan has been to visit several times along with Darren. We haven't gone back in person, and I have stayed away from the phone as much as possible. David and I both have had to field calls from people we barely know, asking about Rylie.

A lady I have seen in service but never actually met accused me of slandering Greg and told me I needed to repent for the good of the school. I was about to drive to the hospital for Rylie's second surgery, so I hung up and blocked her number. I don't think I'll ever answer calls from unknown numbers again.

"We have barbecue left if you want some, Charlotte," my mother-in-law says from the kitchen. I shake my head. That barbecue came from Renee. She begged to bring us dinner until I finally gave in. I remember following her to the kitchen in awkward silence. I still can't wrap my mind around our conversation.

"I'm sorry," she told me as she arranged the pans and boxes on the kitchen counter. "I'm just so sorry, Charlotte." She put a bottle of my favorite lemonade iced tea in the refrigerator and folded the bag for the food into her purse. "I have a problem. I don't even know what to say, but I'm sorry. I've said things about you and Tori..."

"I know."

"I feel horrible, Charlotte. I'm so stupid." She stood against the kitchen counter. "Please forgive me. I should never have talked about you. Or Tori. Or anyone."

"No, you shouldn't."

"Grace said something to me about it, but I didn't listen." She wiped away tears and took a deep breath. "When I heard Rylie was in the hospital..." She bit her tongue and tried again. "I heard that he hurt Tori."

As I watch the wind in the trees from my comfy seat on our couch, that's the moment I keep going back to. I have thought of a hundred things I could have said. I could have yelled at her. I could have kicked her out of my house and told her it was too late.

But I just waited until she realized it herself.

"I'm doing it again, right now, aren't I?" she said. She covered her mouth with one hand. "Casey said I'm the worst gossip he knows. I guess you probably agree with him."

"Yes, I do," I said. I expected arguments and excuses, but she only cried.

"Please forgive me. I'm going to stop," she said, unable to meet my eyes. "Grace is going to keep me accountable. I hate myself so much."

I told her I forgave her, but I don't know if I can trust Renee again for a long time. Maybe never. I believe her apology even if David doesn't. I believe her when she says she wants to change. But since we're moving, she doesn't have much chance to repair the damage she's done.

Darren said something to me in counseling about forgiveness and reconciliation being different things. Morgan told me that Renee isn't talking to Yvonne as much and has been apologizing to other people. That gives me some hope.

I could take a nap, but I need to be productive. I still

haven't touched my studio since I wrecked it. Nana has asked to clean it. My parents also tried to help when they visited, but I told them it was my mess to deal with. I hoist myself off the couch and wander over to the studio to survey the damage.

The Enterprise painting is undamaged except for a small nick on the lower-left corner. I pick at the cracked acrylic paint for a moment before gently hanging the painting back on the wall. I can almost smell the plastic smell of burning acrylic and shudder.

I clear a spot in the center of the studio so I can sit and sort everything into three piles: one for undamaged, one for damaged but repairable, and one for trash. The sorting process makes my heart ache. Some of these were pretty good.

A hand on my shoulder startles me. "Brought you the trash can," David says, sliding the plastic bin next to me.

"Thank you."

"Are you sure you don't want help?" he asks.

"I need to do it myself."

"Okay. The Enterprise is okay?"

"Easy repair," I say, pointing to the cracked corner.

"Good. I want to hang it in my new office."

"I might be able to fix it before we move." I stuff the pile of ruined paintings in the trashcan. "Just need the energy."

"No rush. We'll make sure you have somewhere to paint in Denver." He kneels on the ground next to me and puts an arm over my shoulders. I lean my head against his as we sit in the sun. "You seem...better," he says quietly.

"I hope so." I shiver and see another Charlotte, shimmering like a mirage next to me, painting the Enterprise. Was it a year ago? Two? My hair was still long then.

"Can I ask you something?" David asks. "What changed? Everything fell apart, but you're different."

The Other Me fades.

"David, would you think I'm crazy if I told you..." I hesitate. How do I say what has been following me for so long? "I have been seeing glimpses of memories. All these small moments that I'd forgotten. Mistakes I made." I take a deep breath. "With you and Rylie."

"Me too," David says. "I was actually thinking about that stupid peacock costume."

I shiver and roll my eyes. I don't stand up to look, but I know the Other Me is in the living room, putting moleskin on the itchy places.

"That was a dumb costume. You were right," I start to explain. "But that's not..."

"That's not what I was thinking about," he says.

I pull away from his shoulder and look at him. He has tears in his eyes.

"I was thinking about how she said she was a bad kid," David says. "Because of her grades."

I'd forgotten about that. He sniffs and shifts his legs beneath him.

"Her grades got better after that," I say, patting his arm. "It all got better."

"But she almost quit dancing."

"No, she didn't. She did great."

"She asked me if she could quit the night before that recital."

My mind trips over the sentence like uneven stairs. "You never told me that."

"No, because I told her I wouldn't let her." He breathes in and drops his arm off my shoulder, folding his hands in his lap. His dark hair obscures his eyes, but I know he's crying. "She said that she didn't want to make us fight anymore."

I grab his hand. "Poor Rylie."

"I told her that I wanted her to dance. I wanted to see her be brave and do her whole recital."

This breaks my heart all over again. I was so cruel to him after that performance. No wonder he was so hurt.

"I was so mean," I say.

"You were right, though. I was hard on her. I should have let her be a kid."

He shifts against the wall and kisses my knuckles. "I never told you that I went to see Darren a few times, too."

I don't think it is possible for me to be more shocked than I am right now. I shake my head and clear my throat. "When was this?"

"After we said we were one and done," he said. "I probably should have kept going longer. I knew I had to change things."

How could I see things so completely wrong? He has been trying so hard to break down the wall between us, and I've been building it higher. My heart hurts too much to let me speak.

I pick at the seam of my blouse. "Do you really think she'll be able to dance again?" My voice catches in my throat.

"She's a fighter, Charlie." David says, rubbing my shoulders. "You heard Dr. Wentz, the sports medicine guy? He didn't hurt her ankles. That's the most important thing. You stopped him in time."

"We should go to the lake," I say suddenly.

"With Rylie?"

"She can skip rocks sitting down. We need a normal afternoon, David. We have time before the party tonight."

"I'll go ask her." David goes to tell his mom our plan. She says she'd rather take a nap, but Rylie says the lake is officially the best idea ever. She chatters the whole drive about the ballet studios in Colorado and snow. I'm glad she's excited about moving. It was a battle I wasn't looking forward to fighting. We pass the park where I used to take her as a toddler, and I shiver at memories I can barely see.

David carries her to our favorite seat on the hill above the small rocky beach. Rylie leans her head against my shoulder and half-heartedly tosses a handful of seeds.

"He's staying in jail, right?" she says, watching a duck foraging near our seat. I think she's been afraid to ask what will happen to Greg after all the meetings with the police and lawyers. She's stayed so strong through all of her surgeries and treatments. I hope this means she finally feels safe enough to let her guard down.

"He will."

"Like for sure?"

"He has so many charges against him, honey. There are a lot of things that have to happen, but you were so brave when you talked to the lawyers. I don't think he'll get out of jail for a long time."

"Pinkie square?" she says.

"Pinkie square." I crook my finger and kiss the top of her head.

"I wish I'd never gone to that stupid lock-in." Her breath hitches. "I wish I'd just stayed home."

"I know, honey," I whisper. David sits on the other side of her and hugs her neck.

"What about Aunt Tori?" she asks.

I look at David. We've been trying to shield her from as much as possible, but she has read the news reports online.

"He's in trouble for hurting her, too," David says. "But she's safe."

"She lives with her mom now, right?"

I nod. I haven't spoken to Tori. I sent her a few text messages after the charges were filed against Greg, but they've gone unanswered. Our pastor explained that she'd left Greg when he hit her the night of Rylie's last recital. After years of yelling, threatening, and breaking furniture, he put her hand through a wall and shoved her to the floor. She packed up and left the next morning while he was asleep. I can't imagine how she survived his emotional abuse for so long.

I keep thinking about that day when Tori came to Bible study crying and said the china cabinet fell over and destroyed Grandma Patty's dishes. I'm pretty sure it wasn't because of a cracked leg.

I told her in my messages that I didn't blame her and that she can call me anytime. I hope she believes me. I hope time can heal us somehow.

"Why did God let this happen?" Rylie says, her voice small as if she's scared to ask the question.

I'm afraid to answer her. David shifts on the bench and sniffs away a tear.

"I have spent most of your life asking God that same question," I say slowly. "I kept wishing I could change things and wondering why He let me make all these mistakes instead of stopping me. Or I worried about mistakes I was sure I was going to make. Worrying if I was too strict or not strict enough."

It may not be the right answer, but it's the only one I have.

Rylie looks up at me with surprise. "Really?"

"Yes. Sometimes it was so hard that I couldn't get out of bed." Is it too much for her to hear? I don't think so.

"Your headaches and stuff?" she says.

"Some of them."

Rylie buries her head in my shoulder, fighting tears.

"We can't change what has already happened, no matter how much we might want to." I squeeze her shoulders and wipe the tears that are streaming down my cheeks. "But I don't want to spend my whole life thinking about everything I would change. I don't want to miss what's happening right here, right now. I don't want to lose more time with you and your Daddy."

David wipes his eyes and nods at me. "Your mama is right," he says.

"All I know is," I falter, "we can ask God to show us what He's doing in this big mess."

"Did *you* ask Him?" Rylie looks me in the eyes, searching my face for what I believe.

"Every day."

"What did He say?"

I watch the ducks fight over seeds on the sandy promontory below. "That He's here with us. And He's big enough to heal you. And me. I think that's all I need to know for now." I brush my fingertips against her soft brown hair. "We may not understand all of it until heaven, honey. But I know I wouldn't have been able to save you without Him."

"Love you, Mom," Rylie whispers.

"Love you, too."

We tease and feed the ducks until David signals that we need to go. We hurry back with the excuse that we want to go out for pizza and need to pick up Nana. I sneak into Rylie's room to get her ballet shoes and team jacket for everyone to sign.

Her room is partially packed. The wood floor is scuffed, and the barre is dirty from so many years of hard use. I hope it will be a selling point to new owners anyway. I shiver and watch the ghost of the old Charlotte try to plié and relevé against the barre. I remember Rylie laughing at me and telling me that I needed to listen better. The memory hurts because it didn't happen often enough. I should have played with her more. I should have danced with her. I should have talked to her, especially when Liana stopped being her best friend. I'm grateful we can catch up on lost chats while she does her physical therapy.

The shoes and jacket are in a bag in the closet, so I sneak them back to my room to put them in something less conspicuous. I pass another ghost of myself in the hallway, remembering a day we had nothing but fights over homework. I hated fifth grade.

Even when I don't *see* Her, I *feel* Her. I think I will always feel the Other Charlotte when Rylie gets mad at me or doesn't want to do her homework, Or when my leg hurts. I know She will be hanging over me when Rylie is finally well enough to start pointe. I doubt the cold down my spine will ever go away and never come back, but I think I will learn to keep moving in spite of it.

I look at myself in the bathroom mirror that I've avoided since my infamous haircut. Subtle wrinkles are forming around my mouth and eyes. A few streaks of silver have penetrated my hairline. The years have left their mark.

A shampoo bottle falls in the tub, startling me, and I lean into the shower to pick it up. A shadowy memory of a pregnancy test sends a single pinprick of cold into my hand, and I feel Her right next to me. I'd forgotten that shiver at the first moment I knew about Rylie. The cold doesn't frighten me anymore. It fills me with a sad longing I don't have a name for.

I replace the shampoo bottle and turn off the bathroom light. I walk into the living room and see another Charlotte on the couch. Rylie, David, and my mother-in-law are waiting in the car, but I stand still, unable to leave this memory.

That day was a bad day. I was so depressed and anxious that I couldn't cope with life. I'd thrown up my lunch as nausea gnawed at my stomach, so I claimed I had a migraine. I scared myself then, and the memory scares me now.

I notice a piece of paper sticking out from under the couch and shiver. I gently pull it free and stare at my scrawled handwriting: *Don't let Rylie go!* The tangible crinkle of paper under my fingertips brings tears. I fold the paper in half again and again until it is tiny in my hand.

"I can't fix it," I whisper to the barely visible ghost lying on the couch. "I can't change anything you did. I tried."

I know She can't hear me. She wouldn't believe a word I said even if She could. But I tell Her the truth anyway.

"You have no idea what's coming, and everyone will think you're crazy when it does." I breathe in slowly and close my eyes. "I think maybe you were sometimes. Maybe *I* was."

My heart breaks for that hurting younger me on the couch.

"You were so afraid that you couldn't see straight," I whisper. "You didn't...*I* didn't listen. So many people loved me and tried to help me, but I was in too much pain to hear them. Even now, on the other side of it, I'm still struggling."

I wipe a tear from the corner of my eye and sniff. I've made so many mistakes, but Rylie and David have forgiven me. They've given me grace. I look at the Other Charlotte on the couch and know what I need to tell Her even though She can't hear me.

"I forgive you," I whisper. "For all of it. I forgive you, Charlotte." The ghost shimmers for a moment, lifting Her head as if She heard me. Then She shudders and vanishes like a breath in winter.

AUTHOR'S NOTE

Charlotte's story was written out of my own experiences with postpartum depression, anxiety, and post-traumatic stress. I know firsthand how paralyzing these conditions can be. I was blessed with a supportive husband, a wise counselor, and good doctors who worked to find treatments that were right for me. This story reflects my own mistakes in that I did not seek support for my postpartum issues and suffered unnecessarily. It wasn't until years later after some threats to my physical health that I sought help and treatment. I will always regret that I waited so long.

I believe this needs to be said clearly: You are not "less than" if you need medication to support and regulate your brain's neurotransmitters. God can bring healing and work miracles through a pastor's prayers, a counselor's wisdom, or a psychiatrist's prescriptions.

If you are experiencing symptoms of anxiety or depression, please don't be afraid to ask for help from a counselor or clinician. If you don't know where to start, call the Substance Abuse and Mental Health Services Administration helpline at 1-800-662-HELP (4357) for free, confidential, 24/7, 365-day-a-year treatment referrals and information.

Tori's story of abuse is all too common, even in churches. No one should live in fear of his or her spouse or partner. If you or someone you love has been the victim of domestic violence or spousal abuse, call or text "START" to the National Domestic Violence Hotline at 1-800-799-SAFE (7233) or visit thehotline.org for free 24/7 resources and support.

ACKNOWLEDGMENTS

I would not have interesting characters to write if I did not have so many wonderful friends who inspire me. To Dan and Mendy, Doug and Lori, Daniel and Michelle, Glenn and Mary, Matt and Amy, and Rachael, whatever made you smile or laugh in this story probably came from you (and anything you didn't like came from someone else).

To the Damascus Blades, the Austin Christian Fiction Writers Mastermind group, my awesome beta-readers, the Stellar Stewart Sisters, and everyone at *Lorehaven*, I'm so grateful for your fellowship, encouragement, and goofy memes as I've walked this journey to publication.

Dr. Watson, Dr. Roark, Dr. Longest, and Dr. Camp, your courses taught me how to mess with readers' heads, and I hope you are proud.

Brittany, this is your fault. Thank you for making me submit my manuscript.

S.E. Clancy, I think our matching tattoos should be the crying laughter emoji. Can't wait to hug your neck in real life and celebrate all that God has done.

Corrie, you are my favorite labor and delivery nurse.

Thank you for sharing your medical knowledge and for the blessing of over thirty years of friendship.

Becky, thank you for speaking truth, spurring me toward righteousness, and beta-reading a very messy book. I hope you love the finished version.

CH Ramsey, thank you for opening doors and pushing me to walk through them.

Thank you to the whole team at Monster Ivy who worked so hard to make *That Pale Host* a reality. Every one of you needs a sparkly fairy godsister wand because you made my dreams come true. Cammie, I know I will never again find such a fierce advocate for my vision as a writer, and I cannot thank you enough for your support and advice.

Steve, Diane, Mal, Shauna, Bekah, DiJon, Sarah, and Tim, you're all getting copies of this book for Christmas, so start practicing surprised faces! I'm so glad I married into the McCary Clan.

Mary, thank you for saying my book was art. I hope it doesn't give you nightmares.

Sarah, it means so much that you want to read my book. I hope it doesn't give you nightmares either.

Dad, I'm officially a finisher. You can start busting those buttons now.

Mom, thank you for teaching me to hold a pencil. This book is about a mother's love for her daughter, and without you, this story could not exist.

To my boys whose escapades made Rylie adorably ridiculous, I hope you won't be embarrassed when you can read this for yourselves. And to my precious girl who arrived unexpectedly after I thought Rylie might be my only daughter, I'm so glad God gave me you because He's much more talented at creating little girls.

Caleb, you tolerated an exhausted wife after late nights

of writing, argued me out of quitting countless times, and kept the kids out of my hair so I could finish one last paragraph instead of dinner. You are relentless in giving me grace. You are my favorite, and I love you.

And thank you to my savior, Jesus Christ, who has mended my broken places with gold. I am humbled You entrusted me with the task of telling Charlotte's story. If this book pleases only You, that will be more than enough.

ABOUT THE AUTHOR

L.G. McCary is an old-school Whovian (Fourth Doctor is her Doctor) and a lifelong Trekkie. She has a bachelor's in psychology which means she knows enough to mess with readers' heads but not enough to diagnose their problems. She globe-trots as the wife of an Army chaplain, home-schooling four rambunctious kids along the way.

She writes supernatural and science fiction with intense emotional cores, complex characters, and intricate theological themes. Her Christian faith fuels every creative endeavor, from short fiction and novels to art and music.

Her short story, "A Recipe for Disaster," won Editor's Choice in the 2021 *Sensational* anthology from Havok Publishing. Find L.G. at her website lgmccary.com.

ABOUT THE PUBLISHER

To learn more about Monster Ivy Publishing, the premier Christian publisher of "Edgy, Clean" fiction for kids, teens, and adults, please visit www.monsterivy.com. Don't forget to sign up for their mailing list! And they also absolutely love connecting with readers and reviewers via Facebook, Twitter, and Instagram.